Rebecca Ley grew up in Oxford. She has a degree in History of Art and Philosophy from University College London and a Masters in Creative Writing from City University. Her essays have appeared in *Water Journal* and *Wander Magazine*, a literary magazine she co-founded. She was shortlisted for the Fitzcarraldo Essay Prize 2017. She currently lives in North London.

SWEET FRUIT, SOUR LAND

REBECCA LEY

SANDSTONE PRESS

First published in Great Britain by
Sandstone Press Ltd
Dochcarty Road
Dingwall
Ross-shire
IV15 9UG
Scotland

www.sandstonepress.com

The publisher acknowledges subsidy from Creative Scotland
towards publication of this volume.

ISBN: 978-1-912240-33-3
ISBNe: 978-1-912240-34-0

Cover design by Stuart Brill
Typeset by Iolaire Typography Ltd, Newtonmore
Printed and bound by Totem, Poland

For my parents

Contents

Prologue

I found a lemon yesterday. It was wrinkled and old and down the back of the food cupboard at work, but it had some bounce left in it yet. I wanted to show it to you, even now. I stood in the kitchen in our fifteen-minute break and broke the skin. I laid it out, unwinding it, squeezing what was left of its flesh, and tore it out of itself. I splayed it and scraped its insides out and smelt them – citrus gone bad. I washed the skin, and pricked it with my fingernails, trying to see – or smell, or taste – if there was anything left in the zest. I rinsed it under the tap, and kept the base intact, where the skin meets at its core (do you remember how they work?) and left it to dry out.

I got a needle and thread from my work station. The thread was black but it worked all the same. I sewed it back up together from each bit that I peeled and tore, and it looked quite good like that; it looked like a whole piece of fruit again. But Mathilde came in and laughed at me. She did that to keep the shock of seeing a lemon off her face, I could tell.

'Fruit art?' she said. I didn't think it was art. I thought what would have been art would be the way that you'd have looked at it, if you could see how I'd preserved it. That would be the art, the look on your face, if only you could see it.

On the bad days I think about calling you. Our land-lady has a phone, if you can believe it. It stays on all day,

1

as it needs so little electricity. Did you ever know that? Sometimes when the evenings are quiet I go to her house. I tell her I might make a call, but I only pick it up and listen to the dial tone. I like the tinny electric noise. I hold it fast against my ear and hear the sound even after I've replaced the receiver. I think of dialling in your number. I'm trying to forget the numbers, you see, one by one. I think I've forgotten half of them, but I'm not sure which ones.

Sometimes I look at all this rain coming down and wonder if you ever have a day where you look at the rain, too. I think about the Thames Barrier, and London's little peaks and troughs, and I feel very far away. There's little sun here, so the solar power is mostly useless. Not like in London, where it powered what it could.

If the sun has a kind of sentience, I'd like to apologise to it. If it can remember the beginning of the Earth, maybe it can remember the beginning of man and all that's come with us. I'd like to apologise for what we've done. Or maybe our apology is our suffering for it now.

I think about the beginning because it's better than now. I think about the avocados we used to have. Plenty of them. The vanilla ice cream we added to them; the sugar; the milk. My grandmother blending the mixture and handing it to us in ceramic bowls. The way she held the avocado in her hand and peeled its skin, the way it squished into the blender as we waited expectantly by the counter. I dream of Mama Boga and her basket of avocados. I dream of the Nairobi sun and the dry, kind heat. I imagine taking that avocado from Mama and holding it in my hand. A thing I couldn't dream of touching now: its scaly flesh; its weight, like a small breast of agriculture, a plump divinity.

How strange the things you end up worshipping, that you would never guess.

PART 1

Mathilde
Tender

1

After we came to London, I dreamt of my mother again. She appeared to me fully formed, her dark hair in Velcro rollers and her mouth pulled together in a small smile. I reached out to touch her, wanting to feel the blank surface of her skin, and the folds of her eyelids, and the weight of her shoulders. Then, like all dreamers, I was possessed with supernatural skills and became her. I opened my mouth and her voice came out, and I looked down and saw her perfectly oval nails on my hands. I turned to the window, with our old green shutters, looking out on Rue des Rosiers, and knew, the way you know in a dream, that I was her.

I was a young woman standing above our little cobbled street. I opened the windows, pushing hard against the wood until the glass panes flung before me, and I could smell the *myrtilles* baking in their tarts from the café downstairs.

I walked to our small kitchen, seven floors up from the street, one step from the space of the living room and two from the window, and put the kettle on the hob. I tore up mint leaves with the same dexterity she did. I brought down two blue mugs painted by hand, with small yellow flowers around the rim.

The kettle started to gurgle, and I looked again at my hands, my mother's hands, and in that same alarming state of self-awareness, I knew I had aged, considerably. The folds around my knuckles were pronounced and there were brown spots up my arms. I moved them up and down, like a bird, and felt the fullness of them move with me. I had grown old, and was afraid, and the kettle hadn't boiled yet. I rubbed my hands on a tea towel, which was spattered with old crêpe batter – but crêpes were nowhere to be found – and I sat on my bed, which now appeared in the living room. Just as I sat down, I found I couldn't lift myself from it. I made several attempts, trying desperately, but they only made me weaker until I had to lie back and look at the ceiling. It was cracked and speckled with mould and I remembered how for years we'd been meaning to re-paint it. I lay on my back and the window was still open, and the tart was still baking, and the kettle was still boiling, but I could only watch it, and sense that it was going on without me.

Possessed with that other dreamers' skill, I lifted off, and out through the window – either in body or consciousness it was hard to tell – and now the Paris of Marais cafés and trinket théières was left behind. In my aviation I saw Paris for what it became, later, after my mother died, and we left.

I saw the President's family hiding in the attic of L'Alimentari on Rue des Ecouffes. I saw the rebels, round every corner, with their guns: the towering machine-like things the *gendarmes* once had. And then, in a dreamlike whimsy, I drifted above the whole country, and saw the land for what was left of it: scorched and tropical, parched and cracked, diseased. I don't know if I, as my mother, was surprised or upset. In this floating omniscient state, my only feeling was of being very far away from it all, and only wanting to retire back to the kitchen, put the mint plant back on the windowsill, close the shutters, and drink the tea.

The French community in London would all say the same; they all had dreams of the homes they once had. And they would suggest these dreams were a sign of guilt, that we got out and others didn't. I say this, but I can't be sure. After I left with my grandmother, we moved as far away from French people as we could. I tried to forget my own language, and small French affectations. They took practice to shake.

I should've changed my name, but I couldn't rid myself of it. Because in my dreams, as my mother, I knew I was looking for small infant me. In them, I said my own name, just as she once said it, and you just can't forget a thing like that.

Years afterwards, Mathilde was still my name, and as an adult, I still dreamt of my mother. Years later, after we'd come to London, and fled Paris.

Years after we'd pulled the ladder up after us.

2

Clothes were strung on the branches of the Heath's trees. If I think of anything now, it is the smell of London soap and the sound of slapping cotton in the wind. I would wander to the farm's edges and stare in the windows of the cottages that met me there. I saw a man with a hat tucked neatly over his forehead, asleep against a trunk, leg jutted out in front of him. He was meant to be keeping an eye on his carrots and potatoes at the back of his cottage. I walked along the public meadow and watched them too. Sometimes they gave you leftovers if you looked at them a certain way. If you looked hungry and scared, but not too afraid; civilised with tidy hair but with dirt underneath your fingernails and a smudge against your face.

They were the ones with the food, so they were the ones with the power.

I worked in the sewing shop with my grandmother, which was clean work and difficult in a different sort of way, so before I made it to the cottages I would scrape my hands under the mud on its borders and brush my hair with it, raking it with my fingers.

We'd usually do as well as anyone else with the rations, but it was worth it, in the hope of a few extras. If there was another farmer's strike, it was also best to have more, in case. That day was quiet, and the people there weren't looking for any kind of distraction or charity, and were only bent double all day in their patches, pulling up cabbages. Still, I stopped and watched them, the people with their hands in the soil, who seemed to have so much authority. They've brought the country to its knees, was what Mrs P was always saying. But we were also told that this kind of industry didn't exist far outside of London. There was a reason no one left.

I spent time walking over the once-grazed grass, now manually cut, and imagined the flocks of sheep trotting over it, bleating. My grandmother said you could never quite get close enough to touch them, but you could try. I imagined pressing my fingers into the soft woolly fuzz, patting their solid backs and seeing their heads turn in curiosity towards me. The sheep were long gone when I

8

arrived, but the vegetables remained. After school, most of us worked there. I'd been spared, my grandmother told me, by sewing. She had been spared too, but only after making her way over here with the wave of immigrant labourers recruited after the blackout.

I walked there and imagined I was amongst them, my own hands blackened from soil and bent from picking, trying to stuff an extra mushroom in my pocket, instead of being pinched by a pin and bent by a needle.

I walked up to the fences and put my hands against the wire. Sometimes they looked at me like I was eyeing up the carrots and waiting for them all to go, to scale the allotment walls. But I had no way to tell them I only wanted to be where the people were, and feel a part of it. It wasn't anything more than that.

I was free to go as I liked, which meant walking right to the top of Parliament Hill and looking out at the grey city, the tallest buildings the most crumbled of all of them. I imagined going to them, sitting on top of Big Ben and listening to its loud and reverberating gong, a sound lost to us. But if Big Ben was only the name for the bell, not the clock tower, it became meaningless, I suppose, once it stopped ringing.

It wasn't worth staying for long, meandering on my own and getting too close to Kenwood House where the squatters were. I walked over to the west side of the Heath, past the neat lines of crops and through the woods, out to the village on the other side. I walked down the hill and stopped on the way to check in on the grocers. There were some apples that had turned in the heat, left to rot in their baskets on the side in the hope someone might be desperate enough to buy them. But there were beetroots; one of those valuable things that if you take care of and grow right you can have all year round. You could save

9

them for a while too, in case there was a strike to eat through. I handed the woman at the counter my coupons and clutched the soily jewels to my chest, imagining the earthy sweetness and bright pink juice I'd stare at in the sink after they'd been cut, knowing the tips of my fingers would be stained for hours. I'd put some on my lips and my grandmother would laugh at me.

I rubbed my face in an old shop window, trying to look presentable again before going back. Sometimes I'd come back from the Heath with a few vegetables and pretend the grocer had dropped a little extra in for us. This pleased her.

I walked in and bundled the beetroots on the side. My grandmother raised her eyebrows without saying anything, her mouth full of pins. She held a long trailing dress in her hands (a silver-blue fish of a dress, nothing like I'd ever touched), and she was sitting, hand-sewing each glinting button-like bead onto the material with meticulous care, one after the other. She gestured for me to sit next to her and she pulled the thread up in a deft motion, holding it taut and showing it to me, then threading it back down in a loop. I watched her putting the last glinting sequin onto the skirt long enough for the tallest of women until it fell, complete, around the floor of the workshop, reminding me of a fish I hadn't seen from a sea I hadn't seen.

It had been her life for weeks, and I'd known it. I knew how it hurt her to part with the clothing coupons she was saving for fabric before the client paid her. But these commissions were rare, delicate things, and still there was the old way about them: making the thing first and fitting it, before any questions were asked, any money exchanged. I asked her how she knew the woman would pay and she gestured to her hair. 'She smelled like lavender,' she said, 'Not hard work.'

'And what if she doesn't pay you?' I asked, fingering the slip of paper she kept pinned to the dress's neck with the client's name and telephone number on it.

She threw up her hands in dismay, 'Well, then,' she said. '*C'est la fin des haricots.*'

We laughed about it, but if the woman hadn't shown up and paid us, like we hoped she would, it might as well have been the end of the world. The end of our little world.

The note on the dress read 'Gloria', and I rolled it around my tongue and imagined her. I slipped a hand down the bodice and touched the sleek lining, my dry fingertips snagging on the fabric. I could see her, the Gloria in my head, smelling of lavender and sweet, all red cheeks and waved hair, touching me on the shoulder and laughing with me.

When Gloria arrived to collect the dress at the shop, she was better than all of that. She made an impression on me like a knife in butter. I stood behind my grandmother, afraid to look at her, tall and more beautiful than I could have imagined, and smelling like bergamot. I imagined her rows of perfumes and the choice she made each day, deciding on her scent. I pressed my hair behind my ears and looked at my shoes, the laces dragging along the floor. I touched my hair again.

My grandmother had no such shame with her, thrusting the dress at her and taking the money gladly, not even looking up from her ledger when Gloria exclaimed about the exquisite job she'd done. 'I can't believe it, it's magic. What a talent, Madame.' She held the dress up by its shoulders so that the pink tissue paper slid to the floor. I

11

wanted to pick it up and fold it, save it for another order. She stepped forward and trod on it. 'Oh, what Paris must have been like,' she said.

I looked at my grandmother, afraid, surprised she'd told Gloria where we were from.

'I mean, before,' Gloria said, fiddling with the hem.

My grandmother shrugged. 'It was marvellous, *bien sûr*,' she said, instead of the real thing.

Gloria nodded, accepting the claim. I wanted to open my mouth and gesture to the city outside, and say: I go to the hill almost every day and look at the abandoned crumbling buildings and imagine my Paris like that, but it must be worse. I try and visualise it, but I can't. But logically I know it must be worse than that, all parched and wiped out, with not even the windows left as they are left here, no glass left even in the window frames.

I wanted to ask her if she'd ever marvelled at the glass left unshattered in her windows. But instead, I said quietly, leaning forward towards her, 'You'll look beautiful in it, I'm sure.'

She laughed and folded the dress back up, laying it on the counter. 'And what a treat you are. I must thank you both, you have to come to a little dinner I'm having. How do you say it, *soirée*?' But she said it like *souris,* which could have been a mouse or a smile, but most definitely was not a party.

My grandmother humoured her. 'I don't go to parties, I'm afraid. But my Mathilde would be happy to.'

'Oh, wonderful,' Gloria said, eyes wide and bright and looking me up and down, no doubt realising her mistake. She took my grandmother's pen from her hand without asking, and wrote her address down.

I wondered whether I should ask her what to wear, or tell her I couldn't come because I had nothing suitable.

But she was gone in a blink, tissue paper left strewn and torn on the floor.

Gloria introduced me at the party as the French dress-maker's daughter. I didn't want to correct her: despite her being my grandmother and not my mother, she did mother me; and despite my being perfectly English, I was – at one point, at least on paper – French.

In that giant fairy tale house on the corner of Arkwright Road – with black window frames, crawling ivy, and a red brick wall – I sat at a dining room table with an intricate lace-edged tablecloth placed over it. I studied the place settings, I watched the white plates, I waited with my hands folded. I said very little, but it went unnoticed. All the care and attention that had been put into the arrangement of the crockery was soon dismantled, with people touching the prongs of their forks and swirling their glasses around the table cloth, watching the indentations they made in the linen like ripples forming on the surface of a pool.

It was the first time I ever tasted fish, the real thing, and I asked where they caught it from and they laughed at me. I held onto my linen napkin and fingered the hem. I pressed each individual stitch between my fingers, and touched the starchy whiteness of it. I thought, that's one thing I know. I know how to stitch this, I know how to make something, and maybe they don't. I thought that if I held the napkin it would save me from this dinner party, and transport me to some-where that made more sense, somewhere that had a cosy domesticity about it, or a place where people ate fish whenever they wanted.

I looked into my lap the whole meal, but when I held my napkin like that, that's when the man next to me turned to me and said, 'You have better taste in food no doubt. Tinned tuna is not the height of sophistication.'

He said it like we were sharing a joke, and I looked at my plate and wondered if it was tuna we were eating or if he was referring to something else. I smiled and agreed, and his assuredness gave me a feeling I hadn't had before, and it owned me.

That night, after tasting the fish, I felt an opening in time; one I hadn't known could exist. Gloria worried about me, clearing my plate, at one point stroking my hair from my shoulder. But Gloria's care did not betray an ounce of her knowing what she had done for me. I was not myself. I had an urge to recount my whole life to that man, a stranger. He tapped my cutlery to indicate which utensil to pick up, he gestured here and there, to show me where to stand and what to do.

And when a woman sat down, a stranger then, at the piano, I wanted to cry just from seeing the black and white keys, and her feet moving on pedals I didn't even know pianos had.

I marvelled at the lamps jutting from the walls and wondered how they stayed lit all throughout the evening; their flickering a constant washing over us, taking away the need for waxy candles on the table that would ruin the cloth.

He stood closer to me, to reassure me. That's why I told him, later, for no reason at all, about the recipe books that were in a box in the attic. We found them when we tidied out my mother's house in Paris and sold her things. Condensed her life into two boxes. The pages were worn and stuck together, smatterings of stains littering the pages, covering pictures of things I'd never eaten. But I didn't tell him that I felt resentful of her, so I had thrown them away.

Before I left, my grandmother told me Gloria was married to someone important, a politician whose name I should've known, but didn't. It worried me, and naïve as I was, I spent the evening looking around, waiting for Mrs P herself to enter the room. I worried what they'd think of me, into my twenties and childless – with the policy enforced so strictly those days – but I was struck by how adult that dinner was, in all of its tone and form. It was different from the parties I went to with my own friends, the ones still around. I didn't realise it, until someone presented a bottle of wine halfway through dinner (a symbol of not worrying about your condition), and no one seemed to falter, pause or worry about drinking alcohol, or for that matter, find it in any way surprising to be presented with alcohol at all, especially as it wasn't some homemade concoction, but a wine with a label and a cork yet to be popped.

I didn't touch it, of course, and felt my face radiate as it was offered to me, as though it were a test. The answer was obvious. But the young woman at the piano had a glass that was even refilled and I assumed she wasn't older than twenty-five. After that I concluded this was what wealthy people did as an escape, and their children were all safely at home. But no one hinted at my flat belly, or marital status, and no one even mentioned Mrs P's policy, except as a passing comment as a measure of her strength. I hid my own ambivalence about Mrs P that evening, and realised as I did so that my opinion of our leader was only inherited bias from my grandmother. When people spoke of 'Auntie's strong will' and the way she'd turned the country around after the blackout, I felt that I'd criticised her with my grandmother unfairly. They even joked about the slogan that had brought her into power: 'England isn't eating', in-between gorged mouthfuls. Someone held up a slimy forkful of food and declared, 'Without her putting food into all our mouths, we'd be dust. Auntie Knows Best.'

They also talked about things in front of them: the glasses and where they came from, each item's weighted history; the pieces of the continent they'd been to; the scarf they'd got from Spain, years ago; the cutlery from Prague; all of this without struggle. So much so that as the evening progressed I felt it wouldn't have mattered a great deal if I had touched the wine after all, if it would even have been noted or commented on.

Certainly not by him, sloshing his glass about and explaining to me (as though my polite refusal warranted a lesson in what I was missing) about the taste, the earth the grapes came from – not English earth, presumably – and its legs, which he showed to me with great adoration as he swirled the red liquid around, and watched it fall down the glass.

Gloria stroked my hair and patted my shoulder at intervals, in that intimate way she had. Every so often she'd exclaim, 'The dressmaker's daughter, all ours for the night. We collect people here.'

He smiled, gesturing to the woman at the piano. 'It's true,' he said, 'we do.'

But Gloria stroked everyone's arm, didn't she? I watched her, and her way with people. I listened to her conversations and observed her clinking her glass with a friend who had long hair, waved in the same way Gloria's was.

They stood in confidence, as Gloria nudged her shoulder, 'Oh, Wendy, you strumpet,' laughing heartily, her mouth at her friend's ear.

Her friend's hands pressed to her waist to quell her laughter. 'Stop it, Gloria.'

I smiled after them, not realising I was doing so, and Gloria noticed me from a few steps away. She gestured for me to come over and then wrapped a convivial arm around me, pointing to her friend, 'Wendy Darling, this is the dressmaker's daughter,' she patted her gown appreciatively. 'Mathilde, this is Wendy Darling.'

'Is that really your name?' I said, as she outstretched a hand and suppressed a laugh, eyeing Gloria.

'Second star to the right!' Gloria laughed.

Wendy Darling shook my hand vigorously. 'Gwendolyn,' she said, and made a face as if to say, isn't it awful, it happened quite by accident.

At the end of the night the same man touched my arm and I watched his fingers press my skin and lift as he removed them. He looked at me, puzzled, and I laughed at nothing in particular. I laughed because he was a severe sort of man, with white strands through his dark hair. I laughed because he was oddly formal in every gesture and word he spoke to me. I laughed because of the way he stood and listened to the woman at the piano, and watched as I watched her feet moving about the piano's feet. I laughed because he had touched me with a sense of urgency, and then stopped, as though remembering himself.

He stood at the doorway of Gloria's large house on the corner. 'Is that your bike, Matilda?' He asked me, and I nodded, pleased with the inclusive anglicisation of my name, but embarrassed by the bike's handlebars and the rusty spokes, and the way it would squeak if he stood there and watched me go.

He pulled at his shirt cuffs, standing at the doorstep, and opened his mouth to speak. He was interrupted by Gloria appearing behind him, leaning from his side to speak to me, her perfectly waved red hair falling intimately at his shoulder.

'Don't ruin your dress on that thing,' she called to me. 'Pull your skirt up. Mind your shoes.' She laughed, head held back, satisfied with her joke, and I laughed too, trying to think of something to say to impress her. But she disappeared as soon as she arrived, back into her winding hollow corridor that led to the dining room.

I turned to walk towards my bike, without saying anything. I kept my arms close to my sides, worried that sweat had stained the fabric of my pale blue dress, which I hoped to unpick later and return to the shop. The humidity of the night air clung at my legs. I waded through it. I put my small fabric bag in the basket at the front and pulled the bike towards me. It clicked and whirred as I moved it forward. He was still waiting there, by the front door, pulling at his shirt sleeves.

'Get home quickly now,' he said. 'The watch will be after you.'

I nodded to him, I smiled.

'I'll call on you soon. You're not far are you, in Hampstead?'

'No,' I said, 'just to the west.'

He waved at me, his broad hand towering over his head. 'George,' he said, 'Don't forget. It's George.'

I walked my bike down the drive, out past the stone wall. I walked it far down the length of Arkwright Road, down the sloping hill that rattled the pedals, before stopping and leaning my bike against a wall. It had been papered over with a fresh poster of a black and white graphic of Mrs P's face. I stopped and looked at her eyes,

18

lit from candlelight emanating from over the road. Auntie Knows Best, it read. I pulled my dress up, just as Gloria had said, and rode home in the dark.

3

That week my grandmother brought home a punnet of gooseberries. She rushed to our garden flat and bounced them at me and they rolled about each other. I picked one up by its tail and put it in my mouth. My face pruned pleasurably at the tartness.

She treated them with great care. She used them every way she could; their flesh for flavouring; their skin for fragrant water; she boiled them and watched them burst and split and she used their stinging sweetness carefully. One punnet lasted us days and those gooseberries were a mask for all her melancholia; as long as she had something that had been granted to her, she could hide behind its happiness.

She collected our ration coupons religiously, and was always the first in the village to queue outside the issuing office for them. She was careful never to spend them all and save plenty just in case. Every morning she laid them out on the scrubbed wooden table and counted them. She recorded what we had in her small red notebook, laid its ribbon down as a marker and then snapped it shut. She looked at the coupons like they were a crossword, and she would stare at them in great stillness until she decided what we could eat that would cost us the least amount and last us the longest. On good days she might decide we could have a chicken wing, parcelled up in greasy brown paper and thin on the bone, and only if the queue wasn't too long once word got around; on bad days, it was only vegetables and the grey bread they sold you stale to stop you eating it too quickly. The rest of the day she would hurry to her shop and on the days that I was working, I would follow her. But even when she wasn't at the shop I would come home and find her by the fireplace, leaning over a piece of stitching, pins in her mouth, and pausing to count the logs we had left, or blowing on the fire when it threatened to go out.

If I think of her now, I remember her perfectly like that: quiet and contemplative and always thinking of three things at once, three things to make sure she hadn't dropped one small thing that would affect us, that would mean we would do without. Even in the summer, with the windows blown open and the smell of plant life throughout the village, and the abundance of crops, she would still sit and stitch and count and make sure. I was sure it was because she had a memory of how things fall apart, in the way that I didn't.

That was a good day, shortly after Gloria's dinner party, when she came home with gooseberries. They had a small crop of them come in to the grocers, and no one knew where they came from but no one asked. She said she hadn't seen them for months, years maybe, and she held one up above her head between her fingers as though it was the sun, and she was the small planet below.

'They didn't even cost us that much,' she said, laying out our coupons again and counting them. 'We'll be all right.'

She manically prepared them, splitting them up, deconstructing them, until they looked nothing like food. She sang the whole time, sleeves rolled up and hair pulled from her face, apron tied at her waist (for no reason in particular, other than as a way to feel normal, I imagine, to feel how she used to feel when she had baking ingredients that would spatter about her).

I watched her as I flicked through the orders we had at the shop, and went through her notebooks and looked at the inventory. Cash was always tight but she ran a meticulous and tidy shop in every sense. She knew how to make things work and I admired her greatly for it. And she was reliable; people always chose to come to her, for a knitted jumper in winter or a new house dress, because she knew how to make their clothing coupons go as far as they could.

She finished preparing the gooseberries and wiped her clean hands on her apron. She laid down her knife and put a hand up to her hair. 'I was thinking the other day of crumpets,' she said, without turning around.

I frowned. I couldn't remember them. It was like a test I was constantly failing. 'Crumpets.' I said, with little intonation. I didn't want her to know I didn't know what she meant.

'They were lovely toasted.' She turned to look at me. Now the work with the gooseberries was over her normal contemplative look returned. She moved towards me conspiratorially, bending down to my chair, as though she'd just told me a secret, and then she whispered, 'We had them with butter and jam, when we first got here. Do you remember?'

'Both?' I couldn't imagine it.

She pulled a chair beside me and sat down. She picked up the notebooks I was going through. She looked toward the open windows. I saw sweat forming on her upper lip and around her temples. We had whitewashed the walls

21

and cleared the heavy furniture, taken up the carpets. But in summer it was never enough, we were never prepared for it.

'Margot missed them, of course, such a trivial English thing. But I imagine asking her about them. Margot, these strange little English muffin things, they taste good! But I'm sure she would've laughed at me and asked why I was suddenly besotted with British pastries.'

She did this often. She remembered my mother. She always called her Margot, never 'your mother', an impersonal touch. But it made sense to her, and was a way to remember her, just as she had been. She seemed to be deep under water when she talked like that.

She never talked about the day we left, or what we left behind. She never probed about my aversion to speaking the language, but she went on with it all the same.

'You met someone nice at Gloria's, didn't you?'

'I don't know, grandmother.' I put my hand on hers and looked with her out the window.

'There's nothing wrong with it. Your friends have all done it, better that way, isn't it?'

'I still have a few years,' I said, and removed my hand. I felt angry all of a sudden, of the ease with which she talked about my mother, and my own frivolity.

'Not long when you think about it. And someone like that, you'd be set for life.'

I imagined one of her old jellied pies; the fat that was moulded and cooled and set like that as a barrier so that no meat would leak out from the pastry. Constrained and suffocated and stuck. I tried to taste the fat, that wobbly, shiny, glutinous texture, but I couldn't imagine it.

'Margot and I had a little money once. We had things you wouldn't dream of. I would want that for you, one day. I would want that.' But she said it as though she believed its opposite.

22

We both looked out the window as though we were watching a play, and I don't know what we were waiting to appear at its ledge, with only one other house on the street occupied. But we did that frequently, worried about our empty street. My grandmother stood up and went towards the pane, leaning above the sink. She pressed her nails into the white chipped sill, its blackened edges rotting in the frame. I wanted to prise her fingers from it and move them away.

'Is everything all right?' I said.

'Of course,' she said, but she didn't move her fingers from the sill. 'I just wondered if the neighbours would be out today.'

There were groups of people from the village, scattered about. They marched past our house every so often, on watch. They pushed hand-written notes through the letterbox about supporting Mrs P and standing firm against the farmers' strikes and how they were holding the country to ransom. About how Mrs P had let the country flourish and the nation be fed, how beyond our borders there was nothing, not even within the countries that were once part of our collective Kingdom. They wrote about the dangers of the abandoned buildings that were filled with squatters, most recently Kenwood House. But they only wrote about them stealing our water and scant electricity, hacking the grid. They never mentioned a potential for violence. That threat they internalised.

Of course, part of the watch was to make sure everyone in the village was doing things just as they should.

She started scrubbing the counter. She wiped it furiously, over and over, and I spoke her name but she didn't stop. She wiped her finger against the surface, tasted it. I came and stood beside her.

'Touch it,' she said, 'Can you taste the gooseberries? Can you smell them?'

Of course I could, because it was so foreign. I thought that smell had got into everything. I smelt it for days afterwards, in my bed. I smell it now, still; everywhere and in everything.

I shook my head. I hugged her and soaked up her smell, of parsley she'd planted in the garden. She hoped we'd have enough water that summer that it would survive.

As I pulled away she sniffed again, smelling me for tartness. 'It makes me anxious, sometimes,' she said. 'The people that walk past the house. I always feel like they're looking for something.'

She looked at the scraps of fruit, now in the bin. I knew she was thinking, as she always did, of that day. Years after we'd come to London, and she had the shop. They came straight through our front door, with no warning, into the kitchen. They did it to everyone on our street. They went through everything. Every scrap of food we couldn't account for with our coupons was noted. Everything was taken away; our cards, too. We stood in line for days to be re-issued them, along with everyone else. We were warned about the black market. We were warned about the rules. We could've starved. One more week and we would have.

She bought those gooseberries from the grocer's shop. Little balls of joy. But it was something different, and so it made everyone afraid, having to account for something like that. When the farmers were protesting not being paid fairly for produce, when it was collected by the government to be redistributed, the risk of looking like you'd bought something on the black market was not insignificant.

'It's just different now,' she said, 'You just can't trust

anyone like you used to.' She turned on the tap to wash her hands and the pipes croaked and gurgled and a dribble of water escaped its mouth, then stopped. 'That's it for today, then,' she said, and hit her hand against the tap's neck until another dribble escaped. '*Merde.*'

'It's okay, we've saved enough until tomorrow,' I tried to take the worry out of her, I was always doing that. But I was only a child during the blackout, I couldn't remember it the way she could. She always thought when the water stopped, when the lights turned out, none of it would ever come back on. I didn't believe in that possibility, not then.

'What are you making?' I said.

'*Putain,*' she said, as though I were an irritant, and had reminded her. 'It will have to do without sugar.' She had a small jar of cream she'd managed to buy that day and she sniffed at it. She moved it towards me so I could check it hadn't curdled too.

'Gooseberry fool,' she said.

4

George arrived at my door uninvited. He was dressed smartly in a synthetic jumper that looked knitted by a machine. New, and far too warm for this weather. His shoes were in such good order they looked like they would squeak and press upon his toes. He came with a newspaper under his arm, and sure enough Mrs P's face loomed out of it.

I didn't ask how he got my address or had known my grandmother would be at her shop, but I was sure he'd accounted for it.

I led him into the kitchen and started to clear things from the table. I looked around, desperately, to try and see the house how he would see it, for the first time. It was poky and worn, but it was clean, at least, and my grandmother kept things in the best condition she could.

'Did you see in the paper there's been another outbreak of Dengue?' he said.

'Where?' The north was closed-off and cooler, but I knew nothing of the continent. We'd stopped buying newspapers three years before.

'Spain, what's left of it. They think there'll be another migration to the north.'

'There's nowhere else to go.' Since the blackout, Scandinavia's borders were firmly secured, firmer even than ours.

He looked out the back window, past the chipped gouges of paint on the sill, through the murky glass, out to the parched garden. He looked back at me, at my jeans, my hands in the pockets. I moved my hands up and rubbed them together. I didn't know what he was thinking of. But he made a comment about my pathetic vegetable patch, and how it would dry out to death in this weather. I ignored it because I had to believe I'd be able to grow something.

'It's quiet round here,' he said.

'Same as anywhere.'

I thought of the people in Spain. The sticky air, the arid earth that crunched. I laid awake at night, trying to imagine what might be worse. Dying down there in the heat, the tropical weather torturing you, until the only thing that isn't in drought is the moisture in your own body. Then that leaving you, too.

I thought of what got people here. Trees splitting onto your bicycle, the hot walls beating at you, not built for this weather. Getting E.coli from old rations, things that have been left to spoil. Or starving. That happened to people who weren't alone, who gave all they had to their families, who didn't account for the strikes. Who had children. They tried to account for that, they tried to incentivise you. But if there wasn't enough food, it didn't count for anything.

I thought about it logically, what was worse, and sometimes wrote it down.

That's when he placed something on the work surface. I didn't know what it was. It was an egg shape, something textured and wrinkled. I thought it was a pear.

'I've brought you something,' he said. And I looked at it. 'A fruit?'

He looked at it, he didn't know. 'Or a vegetable?' he said, as though he was asking the thing itself. That's when I knew it really meant something. 'It's an avocado. Have you heard of it?'

I thought about pretending I had, so that he might think I was older than I was, that he might think something good about me. 'No,' I said. 'Have you?'

He laughed, the way he did when he thought I'd just missed the mark. 'I brought it to you didn't I? You can mash it up and cut it open and...'

I didn't think he knew what it was. We both looked at it. I marvelled that he could get hold of things. 'You shouldn't have brought a thing like that,' I said, 'It's not safe, with the watch.'

He laughed. 'They won't come here. I'll make sure of it.' He shrugged his shoulders.

27

'Friends in high places?' I said, as a joke, but I was frightened.

'When you're a Minister you know what's going on, you have some control.'

'You work with Mrs P?' I said. I didn't ask, Minister for what.

He smiled. 'Don't we all?'

I looked at the thread of his jumper and wanted to touch its softness. But I thought it would be unbearably warm in this summer humidity. The thought of it clinging to his arms like that disturbed me. But its neatness gave me the impression he might know the answer to something. He ran his hands through his hair and I watched the grey strands and I watched the dark ones. I watched his fingertips.

He moved closer to me and placed his hand next to mine on the counter. That's the first time we touched, or almost touched, but it mattered all the same. Getting close was just as monumental as the thing itself.

'You're a small bird,' he said, or at least that's what I thought he said, but he murmured it so close to me and I didn't want to ask him to repeat it. That sounds right, though, he would've said that.

'I'm going to help you,' he said, and I didn't know what that meant either. All I knew is that there was a man in my kitchen who was older than me and knew something about the world I didn't. With everything the way it was, it mattered.

'My neighbour died last week,' he said, his hand next to mine.

'Oh, I'm sorry.'

'She used to keep old packets of sugar in drawers around her house. She used to collect them from the old cafés.' His hand moved closer, but didn't touch mine. 'She talked about streetlights, and tiny computers. She said her head was filled with noise.' He laughed, but I think even then I could tell the laugh wasn't sincere. He would have given a lot to have a computer. 'It was peaceful, anyway. She lived a good long while.'

I nodded, wanting to ask what a good long while was, wanting to compare it to my mother's good long while. I tried to imagine his neighbour's face, but couldn't. I thought about where the sugar was now.

He reached into his coat pocket and took out some paper. At first I thought it might be a newspaper clipping, or a picture, and I thought I'd like to see what she looked like. But then he unfolded it and placed it alongside the avocado on the counter. He left it there, arching up at its long indented folds. I pressed it down with my hand.

'You didn't,' I said.

'I want you to have it.'

'But it's fraud.'

'It's not fraud when you have nothing.'

'Debatable.'

That's when his hand did grasp mine, that first time. I wondered why he'd want to touch my hand, and was it in the same way I wanted to touch his.

'There's no point in ethics now. Don't even think of it. Take it.' He raised his voice and stepped towards me. He squeezed my hand, a little too tight. 'You must take it.' He released his hand to place it on my shoulder.

'I can't take it,' I said. 'I feel too bad about it.'

But I didn't, because if I died, I'd want someone to have my ration card. I'd want everyone to have what they wanted. My house, my muddy garden, my plant pots, my kitchen tiles, my eyes, my skin. I'd want them to take it all and use it and put it back into the earth where it

29

belongs. I'd want my body to be fertiliser to grow trees and carrots. I'd do anything.

I didn't feel bad, but I was afraid. 'You know the old saying? Food first, then morals,' he said. He looked at me. 'I'll keep it. If you ever need it, I'll have it.' He nodded towards the garden.

'Thank you,' I said. But I was worried that this gesture was a final thing, and an indication he wouldn't return.

'Of course,' he said, 'I worry about you and your vegetable patch. There but for the grace of God.'

I knew he meant he had more than me, but he didn't owe me anything. I couldn't think of anything to say, wanting to ask if he'd be back, fearing that if I did it would prompt him to never return. Better not to know. So instead I found myself murmuring under my breath the rest of the phrase. He looked at me quizzically as I said, 'Go I.'

I bit into the avocado, and almost immediately spat the whole thing back out. The skin was leathery but the inside moist and slippery. It was sinister. The remnants in the sink stared back at me. The green was sickly; a pale, luminous green, not like a courgette. The flesh was thick and doughy, but not as doughy as a banana: smoother, sleeker, disconcerting.

The mound of the seed rose up at me from the half-cut portion on the chopping board. A large conker of a thing. I tried to prise it out, smushing the flesh surrounding it as I did so, laying perfectly against its round casing. It was just as I remembered kiwis, but not acidic, not transparent, no bite.

This was no fruit. I scraped out what I could from the shells, but didn't eat it in childish delight. I tried

30

to think if I had them once, at dinner maybe. I could place some foods from my young childhood. Odd constructed artificial things, but not this. Perhaps they were early to go. People talked about them, I knew that much; but trying to place them in any context of a meal was impossible. I tried to remember the years of panic, when things started to disappear. Running around supermarkets, my mother's hand clutched round mine, her skin turning white. But I couldn't distinguish the before from the after, not all of it. We were lucky to make it as far as we did, and I was luckier even than my mother. The childhood panic made it hard to remember what was missing now and what was a fantasy. What never existed at all. What I only used to placate myself in dreams.

I brought a small piece to my lips and slowly chewed. It disintegrated easily in my mouth, creamy and mealy. I started to whisk the flesh in a bowl and it became a soft, malleable, thick sauce. I dropped the avocado shells in the food bin. They lay there, curved up on themselves, conspicuous. I took them out and cut them up into mulch with my knife and placed them back. The waste would be collected the next day. I ate the bowl of avocado in one go, even though I was disturbed by the taste of something different. I spent the rest of the day walking around the village, worried I had something green in my teeth. I looked at people and wondered if they could tell. I wanted to ask them if they'd ever had the magical dragon eggs, if they'd felt the pickled, wrinkled, puckered, plummy weight of it in their hands. Or if they'd never even seen one. I imagined holding it out to each person I walked past, and them dismissing it, confused, not knowing what it was.

31

5

George came back, after the avocado. He called on the telephone and said he was glad I answered, that he'd caught me. I didn't tell him I'd been looking out the window at the wilting plants and dehydrated earth and had been waiting for a phone call, too afraid to leave the house in case I'd miss it. I didn't tell him I had spent the afternoon staring at each room when I should have been stitching and cleaning. Counting the boxes of matches and candles and laying them out on the table, only to return them, in the same order. I just said, Yes, and let the silence hang there. He checked my grandmother was busy for the evening, as she routinely was, and told me he was coming to visit.

'I have something for you,' he said. And I laughed, and asked if it was another avocado, and hoped it wasn't, thinking of its wrinkled skin.

'Something else,' he said, 'You'll have to wait and see.'

He brought it round that same evening. It was a box, and it was heavy, I could tell as soon as I opened the door because his leg was pulled up under it, balancing its weight. I helped him carry it to the kitchen table and he smiled at me.

'I hope you know a good recipe,' he said. But I didn't know any.

I opened the top of the box and peered inside. It looked like apples, I looked at him, I said, apples, but he kept smiling and I knew it was something different. Even apples in summer was strange. I touched them and they were furry, they made the skin on the tips of my fingers feel different.

'Peaches,' he said, and I knew that was a term of endearment. Also perhaps a fruit, but not here, not in this country. He took one from the box and handed it to me. I pressed it in-between my fingers and it was soft, not like an apple.

'Should I peel it?' I said, and felt stupid all the same, not knowing how to eat things I hadn't had before.

'No, just bite it,' he said, looking at me expectantly, and I did, too hard against the softness and my teeth crashed together and the skin burst. The juice dripped all over my hand. I only laughed, not out of embarrassment but out of joy because it was so different and sweet. He didn't eat one right away, and I assumed that was because he had his fill when he wanted.

'They're overripe,' he said, 'so we need to do something with them.'

'Eat them?'

'We can't eat them all. We need a recipe for a peach crumble.'

My grandmother had kept one book, the rest I threw away, boxes and boxes of them. I found the cookery books when I cleared out my mother's house. I'd looked through them and felt desperately sad for all the things that she'd known I wouldn't be able to make and had never tried. My grandmother kept one, though, and it was the most worn and spattered. I found it when we unpacked, those first few days in London. It was just a recipe book for cakes, and I think she kept it in hope that if she ever got the right amount of sugar, the right amount of flour, she might be able to make something.

He gestured inside the box, and lifted a few peaches out, and I saw, hidden underneath, a bag of sugar. 'In case you didn't have any,' he said.

He was right, and I looked at it, full and straining and tried to remember the last time I'd seen a bag of sugar like that.

I got the book quite easily from a shelf in the kitchen, and found a recipe for apple crumble, which we used, and tried to amend for peaches. I washed them, holding two or three in my hands at a time, getting the measure of them. I watched them, sitting in my palm and askew on my fingers. I counted them, in my head: one, two, three, and then tried to count the shape of it, but it didn't have a number.

It struck me with food – especially the type that came straight from the earth and that I'd never held before – that everything had a name, and I didn't always know it. That someone, somewhere, would say the word 'peach' and know exactly what a peach was, and it would conjure up the taste and texture of the thing in their mind, even though to me the name peach was just its name and wasn't the thing itself. Maybe to him, peach was the thing itself.

I used to wonder how long it would take for the reference to the thing to actually become the thing. I knew even then that I'd never have enough time to taste everything and put names to them, and learn the names, and know the things themselves as well. It was clear to me, holding the peaches I'd never held in my hands before, that they were abstract things and might remain so. It didn't stop me from cutting them softly, gently, and watching them roll and slop on my chopping board cleared of vegetables. I sometimes squeezed them but mostly just plopped them into the pan and poured all the grains of sugar over them, a thing I did know well, after all.

He sat on the kitchen stool and watched me the entire time. Never offering to help (I noted), but in his watchful gaze a kind of consideration that he must have thought was helpful or at least a contribution towards this act of putting things together in a way I'd never done before. By the time I'd scraped together enough floury and fat crumble for the top, I could smell the sweet syrup the peaches made on their own, and I thought I would recognise the smell of peaches again, if I ever had the fortune to smell them.

He smiled at me as he watched my fascination over the way the syrup bubbled, the way the mixture poured into a baking pan, just like apples, only more glutinous. I thought his smile was endearment, and he was fascinated with me the way I was fascinated with peaches.

I didn't think of why. I didn't think of peaches as a form of something more intricate and delicate and powerful; but I couldn't have known it then.

I sat next to the oven the entire time the crumble baked, so afraid it would burn, or break. I consulted the recipe for apples several times, but it had its limitations, and so did he. He didn't know, and didn't bother to pretend to, and so just watched me watching the pudding, as I held the tea towel firmly between my hands, ready at any moment to retrieve it from the belly of the clanking-iron wood-burning oven. We sweated in the kitchen. All the doors and windows were open, but the smell it conjured made up for the heat.

It was another world.

It was summer, so it didn't get dark until much later. But when it did, just as the crumble was ready to come out, he feigned surprise that there were no electric lights to be turned on. 'All the sockets are there,' he said, and I pretended not to have ever noticed. I pretended I didn't always look at the hanging parts where lightbulbs used to be, and the switches and plugs that used to contain something. He said he could help wire some things up, so I could benefit from that hour of electricity people had as part of Mrs P's fair distribution policy. I didn't know how to tell him, yes you're entitled to that hour, but only if you can afford it. I thought of people like him who got that hour, and wondered what they did with it. If they got it every day, every evening, did they sit and luxuriate under its warmth? Or did they take it for granted, and not think about the light that arrived in the evenings?

I lit the candles and placed them on the table between us. I laid the pan on a tea towel and cut into it, the peachy flesh oozing from its coarse topping. He looked hungrily at it, and that was the first time I saw him want something as much as I did. 'Fascinating,' he said, as I slopped it out onto a dinner plate for him. This would have been an underwhelming exclamation were it not for the look on his face.

'I hope it's okay,' I said, 'I didn't know.' I gestured towards the pan and back to the book. He raised his fork and took a bite and said, matter-of-factly, 'I think you did.' I wasn't sure if it was a compliment or an accusation, but I was too happy to be looking at the mess of peaches to take it into account.

I dug into the crumble in front of me. My mouth soared as I tasted its sweetness, dense and sickly. The peach I held in my hands became the sweetness in my mouth. If my tongue and fingertips were connected it was because of peaches, if my body knew each part of itself and recognised another part, it was because of peaches. If I were a human; a sentient, knowing being, that was one thing, not several, I knew it because of peaches.

I imagined my mother sitting down to her dinner table and eating a tart – apple at least – and knowing myself, finally, what she'd known throughout my entire childhood, and through to the end of her life. It connected me to her, one last time. I missed her, and must have realised then, it was not because she talked about eating peaches, but because she used to say when she was happy, *j'ai la pêche,* I'm peachy, chirpy, I feel great! Maybe to her, peaches was not just a term for joyfulness but also the name was the thing, and when she said she felt peachy, she recollected this fruit in her mind. It made me realise again she was a dearly happy woman.

'Are you okay?' he asked, and I realised my face was a prism of worry. But really it was ecstasy, and the only way it could register upon me.

I smiled. 'Thank you for bringing them to me. They're so wonderful.'

'Good,' he smiled back. 'I thought it might be good. Even in the dark.'

My mind wandered back to him, and wondering what he was doing with me. And the delight of the crumble only made it worse, this not knowing. 'I'm glad I found a recipe,' I said.

'I knew you would. Was it your mother's?'

'Yes.'

'These recipe books are always second generation now, not much going about. You've never used it,' he gathered, 'but you kept it.'

'Doesn't everyone?'

'I suppose so. But maybe they don't talk about it.'

I wanted him to talk about it. I wanted to tell him about that day when she died and I sat with my grandmother in her living room, leafing through all the recipe books and the things she loved, and decided then and there, to

37

get rid of everything that couldn't be used. Except that one book my grandmother kept – did she keep it? Or did I retrieve it later, from the box that was going to be thrown away, my guilt keeping me from pragmatism? I didn't tell him about it, not then. 'They're not much use to most people I suppose, books about cakes. But they're nice to look at.'

'I'm glad I gave you a reason to use it.' He looked at the crumble, and he was pleased.

'I haven't eaten like this for years,' I said, 'Or maybe, ever? I can't remember what it was like when I was a child, before the blackout.' I raised my hand to my forehead as though my fingertips might be able to draw it out. 'I sometimes think my mother's stories are wound up in my own memories. So I can't remember what I did eat, and what she just told me about.'

He smiled. 'If you tell me the thing, I might be able to tell you if it was around.' He looked down, he second guessed himself, 'Or maybe that's a stupid game. What am I? Ten years older than you? I can't remember for you.'

I nodded. But I liked this idea that he might be able to retrieve my own memories for me. That he could tell me what chocolate from purple foil tasted like, or crab meat from its shell. Any shellfish at all, before the water got too warm. Could he tell me what coral looked like? What a reef is and the fish that swam there? Before everything bleached white and died, before the earth boiled itself up. Could he tell me about snowy winters or mild summers, could he remember for me earth that wasn't flooded, people safe in their homes? Had he tasted rice from the Vietnam rice bowl? Or seen electricity burn all day? Had he seen a lift go up and down and those endless escalator stairs and cars stuck in traffic? Or planes, did they used to get stuck in traffic? Could he retrieve for me the taste of caramel, and the sight of it dripping down my mother's chin, and her expression and laugh as she told me she once saw the Pacific Ocean.

'Milka,' I said. 'With the caramel. Milka chocolate.'

'Yes,' he smiled, 'We had Milka here. It's plausible.'

So I did see the caramel then, once, the kind that came already packaged wedged in a chocolate bar. I did see it, and it wasn't just her telling me about it.

He looked at me questioningly. 'You're curious,' he said, 'I like that. Most people don't ask so many questions. I like that about you.' I knew he liked me, then. Not just pity. He grinned when I didn't say anything and he picked up his fork awkwardly. I thought he was thinking about the peaches. 'What do you like about me?'

I felt my throat close up and words disappear from my mind like I'd never had a thought. He must've assumed there wasn't one thing I liked about him. But I liked that he gave me things, I liked that he treated me like I was important, I liked that he treated me any way at all, I liked the shape of his top lip and the freckle on his cheek. I wanted to possess it.

'I don't know,' I said. 'You're kind.'

'Kindness is important.'

He moved his chair over to me, he took my hands.

'Have you ever seen a frog?' I said. I didn't know if he expected me to keep talking. 'I saw one in a story book once, I heard they were gone now.'

'I've never seen a frog.'

'Do you know the noise they made? Have you ever heard it on tape?'

'I've heard it.'

'What a noise.' I was babbling, and his hands clasped mine, firmly, and his eyes were focused on mine, fixed, like he had decided something. I'd decided, too.

'If I could bring you a frog, I would. I'm afraid it might be too late for them though.'

It was too late for everything. 'Yes. You would?'

He kissed me on the cheek, my forehead, my eyebrow, my chin. 'I would.'

My lips parted but I didn't kiss him back.

'I'd bring you whatever you wanted.' He murmured. He kissed my ear, my hair, my neck. 'I'd bring you Milka. I'd bring you a cool icehouse to live in and a floating city above the world. I'd bring you the world itself.'

I did kiss him back then, and as I did so I imagined the world he'd give me, from hundreds of years ago full of colours and textures I'd never seen. I imagined him packaging it up like a box of peaches and my surprise as I opened it. There's my mother's house, I'd say, and there are her lightbulbs and sockets, there's her television box and her video player and her computer. There's a frog, jumping high, making that glottal noise. And there we are sitting on green lush grass in the summer, a cool breeze about our heads.

He gave me that, from the first kiss. He retrieved a memory of something I never saw, something I never knew. That's a kind of world, isn't it?

The first world he gave me was the kindest.

PART 2

Jaminder
Churchgoing

1
_____

London made me hard like the rind of an old grapefruit. In this new country, I'm glad of it. The rind protects me from this life, able to keep the soft pickled flesh of my memories safe underneath. It makes it harder to unpeel and get at them whenever I like.

It's hard to tell if there are more grapefruits left in the world than people. I don't suppose we'll ever know, and I don't suppose it matters. I haven't seen a grapefruit in a long time, but I know that it exists, somewhere, in a different climate. Even if that climate is just in someone's mind.

The argument could also be made that London made me soft. That I was insulated, coddled, that I had access to whatever I wanted. I know you'd make this assessment. I'd like to tell you that you are wrong. We may have had more than some people, but it didn't stand up to much. Isolation can't be measured by the amount of people or the amount of parties. The abundance of food or warmth, or the abundance of physical freedom. Isolation is a state of mind.

The further north we came the less we had. When we arrived there was oatmeal. They made it into porridge for us and we ate the slop like pigs at the trough. We kept going. The rain fell. The vegetables grew rotten and puffy, cabbages were small and slimy. We crossed over into Scotland, a new country. I remember the point where it happened, because we were crossing over a road (it used to be a path for cars, because it was wide and blank and surrounded by barriers), and there was a sign that told us. 'We've done it,' Mathilde said to me. 'We made it.'

'In a sense,' I said.

We kept walking, and the wet of the ground swallowed our shoes. We passed over people, and bodies, and I held my knife close to me.

We arrived here, where the factories are, and Mathilde taught me on the way how to use a needle. I even sewed her wounds when I needed to.

Now there is only oatmeal. Potatoes too, and some vegetables, but it depends on the crop. We split them in half before we eat them, we check. But now oatmeal grants me mercy. It is mundane, but it is also the thin veil between us being here and us not. I pray for oatmeal and I am overcome by it. I bless it, with a prayer I've made up in my head, to no being I know of, that knows of me.

Mathilde comes home to me, she tells me, 'I saw a cat today, I haven't seen one in years.'

I shake her by the shoulders, her head bowed. 'Tell me where it went, where did it go?'

She doesn't want to tell me. She doesn't say anything, she's trying not to cry.

'Tell me,' I say, over and over, until there are finger marks indented on her shoulder. I can feel them forming. I relent.

'Don't, Jaminder,' she says, all the same, as though it will make a difference.

I leave the house with my knife.

Mrs Campbell tells us every day that work is the best antidote to sadness. She announces it, as we collect our bowl food and sit down at the benches on our lunch breaks. She says it as though we have been telling her how

44

sad we are, but I think she might be projecting. I think she's said it so many times it doesn't mean anything to her anymore. I don't think she even registers it. It means something to me.

The first stitch Mathilde taught me was the basic running stitch. She reached into her rucksack and pulled out a small fabric box covered with buttons, and inside were different sized needles, different coloured threads. She passed the end of a piece of black thread between her lips and looked at its tip with one eye closed before she slipped it through the eye, threaded it through the needle, and began.

This little dexterous movement made me feel comforted. For once I felt that she was the one who knew what she was doing, that she could make the decisions. She had blind faith in the power of a stitch. After working on Mrs Campbell's pedal-powered sewing machines these last weeks, I do too.

London made me hard because I had to shield my inner life from all those parties. All those people. I had to shield myself from you. I had to tell myself lies, until they became true. It was only when we arrived here, in this small factory town so far north from where we came, that I started to unpick them. I realised what I knew, and what I told myself I didn't. It is only here that I can see in plain sight all the awful things we left behind. After all these years, it is only here I can finally see it.

London made me soft because I got used to things. Fullness. Satiation. I tell Mathilde the price we've paid for a little freedom is a little hunger. But I'm not sure these things balance each other out. They can't be measured, so I can't persuade her. I hide my hunger from her by tapping my fingernails on the hardcover of the book we read at night, and the work surface on which our sewing machines sit. She hides her hunger from me by sewing, stitch after stitch. She brings her work home with her. At night, after dinner, she mends bits and pieces.

Ruby, our new companion at work, tells us that hunger is a state of mind. Because her children (two boys, both alive) have never known any different, they don't complain. They don't cry about food. The implication there is that we do.

I think about our boy, and how little he complains. I place my hand on his head and wonder, in this washout, how far he'll get.

I rub my stomach after lunch, when Mrs Campbell rings her bell and tells us it's time to get back to work. I try and deduce if I'm still hungry, or if it's just a memory. I unfold the pieces of fabric at my work station and look across at Mathilde. I want to lean over to her, and laugh, and say, do you remember what cheese tastes like? Do you remember melted cheese? I'd laugh because it would be a small joke; because she's French, and surely once in her life her blood was made up of *raclette*. But I've learnt she doesn't appreciate these jokes and would rather not talk about the things we remember, or the things we don't have.

I wish for cigarettes. I wish for the bitter taste of tobacco and the sickening nicotine that would wash away my appetite. I try and forget cheese. I try and forget hunger. I'm not dying, I tell myself. I won't die without cheese. But some days, as trivial and insignificant as it sounds compared with everything else, it does feel that way. On those days I make sure I walk about the streets of the town before it gets dark, and look in the windows, and remind myself how lucky we are. I try, I promise, to remind myself.

I'm not promising anything to you, I hope you

understand. I don't feel I owe you that. In a sense, it's the opposite: I promise it to all those women. It's them I owe it to.

Perhaps the gap that cheese leaves is the gap that God might fall into. Hunger gives you some false association with something godly, because there's nothing else to plug that hole. Hunger is a form of meditation, a form of concentration. That could just be what I tell myself when I think of that hunk of British cheddar, or straining paneer with my grandmother, or whatever else I might miss. It could just be what I tell myself because of all those years in that Catholic school on the Euston Road. Most of us were brown and few of us were Catholic, but it still had the power to get under your skin. I still think of being thirteen and being laughed at in English class for not shaving my legs, the hair thick and dark, hiding them under the folding table. I still remember the things the Sisters said to us, even though I never believed them. It started a narrative in my head I don't think I ever forgot.

The truth is, we were once Gods. We once had the power to eat as we liked, whenever we wanted (and what was more difficult, and sought after, was a kind of restraint). We engineered our entire lives, the worlds we lived in. We made them warm, we made them cool. I remember the feeling so vividly of kulfi, the ice cream my grandmother made. I would arrive home and she'd gesture extravagantly to the freezer, giddy with her surprise for me. She spent the afternoon boiling the cream and condensed milk, adding the cardamom and spices, sprinkling on almonds and pistachios and freezing them in moulds, until they became the thing that I adored.

What was that other than godly? There is nothing more holy than the power to make something from its individual parts, and give it to someone in a gesture of love.

47

In the absence of our own godly power, it's easier to think that you might be able to hear the voice of the divine.

I hear your voice too, but that is nothing like God.

Sometimes, as I walk about this small town, with its dwindling population, reliant entirely on the trade Mrs Campbell has set up, I say the words, out loud. I don't say it to God, or even to you, but just to myself, just so I can hear it. I'll say it, in the gloomy light, over and over again. And as I say it, I'll imagine the things I'm saying are real, and that imagining is a small satiation. So that when I return home, to my Mathilde, I won't have to say it to her. I won't have to make it real for her.

Cheese, I'll say, chicken curry, cheese toasties with leeks, creamy dhal. Squeaky aubergines and blueberries. Beef, bone marrow, ghee. Kulfi. Creamy kulfi. Saintly kulfi.

It's a way to stay sane, so as not to forget. It's a plea, but the hopeful kind. I feast on it.

Mathilde asks me what I've been doing and I say I was praying.

I don't know if this answer upsets her more than the truth.

2

_____

I walk along the path by the river to get to the factory. I wear my overalls and cover my head with my jacket.

The rain never ceases up here, and carries with it a kind of mysticism that it never had in London. That might be attributing too much romanticism to it. It is unending, relentless. It gives life to us, and feeds us, but it washes as much away.

The mist rises from the river and meets the rain in a fog. I'm drowned in it. I hold my fingers out and the rain pats them. I slip them back into my pockets. It's getting colder. My boots are sucked into the path, encased in mud. But the walk is comforting. This place shows no signs of ever having housed cars or lights or restaurants with terraces and gas ovens. It shows no sign of anything. Nothing echoes here, nothing speaks of a lost time. I find it matters less and less.

As I walk along, I imagine my life as a palimpsest of before. I think of all the ways Mathilde and I talk to each other, with our words and our hands, and how artificial they are. They speak only of a memory. I imagine this is why Mathilde stopped speaking French, as a way to let go of the things that no longer exist. Even the way I look is an echo, and there is not much left of it here. There is no other marker to make me different.

We've been equalised. We all live the same lives. We all have nothing.

There's a lump on the side of the road, further ahead. I will walk past it. I look at my boots. I tread firmly. I squeeze my hands in my pockets, checking their numbness. I could circle back, and go around. But this is the quickest way. It might be nothing. I wish for Mathilde to be next to me, but I know she manages to walk this path alone, too. It looks like some abandoned heap, a piece of tarp. Less likely is that it's something. Some clothes. A package.

I tell Mathilde there's nothing to be scared of all the

way up here. Apart from the obvious: the weather and the food and the people we don't know. I said it to her several times when we first arrived, put our rucksacks down at the nearest place, dried our hair on the towels they gave us. They looked at our clothes and called us rich kids from the big smoke. A name that stuck even after all that smoke went. Even though London isn't that well thought of up here, they couldn't fathom why we left, not with the power down there, and Mrs P's distribution of energy. We all bundled into bed that first night, while we decided what to do, and I said it, over and over again: you don't have to be afraid, you don't have to be afraid. I think I was afraid, and I was trying to convince myself, but I was convincing her. I look after her.

What I didn't say was, you don't have to be afraid of him. Even if that's what I meant.

I repeat it to myself like a mantra. Even as I repeat it, I think of the words I choose to use. I think of the way we have chosen them to mean something, and that is the way we identify with each other now. Every word we speak in our little London way has little to do with now. They are the only markers we have that show we once existed in a different form, in a different place. That we were once different people.

Sometimes I look at Mathilde, and think, would I recognise her if I hadn't travelled all this way with her? Are there any signs that she is still the same person? That she once loved lemons, and she was once French, that she was once a young woman, and that was all she was. I don't think I would. Except for that small turn of phrase, a strange way she says, 'It's pissing it down', with a very un-English lilt, a very awkward turn of the head. That and the part in her hair, the wave at her crown.

The rainy fog is blinding so that I can't see very far in

front of me, and I can never see beneath the water in the river. But I can just make out that lump ahead of me. I get closer. It's not a package, it's not tied up. It looks like a piece of tarp, which means there might be something underneath it. I pulse my fingers in my pocket, they reach for the knife that I keep there. Mathilde won't carry one, but I do.

I get closer to the tarp. I snatch the knife out of my pocket, I hold it out in front of me. I look behind me, I can see a few feet back, but that's all. The rain pounds behind and pounds ahead. The rain is a heartbeat. The pulse of the earth. Without the rain, that would be the last sign, I think. The world's last, great breath. A flood shows it's still breathing. A drought sucks the life out of everything and swallows it.

I wave the knife. I hear myself calling out your name, but I don't know why. The lump doesn't move. But would I see it? Would I hear it, if it did?

I rub my eyes. My whole face is wet.

It moves. A shiver. I stop. I turn around, but there is nothing, just the wind. It's late enough in the morning that there is a glint of light in the sky, but it is buried under this rain. I hear your name again from my mouth. I'm approaching it. A few steps, and I'll be able to touch it. I call out to it, Hey, I say, Hey, hey, hey. My voice is a small crack of noise. It doesn't move.

I tell myself, Mathilde wouldn't think I was afraid, even if she was. I have to be brave for the both of us. She'd expect me to sneak up on it; to slip inside the rain and let it hide me. But I only stand in it, and let it wash over me.

I'm upon it. It's a large tarp, and I breathe out, relieved. I open my mouth to let my fear out, but it doesn't go anywhere. I know what I have to do. I put the knife back in my pocket. My hands are vibrating nervously, so

I shake them, smacking them together, press them into each other, to still them. I bellow a name, your name, as I pull back the tarp to reveal what's underneath.

It's a man. He must have been here for days. His cheeks are hollows, and his mouth is an open question. I know he is a man, because he has a face, and a body, and he wears clothes. But he is also not a man, because he is a body. He is the parts of a man. But the man is gone. I prod him with my shoe. I have to make sure my eyes aren't deceiving me. I have to make sure because we've seen bodies like this before that turn out to be people. People who are alive and resent being found. I have to be sure because those people remember your face, and they will follow you. And they look for you, and they'll smell you, and they'll find your food and take it, and they'll find you and take you.

He's cold, and has been for a while. I had to find him first before he found me, and came up behind me. I have to make sure because he's lying sprawled over a bicycle, the likes of which I've never seen up here. He must have covered himself in the tarp and laid here. He must have known.

I don't look in his pockets, but I could do. People do that. I see the wheel and the spokes underneath him and it is something, after all.

He's heavy, and it takes me a long while to pull his weight off. The bicycle is still intact. I heave it upright and press down on the pedal and it zings round. It click clicks, and so the chain isn't broken. I cover him back over with the tarp. I did try to be kind to him. He wasn't a man anyway, he was just the body, and the man was gone.

I adjust the seat, and the whole frame creaks. I steady myself. I put my feet on the pedals and my legs remember how it works, and my torso. It balances and I push, and even through the rain, the bike zings and clicks and whirs and I move forward. The rain rushes past me, and I feel for the first time in a long time outside of myself. The tarp is far behind me, and I don't look back. It's nothing, it's really nothing. I'm a child that can rush and sprint and jolt through the days, its hours, through the dark. I laugh, because I am cycling, and I am new. And maybe today, I have something that is my marker. I have a bike, I cycle just as I did once before, and I recognise it.

I don't think about why I called your name, bellowed it, before knowing what I would find. I don't think about why I said it like that, desperately afraid: George, George, George.

The rain slips around my hair and down my back and covers me. When I get to the factory I park my bike outside. I notice that it is blue, and plain, and rusted.

Ruby sees it, as she arrives at work just behind me. 'A bicycle!' she says.

'Yes,' I say. 'We bought a bicycle.'

She laughs. 'Fancy, fancy Londoners. Look at that,' she says. 'Wow.'

My heart drops for a short moment, when I think that man might have had taste and money and southern roots once, when he bought this bicycle. He was a man once, and he had a bicycle. He was the man with the bicycle.

I always tell myself I'm not afraid, because Mathilde wouldn't want me to be. I repeat it to myself, like a mantra, and it becomes true. I'm not afraid when I arrive home at the end of the day. I'm not afraid because I don't tell Mathilde about what I saw or what I found. I don't tell her, because then it doesn't exist. I replace the bicycle on my way home, dump it by the river, for someone else to find. Even though he had probably stolen

53

it too, I couldn't think of it. I find I am less afraid once I've left the bicycle, once I am just as before.

Mathilde is not afraid, because she looks to me for reassurance. I walk that path by the river every day. And I think of her and our boy, and I can do it, I can make it all the way. I walk the path for them.

3

I went into the chicken coop this morning to do the usual clear out and found the last of the chickens dead. We bought her when we arrived here, only weeks ago, but they said it was all they had left and they'd stopped living out the day. She stopped laying a few days ago, but I hoped it was just a spell. I know she was just a squawking thing, but I gave her a name. I know she didn't have the brain capacity to understand it which makes me question why I thought of it at all.

I pick her up and bring her into the house, not knowing what to do with her. I think about burying her (and for who? For what?), but then realise this would be a romanticised notion of the highest order. It's a stupid thing to be so sentimental about with the rain crashing down and little growing, when what is left costs all you have. But I am. I'd like to believe that's human spirit (not cowardice) to remember something worth being kind about. Still, after wrapping her in brown paper and putting her in the old warm fridge, I lay her on the countertop and pluck her feathers out handfuls at a time, and gut her, and boil every ounce of her. Later, I roast her over the fire in the kitchen.

My grandmother used to be a vegetarian. She used to labour over paneer and leave bowls of whey on the countertop. I think about it a lot, this choice. I look at the bird, its decapitated head on the side I will boil in a pan for stock. She will last us days. I don't feel sorry for it. I try to imagine if things were different, if I would.

My small life has mainly comprised of eating, the conquests of finding things and doing without. I don't think I'll eat any of that stuff again so I can't regret the beef and duck and lamb, because just to have tried it changes things. I still think about that meat, and my grandmother. These things are connected because I think about them often and they are both impossible.

I take the roast chicken off the spit when it's ready and Mathilde sniffs it out straight away (nose like a bloodhound). I say this to her, and she shrugs. 'Have you ever seen a bloodhound? Do you know what one is?'

'It's a dog,' I say, but she looks at me like she's not sure, like she doesn't remember. She picks at the chicken, though I haven't served it up yet. 'Don't see many dogs around,' she says, and I try and think of all the dogs I've seen recently, but they do not include a bloodhound, and I may not have always seen them with my eyes but just inside my head. That makes them no less real. I know that they are there.

We say goodbye to our landlady in the morning and take our leftover chicken with us to work. We separate it out onto plates and into the fridge before we start work for the day. Mrs Campbell comes in, admonishing us, telling us she pays us too much, but looking at the chicken, getting an eyeful of it, before she snaps and calls us girls (even though we left girlhood many years before). We sit down at our stations. We click-clack like that for hours, sewing everything from bed linens to coats – never asking who they go to eventually – until lunchtime, rhythmically moving the pedal of the machine with our feet, varying the pressure, and pushing fabric along the bobbing needle. Sometimes we get to finish things off by hand, and there's a quietness to that I enjoy, but more often, like today, it all needs to be churned out quickly. 'I'm not sure about the chicken,' Mathilde says at lunch, fingering her lump of meat.

'She was old,' I say, but I don't want to tell her how old, how cheaply I bought her for us at the market.

I'm grateful for Mathilde for coming with me here, though you might not understand that. I don't think it would be the same without her.

She was the only one who listened to the music I played at those parties. She was the only one who saw me there. After all that fell through she said the memory of my playing the piano made her sad and my fingers must be restless, so she taught me how to sew. I tell her it is silent torture, but it's better than nothing. I like the tunelessness of it. 'I say it's a good thing. Roast chicken is better than the two eggs we'd have got from her a year, or whatever it was. Bafflingly inefficient,' I say.

'I don't know, maybe we need the company.'

'It's an improvement on the kind we used to keep.'

I laugh. I would say your name but it horrifies me. I'm trying to forget that too. It's only six letters, small and unappealing, so I might be able to do it. But it's everywhere and in everything. I think about how the rain has washed out crops, countries and people, but it won't make a mark on you.

I poke the chicken on my plate. Mathilde follows my

eyes to the meat and raises her eyebrows. She sighs, 'A few eggs might have been nice.'

I clatter my fork to the table in a deliberate gesture. 'What did we need them for anyway, it's not like we're going to make a bloody meringue.' I try to remember if I've ever eaten a meringue, or remember what it is. It was the kind of English thing that held a lot of promise when we first moved to London, but once you had it at an awkward schoolmate's birthday party, stood in the corner with a plastic fork clacking about your teeth, you realised it wasn't worth the effort.

'You're just being short-sighted,' she says.

'Oh and you have a big long-term plan do you?' I say, a teasing lilt to my voice. 'You know as well as I do that it's better we enjoy the chicken while we can. Because in five years, poof,' I make an exploding sign with my hands, 'We could all be under water.' I raise my eyebrows pointedly. 'Or underground.'

'You don't mean that,' she says. 'You don't know. What about Hugo?'

We all think of it. Sometimes I wonder if I'd give all this up, just to have my hands occupied again, just to hear the piano play. Playing at Gloria's house was the only work I could get with my music, the only way I could ever make money from it, and that had been enough. That's all I wanted, then. It was enough to be in my mouldy Kilburn flat, water streaming in from the ceiling, the corners of every room black and my feet permanently cold, because I knew most evenings I'd scramble up to Hampstead, and I'd get to play that Steinway I had no other chance of playing. After a while, it wasn't just the piano, it was seeing her face, as lost as my own, night after night.

If I could show you her face, I would: my lovely Mathilde. I'd put it next to the memory of her face as

57

I watched her from my piano and you'd see how it's changed. You'd see what got away from you; you'd know in an instant. But then, maybe you do know. I'm not sure it matters either way.

What I don't tell her is how I regret the death of that one chicken, because of the hope, not the eggs. Because of the noise she made and the sound of life; the squawking and chattering that covered up the sound of you saying my name, Jaminder, and drawing it out, Jamiiiiiiinder, that I hear and see in my head all through the night and all through the day.

4

When we take a break from our machines we pick at our oatmeal with teaspoons. I stretch my fingers out, and look at the older women with arthritis. I won't be here long enough to let that happen. But I imagine they all told themselves that at one point, and I remember how I'd told myself that in London, over and over again, before the blackout, as I stood at the traffic lights on Kilburn High Road when the rain had got into my shoes. Moments like that lasted longer than I thought.

Mathilde takes large spoonfuls into her mouth, gleeful. I can taste the absence of sugar. It has a flavour.

It's Ruby's birthday today. We brought her wildflowers we found in the nearby fields. They might even be weeds but to us they are beautiful. Ruby's the one with two children but no husband. Ruby told us she was named after her birthstone, and I find this an oddly superstitious thing to be named after – meaningless, and comforting. I've never seen a ruby but I know they are red. I imagine them to be a red as dark as blood, but I can't be sure.

Ruby gets extra food for her children because she has two. Even though he is absent, she talks about her husband, enough for us to know his name, which is Charles. Was Charles.

'My boys love the oatmeal,' she tells us, though she isn't eating any, and we feel no obligation of politeness to wait for her. 'You wouldn't think it, but they do.'

'They're hungry,' I snort, shovelling. She stops and lowers her spoon. I look at her fingers, I check them. But it's only been a few months of work. 'I mean.'

Ruby smiles, and it's a relief. 'You're right.' She looks me up and down, she looks at her fingers, too, poised above the bowl. 'Children are better at it than adults.'

I shrug, licking my fingers. 'They don't know any different.'

'Charles had chocolate sometimes. He used to bring it back from work.'

We didn't ask her, but she told us. Charles died on a boat. They were looking for things. They were on an expedition. Charles got a fever but we don't know why. There was no way for Charles to get back to land in time. We also know, and have told her, this isn't something to worry about. There is nothing on land that could have helped him.

Ruby changes the subject as quickly as she brings it up, to give us the impression his name is of little consequence to her. She's older than us, but not by much. Enough for her hands to be more crooked than ours. Ten years, that's all it might take.

'You girls should come along to the church on Friday.' She gestures to me and Mathilde, because we're the new

59

girls. 'There's music.' She's watching my oatmeal disappear. 'I help organise the thing, nice place to take the kids.' We nod, politely. I think of last weekend where we holed up at home. We tried to light a fire in the old fireplace and burnt the rug. We hung our clothes by it to dry. We blew on the wood to keep it lit. We huddled by it and told each other stories about the future.

Ruby raises her eyebrows, 'There's heating.'

'There is?' I clatter my spoon into my bowl. 'We're there.'

Ruby takes my hand and I try not to touch her crooked knuckles. I don't want to feel them, because I know I'll think about them. They curl around my fingers, and I realise it is joy that makes her do this. 'There's booze too.' She whispers, close to me. 'If you ask the priest right, for communion.' She makes a glugging motion with her hands and mouth. It isn't that hard to find drink, but it is expensive. It helps with the cold.

Ruby has red painted nails as red as her name. I ask her where she gets her cosmetics. I find it such a jarring thing to bother with. Especially with her fingers, but also for the fact that there's nowhere to go. What a thing to spend money on. She said she made a trip, a few years ago, to the nearest town. She found some leftover things there. The nail varnish has hardened in its bottle now, and she tells us she has to hold it over the fireplace to warm it up before she can paint with it.

'It's called "Affair in Red Square". Do you remember how nail varnish had names like that?'

I laugh. 'I remember,' I say, 'God, how stupid. How perfectly stupid. You could be a nail varnish: "Ruby with her red nails", that's what they call her.' I think it sounds like freedom.

I know we will both spend the afternoon thinking of the

warmth, and the bodies, and how like London that might be. How we have nothing to wear that we might have worn then. Nothing but overalls and blue jeans that gather around the bum and the knees, that we have to wear with men's belts we find in seconds shops, belts once worn by people who looked smart in them. The kind of belt my grandfather bought when he moved to Kenya and subsumed himself into Britishness: the belt that landed him in the paper with his immaculate suit and turban under the list of 'best-dressed'. The belt that my grandmother fretted about him wearing at my mother's wedding, when he should have been in traditional dress. The kind of belt that once acted as a symbol and a set of signs; that once designated a kind of culture and a language. The kind of belt that once started arguments, and once made someone happy.

Now the belt means nothing.

I think about Ruby's red nails, and the shiny lacquer of Affair in Red Square, not even chipped. I look at them, and remember the process of pushing cuticles back, removing the skin, shaping them, holding your extremities as decoration. I wonder about her house and how she lives. Even with the children, she must have acetone about the house. She must, because she must remove the polish, neatly, and reapply it. I am so struck by this thought of a bottle of acetone sitting in her bathroom cupboard that I see it in front of me, as if it were there: the lilac colour of the bottle, and its smell. It's positioning in the cupboard in the corner, its winkingly glossy, clear liquid, label turned away, bottle turned towards me.

It makes me think of Gloria and that last party we went to. I can't remember if her nails were painted (even though Mathilde asked me afterwards, several times, as though it might have made a difference). But I do remember what she

61

said, half-sitting on the window ledge, her legs tucked over one another, casually. Wearing her jeans, one hand jutted out from her body, dangling a cigarette, the paper burning through to nothing without her having taken a drag.

This is such a bore! she said, and she laughed, gladly. But she did also look out of the window and stop laughing. And said, turned away from me, We're all such bores, even now.

Thinking about Ruby's nails and knowing about that bottle of acetone makes me just as excited as I was at that party, when we had everything. Strange, that it excites me now, when at that party all those women could have had painted nails, and I wouldn't have noticed.

That was the beginning, I think, another beginning: that party. That last day. When Gloria, who may or may not have had painted nails, but definitely had 100% pure acetone, went to the bathroom and drank said bottle of acetone. She drank it like it was a martini and might have bequeathed her a light head but that was all; might have had an olive in it, but that was all.

It was bloody murder in the bathroom when I found her, and too late by then, but we decided she might have said she thought she'd been drinking a cocktail, and that was all.

Of all the much easier ways to do it in the world we lived, even then, it was a strange choice, a choice I thought about often, of all the choices you could make. Maybe there weren't many, but there were some, and that was one. Even with the open window, she'd made that choice.

But it wasn't so strange that we didn't understand, not so strange that we couldn't explain it when we found her. Not so strange we didn't look at women's painted nails after that and wonder about their acetone. Or toilet bleach, or furniture polish. Or whatever else women still had in their houses and thought about.

'What about our son?' Mathilde says. 'Can we bring him?'

Ruby looks at us, surprised. She is clearing away our bowls, as we are ready to start our last shift.

'You have a child?' she asks, amazed.

'Yes we do,' I say, 'Is that okay?'

Ruby looks from one of us to the other, hoping for more explanation. 'I'm sorry,' she says. 'It's just, you've been here for weeks now and you hadn't mentioned.' A smile overwhelms her face. 'What a relief for you, with the child policy in London. What a relief that must have been.'

They've heard about it then. Despite that tenuous border and all that rain separating them from Mrs P, they know about the policy.

She looks searchingly from one of us to the other, as though to ascertain who she should be relieved for. 'Do you mind me asking?'

'He's both of ours,' Mathilde says, then looks at me.

'We raise him together,' I say.

'Oh,' Ruby says, and raises her eyebrows and smiles. She might assume that together means that we are romantically together, and neither of us counters her assumption. It matters little, either way, especially when I think we are together in nearly every sense. There is only the three of us. I think of us crawling up under our blanket on our one bed, trying to stoke the fire with our feet.

'And you didn't want any more?' She looks between us, as though wondering who she should feel sorry for, as she had felt sorry for the both of us, thinking us childless, only moments ago.

'Oh, no,' I say, my face straight, 'One was enough to almost kill us.'

I break a smile and Ruby exhales. She laughs, but it is out of pity.

I remember Hugo's birth vividly, we both do; the pain on our faces and the horrible energy of it. It was just the two of us; and then, suddenly, three. We gawped at the responsibility of another life when we hadn't always taken our own seriously. We had to immediately care for him more than we'd ever cared for ourselves. We knew he was going to see the world through our eyes so we had to work out what that meant.

Almost six years have passed since then.

We arrive home, together today, and collect him from our landlady in the flat above us.

'Was he good?' Mathilde says. 'Were you good?' she asks him.

Hugo looks up at her. 'Yes, Maman,' he says, surprised.

'He was fascinated by the jars in my cupboard, so I gave him one.' Mrs Donald says. She gestures to the jar he clutches in his hands. I bend down and squeeze it out of his, to look at it. His face breaks and he starts to cry.

'Come on, Hugo,' Mathilde says, soothingly. I take little notice, and hand the jar to her. It has a label on it, Strawberry Jam. 'Oh, Mrs Donald, no, we can't accept this.'

'He'll like it,' she says, bending down and rubbing his back to try and stop his crying.

He stops abruptly when she touches him, and looks at Mathilde, arms outstretched. 'It's time to go home now, isn't it, Maman?'

She nods at him. 'We can have it after dinner.' She places the jar back in his hands and he laughs gleefully.

'How did the food get in the jar?' He says, holding it up to his face. He shakes it. 'Did it come from here?'

'Thursday, then?' Mrs Donald says, straightening up and trying to regain her detached air of indifference towards him that always manages to slip. 'Little boys shouldn't cry,' she says to Hugo, as though warning him. He reaches out for my hand and we start to walk down to our flat.

'Thursday,' I call out, in agreement.

As we get to the door I say to him, 'Boys can cry as much as girls.'

'I don't want to be a girl,' he says.

'And you're not,' I say. 'But you can cry.' I look at Mathilde, waiting for her to agree.

'We can all cry as much as we like,' she says, gleefully, opening the front door. She picks Hugo up and brings his face to hers, as we walk into the kitchen. 'Let's wail and wail until Mrs Donald tells us off.' He starts to laugh, and wriggles his legs.

'What's for supper?' I say.

As soon as Mathilde puts him down, he runs up to me and showers me with kisses. I hold out my arms for him and swoop him up. 'I'm a boy, aren't I, Mummy?'

'In a sense, Hugo,' I say.

'Do you cry, Mummy?'

'Only when it matters.'

'When I grow up I don't think I'll cry.'

'Big words,' I say, and pat his belly, 'Big words.'

After we've eaten some potatoes and cabbage, all three of us bundle into bed. We submerge under the blanket, and Mathilde takes out her worn copy of Peter Pan. We found it in an old shop months ago, and the sight of it warmed us, in a way. It made us feel close to Gloria and Gwendolyn again, as though we were laughing with them as we turned the pages.

We told Hugo it was a book for older children and so he flicked through it to make a point. We relented, recently, and have started reading it to him as part of our nightly routine. But there's so much about it he doesn't understand. We have to explain Nana the dog to him, and mermaids, and fairies, but not thimbles or sewing. He understands why Wendy must sew Peter's shadow onto his feet. And he understands imagination, and how time passes in strange ways in Neverland.

Mathilde does the reading. She tests him, to see if he can remember. 'Who's Wendy?' She says, and he'll reply as best he can.

'She's the lady, she's the Lost Boys' mother,' he says.

'And where do they live?'

'Neverland.'

I see her look at him, deciding on the kind of child he is. And I think she likes to say the names again; Wendy Darling, and Peter Pan, and Hook.

She encourages his questioning, even when it becomes relentless. 'Why aren't there pictures in grown-up books? Don't grown-ups like pictures?' he says, as we bundle down and Mathilde reads him the first sentence.

'They do,' she says, pleased with him. 'But when you get older you like to focus on the words more.'

'Are words better than pictures?'

She smiles. 'Neither is better. But words make pictures. I say a word and you see a picture in your head, don't you? So you don't need to have someone draw it and tell you what the picture in their head is like.'

He muses on this for a second, before saying, 'But I can't imagine Neverland on my own. It's not like here.'

'That's true,' she says, 'but you can try.'

'It's okay, Maman, I'll find it for us. Second star to the

right and straight on 'til morning.' He pauses, he looks at her and I start stroking his head. 'You can keep reading now,' he says, as though it's obvious. We always start from the beginning as soon as we reach the end, and he enjoys the repetition of it, as though he finds something new in it each time.

'Back to Mrs Darling,' Mathilde says, turning to the first page, and reading:

'She was a lovely lady, with a romantic mind and such a sweet mocking mouth. Her romantic mind was like the tiny boxes, one within the other, that come from the puzzling East, however many you discover there is always one more; and her sweet mocking mouth had one kiss on it that Wendy could never get, though there it was, perfectly conspicuous in the right-hand corner.'

Out of the three of us, he falls asleep first, sandwiched in the middle. Mathilde and I look at each other over the top of him in the dark. She keeps reading at first:

'Mr Darling got all of her, except the innermost box and the innermost kiss. He never knew about the box, and in time he gave up trying for the kiss.'

I look at her, and down at Hugo, now sound asleep. 'He'll understand it better in a way,' I say, 'when he's older.' I look up at her again but she breaks my gaze.

'We need another book,' Mathilde says, 'We can't read Peter Pan until he's twenty-one.'

'We could try find *Treasure Island*.'

'Funny,' Mathilde says. 'I'm serious.'

'So am I,' I whisper as Hugo lets out a heavy breath. 'Another book would keep us going for years.'

'I'm going to ask Ruby,' she says. 'She must have books.'

I look at Hugo's small ear, turned towards me, perfectly formed in miniature. We didn't have to do anything for that structure to form, intact, impeccably rendered. I don't want to think about what happens when we finish *Peter Pan*, or any other book. I want him to stay like this.

'I'm not sure she cares about books,' I say.

'She might know about a school, though.'

I prop myself up on my elbow. 'People at schools ask questions.'

'We can't keep him here. We don't have enough to teach him with.'

'But that was the plan.'

'He's clever,' she says, a tone of desperation in her voice. 'He needs to go to a school.'

I look at him. He is grasping Mrs Donald's jam jar in his sleep. 'Do you think he knows there was jam in that once?'

'Mrs Donald would have told him. She might have explained what it was.'

'I remember raspberry seeds. That got stuck in your teeth.'

'I don't remember,' she says.

'You do, it was sweet.'

'I don't remember.'

'He pretended to, after dinner. Did you see? He pretended to remember. He ate air out of the jar with a spoon.'

'She must have told him, but he can't imagine. He doesn't know.'

'No. You can't imagine a thing like that.' I look at her, I whisper.

'So maybe it's better not to try and make him. It will only hurt him. He shouldn't try and imagine. He shouldn't have to. We shouldn't have to.' She looks at me, pointedly, 'It will only break your heart.'

She tilts her head towards me, pleading. I have no way to tell her we're too far gone for that.

5

_____

On Sundays we go to the market in town. Hugo can barely contain his excitement as people plonk things they don't want on makeshift tables. The bulk of stalls are made up of Mrs Campbell's rejects, which means everyone has built up a substantial collection of blankets and warm gear; odd clothing with bad stitching and holes (easily mended) and awkward squares of fabric (good enough for anything).

This is the third time we've come, and I marvel, as I look across at this drizzly sight of vendors, that Hugo is excited about these items. It's the experience of looking at things he's never seen before, holding them in his hands, and asking me about them that matters. Even if they're only forgotten toys with no batteries, wool jumpers that have shrunk and collapsed, old door handles and wires that have no earthly value. Not now.

The last time we came, he surprised me by picking up an old calculator, one which would never work because there would never be the batteries to power it. I held it up to the sky to check if it was solar powered, but realised that was futile too.

'I don't think it works,' I said, and he looked so disappointed I bought it for him anyway, and he carried it along pressing the numbers until his fingers grew sore and he had to wiggle them about in front of him. I laughed at him, watching these hours of fascination, until he eventually looked up at me and said, 'What's it for?'

My stomach fell with guilt, that I hadn't explained it to him. That I assumed he knew. I felt terrible that a thing he didn't even understand brought him such joy.

'Don't cry, Mummy,' he said, and I laughed it off. But he put the calculator down after that.

I look for things too, but it's a different sort of looking. His is discovery, enchantment and a world of endless possibility. Mine is the pointless hope of recovery. I look for books, but there are never many. I look for anything that might have a musical note on it. I look for parts of a piano – parts, because who wouldn't have ripped it in pieces if they found one, to use for firewood. I look for old newspapers to check, afraid, for any sign of us, or them. I look for anything that is recognisable, anything that's familiar. I look for anything that I could hold up to him and say: look, this is what we left behind. Mathilde doesn't come with us, and I know it is because it is easier for her not to pretend there might be something worth giving to Hugo, there might be something worth finding. When he brings home another pointless object, the letter Q from an old keyboard, I am the one who tries to explain to him what qwerty is, and she is the one who looks into her lap and continues sewing. She resists telling me to be quiet, but I turn quiet eventually, anyway.

It's easier for us to go alone and have these conversations away from her, so as not to trouble her. I savour these walks, knowing that whatever I tell him he'll keep and turn over in his head in amazement. Whatever I tell him might not have a solid image to go with it, and might only be an imagining, but I like to think it helps with his monotony.

We pick up a few potatoes before we get to the other stalls, and the woman behind the table tells us they've run out of green beans, the string kind that you used to top and tail, before it became wasteful. I laugh, jubilant, and she looks at me, surprised.

'It's the end of the world,' I say, expectantly, and she furrows her brow and turns to someone else.

'What's wrong,' Hugo says, and he tugs at my coat sleeve and pulls me in the opposite direction of the food.

'It's a French expression,' I say, 'Maman taught me once. *C'est la fin des haricots*. It's the end of beans. When all you have left are beans, and then they're gone, you've had it. It can't get worse. It's the end of the world.'

'I don't get it,' he says, and I repeat it to him, pronouncing it badly. He looks at me, confused.

I wish I could say something to Mathilde. I wish I could say to her: maybe we've reached rock bottom. Maybe it's a sign, maybe that's it. And laugh with her. But she doesn't acknowledge even these little expressions anymore, as though she's forgotten them, as though the whole language doesn't exist. So I remember them for her, and say them out loud for her. And tell Hugo for her, just in case one day he might want to know. In case one day a few French words might be familiar to him. But I urge him not to repeat them, not to say anything. I can't explain why, and this confuses him more.

'Is it really the end of the world?' he says, pulling me towards a table full of broken down telephones and shiny metal things. I know he can't conceive of what he's asking. Because if he knew, he might not ask. He might think his question answered.

Still, I say, 'No. It's not. We're still here aren't we?' I hand him a small portable block phone, that will never switch on again, that once contained someone's whole life; their messages, their thoughts, their plans, their pictures.

He looks at the blank screen. 'Where is everyone else?' But he's not listening, not even to his own question, as he strains, mesmerised at his faded reflection in the black glass.

The next day I pull on Hugo's small wellington boots. A godsend, a thing like that, up here. Ruby had them from when her boys were smaller, and gave them to us. We have nothing to give back, and no way to thank her. Ruby says she has more things to give us, and we are reluctant to take them. We are desperate to get our hands on anything like that, anything unusual that we could give to Hugo and make him happier. But we know we can never repay her, and so pretend we have a mixture of pride about it and let her assume that because we are from London we have things. That we have anything.

We make our way to the church, which isn't too far from our flat, so we are able to shield ourselves from the rain. We hold each of Hugo's hands in ours and swing him forwards over the deepest of puddles. He shrieks with delight, as the rain sodden earth is his playground, and he revels in it.

It is Mathilde who is agitated as we reach the church with its low stone wall and worn away graves. Religion wasn't encouraged where she was, she never got used to it. She had another kind of guilt to get used to.

Even though I spent much of my early years in temples rather than churches, I am just as comfortable here as anywhere else. London made me like that. I know stories from the Bible and I know the symbols they use and I know that light is as important for Christians as for Sikhs. Peace, too. I know they have God and we have God. I know not everyone believes in God and that feeling is not particular to any religion at all.

We see the light from the church as we approach it. The way the candles flicker out from the old stained-glass windows. It's a magical thing and it silences Hugo. We haven't taken him anywhere like this since he was a baby, when he was too small to remember.

'Is this where God lives?' he asks, and Mathilde sighs as we walk up the gravel path to the wooden door.

'If he lives anywhere,' I say, gesturing around us, my arm becoming wet. 'It would be here.'

Mathilde shushes me. 'He can decide about all that later.'

I bend down to him, 'Or decide about it never.'

'Have you not decided?' he says, looking at the church now with a mixture of anticipation and fear, and back to me as though I will give him the right answer.

Mathilde gives me a warning look.

'We want you to make up your own mind. We want you to think for yourself,' I say.

He puzzles over this, and forgets it as soon as Mathilde pushes on the old door and it reveals a shining radiant pocket of people and warmth inside. There are candles everywhere, and there is Ruby and her two boys, by a low table. There are drinks too, small amounts of old spirits and wines. And there are potato wafers, for communion, presumably, but now a snack. The church has provided a feast.

Hugo pulls instantly towards the table of food, laden with perceived treats, but we pull him towards Ruby, politely. Once he notices her children he forgets the wafers, jubilant. He has seen so few other small children to play with.

Ruby exclaims, delighted, and pulls herself to her feet and introduces the boys (Jacob and Tommy) and Hugo introduces himself right back, stomping his feet in his wellington boots and thanking Ruby for his new shoes. I look to Mathilde and she is radiant with joy at his politeness. She laughs at Ruby, 'We didn't even tell him to say that,' and Ruby laughs back.

We leave the children with their small lead pencils and mish-mash of old plastic toys. Ruby leads us over to the priest. He is standing serving drinks at a table in his black robe and collar, just the same as in London. This consistency pleases me.

'Father Anthony,' Ruby says, 'I want to introduce you to the two new girls in the village. This is Mathilde, and Jaminder, and their son – over there – is Hugo.'

'Delighted,' he says, extending his hand gratefully. And he does seem genuinely pleased, so much so that we are taken aback and cold until Ruby nods at us and we extend our hands, in turn, and shake them, exaggeratedly, to compensate.

'It's wonderful here,' I say, gesturing to the lights and the wafers and the people.

'We work hard to remain at the centre of the community. Especially if you're one of Mrs Campbell's. But everyone is welcome. You are most welcome.' He smiles, and I try and look behind it, I wonder about it. I wonder what it must be like for him to sit in this privileged position, funded by the government and our garment trade, protected, fed and warmed.

He rummages about below the table and retrieves a couple of inky printed leaflets. I examine the faded black letters and drag my finger across them, I wonder how he prints them. They smudge.

'We have oatmeal here, every day, for our residents. If you show us your pay slips we will subsidise what you have.' He points to the leaflet, which lays out the points as he runs through them. 'We have blankets, and welcome people to come here whenever they need. We are open late sometimes, for special occasions. Midnight Mass, Easter Vigil. We are always here for shelter, and counsel. And we school the children here, every morning. Should you wish to enrol your son.'

Mathilde livens up at this suggestion, and makes an appreciative noise.

'Who teaches them?' I ask, wearily.

'Oh,' he says, smiling broadly, 'I do. It's not just religious studies, it's everything I can offer. Can Hugo read and write?'

'Yes,' I say, proudly. 'We taught him.'

'I tailor my teaching to different pupils. There are so few of them, I'm glad of it.'

'Why are you glad of it?' Mathilde says, a sharp tone in her voice.

Father Anthony lays the leaflets down in front of us. He smiles awkwardly as someone approaches the table for a drink. He hands it to them and then looks back at us. 'I can assure you,' he says, 'they are well looked after.' He smiles, but the sincerity of it has disappeared. I can see he is hurt by the accusation.

Ruby picks up the leaflets and puts them in her bag. 'Fantastic,' she says, 'He's a fantastic teacher. Hugo should join, along with my two. They really do enjoy it. And what else do they have to do?'

She can't imagine another way. She can't imagine where we've come from. And I note that Father Anthony doesn't ask us – and doesn't seem to mind – why we have travelled to this place and what for. Why our accents are so southern. He doesn't ask (as I was so often asked in London, for no particular reason), if I am Indian, if I am Muslim, if I am something they can understand. It seems enough for him, just that we are people, and we are here, and it doesn't seem to matter how far we've come, or why, what we have run from. It doesn't matter to him that he can't imagine what London is like, or what France was or Kenya, or that we have known many other worlds before this meeting.

All that seems to matter is that we have ended up in the same place, and have met here, and he can offer us something. I am glad of his enthusiasm, which washes away our scepticism from our journey up here. I am glad for Hugo, not to be asked why he has two mothers, and for him not to know the answer. I know from the way he has dealt with us that he will never ask, and Hugo will be safe. I nod to Mathilde, and she nods at me. I know she is pleased, too. I pick up a small wafer, grateful to hold it in my hands.

'We'd love for him to come to school,' Mathilde says, and shakes his hand again, an awkwardly formal gesture, which I can only imagine she thinks is a way of being grateful to this Christian man in a language he might understand.

6

The thought of you was unavoidable, entering that church for the first time. I looked up at the crucifix and saw Jesus' white, bony body hanging there; not in that bloody, visceral, Catholic way, but hanging there all the same. With that grimace on his face and that expression of pain. I wondered if you felt pain, too. I wondered if that's what we had done: made a sacrifice.

Of course, I worry for our boy. If he should belong to a church that is not a home for either of us. But we don't really have a choice. Mathilde and I watch each other's faces to look for the right thing to do. We don't have to tell each other, after these long years, we just look at each other and know. In every passing comment, or moment of anger, any time she clangs her cup down or slams the door, I know she only does it out of love. I know that after all these years, that is what she has built up. I am working on it, too. But I also do things that aren't motivated out of love. I look back.

Mathilde is only glad to have got this far. I find it more difficult to be glad of it.

I tell Mathilde, as a kindness, that I will take Hugo to school on his first day. I know she worries about it, and doesn't want him to be afraid, or miss us, or miss Mrs Donald, or cry. But I find as I walk him to the church, his hand in mine, that he is only bouncing along on his feet. Maybe this is what he has wanted all along.

'It's okay to be scared,' I tell him. 'I was on my first proper day of school.'

'Was your school in a church?'

'No,' I say. 'It was in a building of its own because there were so many children.'

'How many?' He looks up at me, his brown eyes wide and wondrous, as though he is counting the imaginary children in his head.

'I don't know, Hugo, maybe a thousand?'

'A thousand!' He breathes the word out in great exclamation. 'How did you all fit?'

I laugh. 'We squeezed in like sardines, our eyes popping out.'

'What's a sardine? Were you scared?'

I think about this. I was scared of many things, but

that wasn't it. How could a child who hasn't known any different understand that all I was scared of was leaving my grandparents, fearful that they might disappear while I wasn't around to watch them? That they might forget me, or leave me there, that maybe that was their secret intention?

'I wasn't scared of all the children,' I say. 'Just one.'

'Who?'

'His name was Boris. He went around asking everyone for their Lego, and if you didn't give him your Lego, he'd bite you. I waited, knowing he would come to me eventually. And I wouldn't give him my Lego so he bit me.'

He swings my hand forwards and back, a sign of entrancement with the story.

'I told Ms Sheeran and she took us outside the classroom. And she said that if I wanted, I could bite him back.'

'Did you bite him?' Hugo says, horrified.

'Yes, I did. And Ms Sheeran went and got ice for my arm and left him outside. She was making a point.'

Hugo stops swinging my arm and we walk quietly towards the church. I think he might be deciding what point Ms Sheeran was trying to make, and maybe I am still deciding too. But instead he just looks up at me as we approach the church's low stone wall and says, 'Mummy, what's Lego?'

We open the church door and the heat hits us like stepping into another country. It's heat left over from the nights of parties and drinking and bodies and the small amount of heating the church can get. It reminds me of stepping off a plane and walking across the shiny tarmac and being hit by that wave of heat and that smell – red, dry earth, and frangipanes in Mombasa, by the coast. Coconuts and salt air.

I try, but I can't smell it now. It is only that old English smell of damp and dust, stale bread, and thick, padded, prayer cushions sewn together decades ago.

Father Anthony greets us, and leads us to the back room where the children are sitting around low tables, quietly contemplating their sheets of paper. They are well behaved, and it is nothing like a school I once knew. There is no screeching and wailing and excited movement and bodies thrumming together in a small space, anticipating the day. They are fascinated by the things given to them, in miraculous contemplation. Maybe for this reason I am reticent about releasing Hugo's hand and letting him join them. We can't know what this will do, how this might change him. The company of other children is a wonderful delight, but the rest. I am anxious and look around the room, studying the walls and trying to locate some sense of normality pinned upon them.

I let go to pull out his small chair for him at the table, next to another girl who is older than him. There seems to be little segregation of ability here and I wonder that anyone this far north has been schooled at all. But age would have no impact on what they might have learnt. Some children may have learnt nothing in their lives but how to thread a needle.

'Can I see what you're teaching them?' I ask Father.

'Of course,' he smiles at me, and hands me a few sheets of paper that are handwritten. The paper is thick: that old recycled stuff they stopped circulating years before. But I imagine it is all they have. There's basic arithmetic and reading. There are sheets of words, bringing me back to being young, when words like that were difficult and had to be spoken first inside your head. I feel that Hugo might be beyond this, but I'm not sure. We have never been able to challenge him as much as we'd have liked.

79

'Can I keep this one?' I say, holding up the page of sums.

He doesn't question me on it. 'Absolutely.' I think about studying maths in school all those years ago and how I knew more then than I do now. I want to test myself.

'I'll bring it back if you need it.' I fold it up and put it in my pocket.

He tells me he'll feed them something for lunch, and then we can pick him up afterwards. I'm grateful for this, and find it a marvel that there is somewhere where we can guarantee he will be fed, at least once a day, and that one worry is catered for.

I leave him, and Hugo doesn't cry at my departure, in fact barely glances up at me. But I know I will feel guilty about leaving him there all day. I know I will think of him, every minute, and feel my stomach lurch, and worry that he is safe. Worry that he fears I may not come back and collect him, worry that I have left him, abandoned – in a church! A foreign place, even to me, even now.

As soon as I walk from the room I feel guilty for my singularity, that I am on my own and the people I love are occupied. I am free to do as I please until lunchtime, on my day off, with no one to look after. It's a strange kind of luxury, and one that I haven't had or known what to do with for years. Even before we had Hugo, our free time never seemed to be our own, not really, not in the sense that we could move about as we pleased and be in our own bodies as we pleased. You made sure of that.

I wonder what you would think about Mathilde's son in school, almost five years old, my son (yes, he is mine, too) as beautiful as anything that was ever born of man. That was ever born at all.

I try to extinguish the crushing weight of your face from

my mind, and find that I can't. I look up involuntarily to that Jesus, hanging there, his arms pulled up in a perfect arc of pain and I see you again, your arms on Mathilde, your arms everywhere.

That's when I notice it, more perfect than anything I've seen in years. I stop, dazzled by it, afraid. I imagine myself at it, my feet moving, and my hands, and the peace that they search for. The peace that I might find in light, but not in a church. I imagine the music, and the slippery keys, and I imagine that this is what people speak of when they say Jesus died for something. That all of us die for something.

A sentiment that is used to placate a whole people, but I still wish it to be true. I can try and let myself think it is, looking at that thing. If any of it is true, that would be something to die for. It would be music; the humanity of people; the beauty of pain; the melancholy of hearing a note. It would be all of suffering: it would be a piano.

PART 3

Mathilde
Stitches

1

The one thing I liked about going to the hospital was listening to the radio. They had one in the waiting area, along with the newspapers. There was something other-worldly about the all-day electricity there.

The sound of the radio was tinny and it crackled, and the receptionist rarely got the frequency right, but people were mesmerised by it. It was used as an alternative therapy in private rooms, as though music could take the place of redundant antibiotics.

The best visits were the ones where there was music playing; old records piped through, classical tunes and recognisable songs. Some people, like Gloria, had their own players at home. But for most, this was as good as it would get. And those few minutes where you hoped your name wouldn't be called, where you could sit and listen for as long as your wait allowed, were as good as any you'd ever get.

Sometimes there wouldn't be music, sometimes there'd only be Mrs P. No one dared or no one bothered to change the frequency, and so we would sit and listen to her, and look at her face on the newspapers, the same image on every paper, shot from the same angle, by one person with a good camera. She gave her regular sermons on BBC's Auntie's Hour, a leftover from when she was the head of the broadcasting company. As we came in for my appointment that day, her voice echoed throughout the room. We sat down and my grandmother sighed audibly. 'That's how she did it,' my grandmother said, 'She ruled the waves. "England isn't eating" blasted out of every room.'

I tried to shush her, looking about me to see if anyone was listening. 'The country was on its knees,' I said.

She scoffed.

'She got us out of the blackout,' I said.

My grandmother laughed. 'And what do you know about that?'

'It's better now,' I said, bolstered by the people I had met at Gloria's dinner party. 'There's more food, and energy.'

My grandmother grabbed my hand, and slowly squeezed my fingers, like she was holding an apple firmly in her grasp, about to bite. 'We live in the same house don't we? We're both here, aren't we?'

'I know, grandmother,' I said, pulling my hand free. 'All I'm saying is it's better now.'

We came to these appointments, anxiously, twice a year. My grandmother saw the other worried women with their daughters, their very young daughters. But the older, the more anxious, of course.

'—*We've seen picketing that threatens to bring the country to its knees once again, endangering our farms and choking our food supplies. An attempt to strangle the country*—'

Mrs P's voice reverberated about the room. Someone coughed into their newspaper, shuffling the papers. The receptionist stared at her appointment list.

'—*Despite our problems and our failures, this is still a good land to live in and bring up a family. It is a land of great natural riches*—'

A woman walked through after her appointment with her husband. 'People are starving!' she screamed at the radio. 'You let them starve!' Her husband grabbed her arm and pulled her out of the hospital as quickly as he could.

'—*There are wreckers among us who don't believe this. But I am talking to you, the majority. I am an Auntie to you all, our regime is here to help you flourish, to nurture England's green land, to bring you the fruits of your labour. Those who seek to disrupt our agricultural industry disrupt the nation. Those who choose not to replenish our population, crush our country*—'

'Regime,' my grandmother scoffed. '*Oui, Ancien Régime*, but where is *la Révolution*?'

I shushed her. It was better when we didn't talk about France, when we pretended it wasn't there. Which it wasn't, I always tried to tell her, in every sense that mattered. But maybe she lived there long enough that it wasn't just the culture and language and people that mattered, and that she missed; it was the ground and the streets and maybe even the stone and the glass in the buildings, if they hadn't got to that yet.

'There's a Sainte Chapelle in my heart,' I said one day, when she lamented the inevitably broken Christian stained glass of the chapel.

'That won't outlive you, Mathilde,' she said. 'That won't go on without you.' I suppose she was right.

As we sat listening to the radio, we were handed the same set of forms, and I completed them, the same as I always did.

'—*my nationalisation of the grid gave you a gift of shared energy, and rationing means that no one will starve, and no one will have more than another. This is fair and equal. We must never return to the days of the blackout. We must not be held to ransom by farmers as we once were by private energy corporates, who served only the wealthy*—'

The nurse called me over as my grandmother took up the paper, one of her few chances to read it. Mrs P's face gleamed from the front page, some article included inside about her sartorial choices – bestowing her with the impression of frivolity and benevolence – which my grandmother turned to immediately. 'Twenty years,' my grandmother said. 'And we still think just because it could be worse, that's enough.'

'—*I will not be swayed. I will not turn back to those dark days.*'

Applause filled the room from the radio. Someone lowered their newspaper and said cheerfully: 'Auntie knows best!'

My grandmother murmured to me, 'My Aunt was bombed in her bathtub in Lyon. What a phrase.'

They led me towards a scale. They took my weight with my shoes on (so I always wore the same out of the two pairs I had, as though consistency was key), and my height, where they claimed I'd gained a centimetre, and I laughed. Then there were blood tests, and finally, the room.

My grandmother followed me. The doctor was the same man I always saw. I attributed to him a kindness, as he had a friendly way of sitting, and putting the curtain around, and looking at me over his glasses. I could imagine him as the sort of person who would be at Gloria's dinner party, and for a moment, wanted to tell him about what I'd experienced, to explain I was different, not in body, but in other ways.

'Change behind the curtain,' he said, as my grandmother sat down, and he made a comment on the weather. She remained silent. He shuffled paper – my results – as I came from behind the curtain, positioning myself on the chair, placing my feet on the stirrups, my legs widely spread.

'You're almost twenty-two,' he said, questioningly,

and I agreed. He checked my notes. 'And your results here still put you in great health, top percentile.' He smiled, joyously. 'Let's have a look then.'

He swivelled his chair towards me and positioned himself in front of me. He pulled his plate of instruments towards him and I looked at my grandmother; as though looking away from him helped. I directed my speech to my grandmother, my head turned that way, and I watched her hands fiddle with her shirt, counting the stitches on the cuff of her sleeve. I sucked in a gasp of breath. He forced me open, without warning, and it was cool and uncomfortable, if not painful. He swabbed and prodded and my stomach tensed, though it was nothing to do with my stomach.

'Are you trying for a child?' he said.

'No,' I said.

He stopped the prodding and I counted the stitches with her. One loop, two loops, three. I heard paper shuffling again, he was consulting his chart. 'You're twenty-one,' he said, 'Fairly unusual in your state not to be trying or planning.'

'I'm not ready yet,' I said, which was foolish.

He laughed, heartily, like he was in on a good joke. 'Everyone is ready. There is only ready.'

The prodding hadn't resumed. I waited for it, and the waiting was almost as bad as the thing itself.

'I would start soon,' he said, prodding more forcefully now. 'I wouldn't want to report otherwise.' Prod. 'And if you miss your window, a girl like you,' ceasing now. 'It doesn't bear thinking about. Look at me,' he said, and I turned my head from the stitches to him and he slowly pulled out the thing that pulled me apart. 'Now,' he said, 'Do it now. If there is no partner, we can supply the necessary aids.'

I had nothing else. I saw my future closing in front of me; me, my grandmother, and a baby, to propagate this earth with one more. What did one more count for? It counted for something, to them, to Mrs P. And yet, as we were one, a singular, an individual, we counted for little. And then there was him, and the dinner party, and the gooseberries, and it seemed miles away.

'Technically you have four years, to try on your own.' He chuckled. 'But that's not an eternity.'

I released my feet from the stirrups without him telling me so. 'Yes,' I said.

'It's getting worse,' he said. He looked out the window, at the sun shining brightly. 'The heat is almost tropical. We're lucky Dengue isn't here yet,' he said, 'Lucky we closed our borders when we did.' He gestured to my swabs in the container. 'I'll get these checked, but if all's well, I'd hope you don't let it get urgent. The interventions.'

I thought of the wine at the dinner party, I smelt it, didn't I? But I didn't drink it then. I regretted it. I regretted it so much as I dressed back into my clothes that I could almost taste it. An iron, clanging, bitter taste. No, it was just blood, from where I'd caught my lip. The cramps started, forcefully, and I felt I could taste them too.

He looked at me, frustrated, as though I were a child in school that wasn't paying attention. 'I'll walk you out,' he said. My grandmother looked at him with eyebrows raised, but followed him, gesturing for me to come along, out the door. He turned away from the reception and through to a different ward, commenting on how this hospital was the most prestigious in the country, Auntie said so herself. We got to a set of double doors and he punched in a code on a keypad, and with a strange electronic whirring, the kind of noise that was alien to me, the door clicked open. He held it open for us as we stepped through, and then led us down another corridor that smelt of clinical disinfectant and a foreign cleanliness.

'Better to go out this way,' he said, walking more slowly now. The doors to the rooms on the ward were open, and I could see inside seven or eight beds neatly lined up together. They were all full, but not with the quiet melancholy of the frail and infirm, but a sick writhing of people feverish and restless, whose minds didn't want to be there. I listened to their moans as they wrestled with their sheets and shuffled their limbs.

The doctor kept walking. We went past room after room. I looked at my grandmother and she shook her head at me as though to say: Just act normal.

I realised as I passed these people, and the noises got more and more sickening, that there were only women. I wanted to ask the doctor what was wrong with them, but before I could he stopped abruptly outside one door. It was a room of about ten or so beds, so close together that each person could have reached out and touched the other if they wanted. From inside this room was a visceral screaming, and I tried to step away and keep walking, but the doctor took me by the wrist.

'You have to be careful,' he said, holding me towards the open door, as though I were a hen's egg, unseen and rare, in the oval dip of someone's palm.

Inside, amongst the writhing women with saline drips, was one in particular who was being held down forcibly, her arms and legs strapped to the bed, a sheet draped over her middle. She woozily rocked her head from side to side, and a screaming gurgle escaped her lips as a nurse rubbed her arm and walked towards her feet. As she reached under the sheet I thought for a moment that she was in labour, and we had ended up in the delivery suite. But after a few movements, the nurse left, syringe in hand. She walked past us out of the room, and said casually to another nurse: 'Tell her to keep her legs elevated.'

The doctor let go of my wrist. He turned and carried on walking, gesturing for us to follow, as though nothing had happened. We walked in silence behind him until he led us to another door to exit the hospital. He clicked it open and held it for us to walk through.

'It's important that you saw that,' he said. 'She was almost thirty. Something had to be done.'

Neither of us said anything, but nodded, and walked from the hospital in silence, until the building and its sour clinical stench was well behind us.

'If I do it,' I said, 'we'll have more money. And I'll have to do it eventually, won't I. So maybe it should be now.'

It was a long, hot walk home, up Pond Street and down through Hampstead (past Gloria's house), which we took slowly. My own fragility after seeing the doctor was mirrored by my grandmother. She was quiet, and almost angry, and I took that anger as directed at me.

'There are other ways, you know there are,' she said. We didn't look at each other. 'Margot and I didn't want that lonely life for you. We decided, when it was only a whisper of an idea. When you were nine years old. If you met someone, fine. If not,' she shook her head, 'you are not cattle.'

What we heard about cattle around the village now was cattle starving to death, cattle dying of heat exhaustion, cattle flooded out of their fields, their homes. I thought we sounded exactly like cattle.

'Everyone else has done it,' I said, trying to convince myself.

'We could wait. There's still time for Mrs P to step down. She won't be in office forever. It will happen eventually.' I'd never considered this was because of our President; it was just the law that everyone agreed with, to boost the population. Even now I would think it reductive to say that without Mrs P there would be no policy.

'No,' I said. 'It won't change.'

'Is this what you want? Hungry baby in our tiny house, the three of us, collecting coupons for the rest of our lives?' Her voice was raised, and her head was turned towards me.

I felt my throat closing. I wondered what my mother would say. 'What else though? Refuse? End up in prison and die while I'm at it?'

She softened her tone, apologetic. 'It was a choice for me.'

'I know.'

We both stopped walking after that and looked at one another. It had never occurred to me, I'm sure wouldn't occur to people, that it had once been that easy. 'I wish I could give you that,' she said. '*La liberté.*'

I wanted to tell her about the meetings I'd had with George, but I sensed a great deal of ambivalence on her part. On the one hand she had encouraged me. Money, which was running in his circles, meant freedom. On the other, I'm sure she was afraid of his power, personal and political, and would rather I was well away from it.

'If you were needed somewhere,' she said. 'In a role, a job, somewhere important, if you had to be away, you'd be exempt.'

'Where am I needed?' I said. 'Nowhere. The only thing I can do is sew, you made sure of that.' I regretted the

93

words, instantly. 'I'm sorry, this isn't your fault.'

'No,' she said, not looking at me. 'You're right. I should've done more.'

We continued walking. I rubbed my lower belly, the cramping started to cease. Did I yearn, for a moment, for that vessel to be filled? They told me I was empty. But my grandmother assured me against that feeling. She gave me the illusion of choice.

'Then the only other answer is money,' she said. 'Either you pay off a doctor to sign you something, to say you can't have children, or someone else pays. I know it's done. I know they do it.'

'It's death,' I said, 'You know how people disappear.'

'Bearing a child is death, too, Mathilde. How many young women are lost to it? It's too dangerous. Without drugs, without enough doctors. And if you make it through, then what? Your child dies at three years old of the flu and you may be exempt then, but you are left with nothing. No funding, no life, only heartbreak. Or you run out of food, and one more mouth to feed kills us all. How many friends have you lost to this insanity? To this crazy notion that even though there's not enough for the living, we should make as much room as we can for the unborn?'

I didn't want to count them. I had stopped counting. Some had left children behind, others had not. I gave myself tunnel vision, on purpose. I pretended we weren't friends to begin with.

'Why did Maman have me then?' I said. 'Did she choose it?'

My grandmother looked at me, as we tapped lightly down Netherhall Gardens, past the empty, forgotten giantess houses; broken windows and overgrown lawns, brick walls higher than our heads, buildings dark, oppressive. They'd stood empty for years.

'It was different then, Mathilde. She chose you because she wanted you and loved you and there was a life to be had for you. Now, there is nothing.' She lowered her voice as she spotted a woman on the other side of the street. 'To bring a child into this nothing is cruel. It is a drop in the ocean.'

I nodded. I agreed with her. But I did also think that the world could continue on without us, for longer than we imagined.

I knew that the only thing that kept us going was the other. Or maybe the gooseberries that had once grown on bushes, and the parsley that we could just about get to live. It was the chicken we might nurture and respect and then eat, glad of the small system that still existed in the world that allowed us to do this. What the weather blotted out, we fought against. I fought against this invasion of my body, but I also imagined that somewhere, that ocean she spoke of was a presence and a force, a force that might have brought us to this point, and this earth we lived on. I had a strong sense of this ocean of people and the drops we were within it. I still had a strong sense that I was a woman second, and a human first.

Which is why I chose the way I did.

2

I thought often about kissing George in the days after our meeting. I thought of the shape of his mouth, and tried to remember the exact order of conversation that we had, which I have now recounted but cannot claim is entirely accurate.

My grandmother pulled me into the shop regularly, for some basic mending and working on simple patterns. But with every stitch I thought only of him and my body in turn, and the decisions I had to make. I wanted to enter his world and be rid of mine, desperately, but in my mind I also wanted to be rid of my body; I wanted to re-enter it as though it were an item of clothing I could slip into, for decoration, with nothing practical hidden underneath.

I was afraid his intentions didn't align with my own, but I knew that this mattered little. Whether I had to have a child or I had to get out of it, the answer always came back to him.

That I attributed to him at this time my entire future existence never occurred to me. In reality, the seriousness of it didn't settle down on me. I couldn't imagine myself with a child, or without, I couldn't imagine a future at all; I stitched and stitched to keep myself in quiet occupied solitude. Between my meetings with him there seemed to be only stitches, small and uniform and repetitive. It was a meditation on his mouth, one stitch upper lip, one stitch freckle. It was a meditation on the peaches, one stitch sugar, one stitch crumble. It was a meditation on myself around him, one stitch pull me in, one stitch let me go. When I finished all my stitches, the last being pulling together pieces of fabric to wear as a dress myself (which would be unpicked and returned to the shop later), I felt I had imagined him. But I wore it to the party he invited me to, and when he came to my door and noted it, I looked at his mouth and stroked the fabric of my dress. It felt exactly like his mouth, and his body, and even the transcendent feeling that I had imagined, completely,

96

paled in comparison to the real thing; of him, of his people, of his world.

George could have been anyone, in the sense that he could have done anything; whatever he put his mind to, in his singular way, he would have been compelling enough to achieve.

He could not have been anyone in the way he captured my imagination, as others had now and again attempted, leaving me cold. It was the way he watched me as I turned my head away from him. His gaze would fix, examining my neck or whatever part of me I'd left exposed, so that when I returned I'd always meet his eyes again.

It was an intoxicating thing to be noticed the way he purposefully noticed me. And at that second party of Gloria's, amongst all that food, that room, amongst people like Gloria herself, it was my shoulder he squeezed and my tread he followed over the plum-coloured carpet. Even on our way there, over the pot-holed streets of Hampstead, he placed a hand on my back as we crossed the desolate four-lane Finchley Road, leading me on.

George introduced me to Gloria again and she pretended to remember me. I was intimidated by her. She was a tall woman, taller than the men, and she held herself that way. Everything about her was tall: her graciousness and her openness, her frivolity and her seriousness. She was imposing and inclusive, and you always felt like you were in on a good secret when you were around her.

'Your new squeeze, Georgey?' she asked him, after introductions. She didn't move her eyes away from him, waiting for his answer.

'Quite,' he said.

She looped her arm in mine and pulled me up the stairs to the first floor. I could hear the piano as we approached the drawing room, and with each step that we took, I wondered if it was real. I looked at Gloria, to see if she had any sign of surprise in her face, but it was as if she didn't hear the music at all.

'You should be careful with him, you know,' she said, holding my arm fiercely as he lagged behind. 'A cad. Even when he brings the good champagne, we all know he's a terror.'

I couldn't detect whether she was serious or not; even her tone of voice was unlike anything I'd heard before. For a moment I didn't want to speak, so afraid her voice didn't match my own.

'Can you hear that?' I said, and I think my arm was shaking just to hear it again. We approached the landing and she pushed open the drawing room door. The piano was at the back of the room, large and black, a beast with its lid propped open. The woman there was furiously pedalling and playing, and I stood, astonished at it, greater than any animal I had once seen, or any man-made thing. I wanted to touch it. I wanted to make a sound.

'That?' Gloria pointed to the piano. 'That's just Jaminder,' she said. 'We hired her to play. She's become quite the fixture around here. She's like wallpaper.'

I looked at Jaminder, and I thought she was the most magnificent thing I'd ever seen. She was different from the others. Darker skin and longer hair and fixed with purpose. 'Oh?' I said. 'I suppose she does decorate the room.'

Gloria looked across to him with a smirk. 'Oh, George, where do you find them? How droll.'

He put a hand behind my back and we snaked in-between groups of people to a table laden with drinks. I'd never seen so many well-groomed people in all my life. Women with styled hair, men with scrubbed skin. And suits and gold rings and polished leather shoes. Everything looked so new.

'Don't mind Gloria,' he said, passing me a drink that frothed at its edges. 'She's a drunk.'

I raised it to my mouth to take a sip, and was greeted with a sweet and bitter assault on my tongue. It was clanging and fizzy. It slipped down my throat and I coughed; it was vile.

'What is this?' I asked.

He laughed. 'Champagne.'

I looked to Gloria, holding her arms out to every person who entered the room, glass in one hand, cigarette in the other. I grimaced. 'She gets drunk on this?'

'Amongst other things,' he said.

I watched her floating about the room, with a deft, insistent way about her. She leaned forward with purpose to everyone she came across, and people felt at ease around her. You could tell because of the way they'd forget themselves, loosen their arms and not wonder about where to put them, touch her shoulder. She held everyone's attention, and they welcomed it.

I held my champagne glass at its top, rather than its stem – even though I could tell this wasn't right – because I was afraid it would topple over. I took another sip and the liquid had warmed beneath my hand. I watched a man move between people, filling up their glasses. He stopped by one group of people and put a hand on Gloria's waist and then through her hair, reaching towards her neck. 'Who's that?' I asked George.

'Frank,' he said, 'they're practically one person. Always have been like that.'

'Oh?'

'Yes, married for years.'

99

'Children?' I said.

'No, not yet,' he took a slug of his drink and shrugged.

Gloria turned her face towards Frank and it was a look I didn't recognise. Her attention from hosting was lost. The group of people around her smiled at each other, but crossed their arms awkwardly, waiting for her focus to return. The glance was brief, and she returned to her guests with an anecdote which made them laugh. Frank moved away and she watched him go, I thought, from the way she angled her head towards him. The couple's movements towards each other reassured me, because they were intimate and kind.

The levity in the room made the place feel timeless. It made me feel like a person who belonged to the real world again. Because wasn't this the real world? Feeling present, letting yourself forget about your little vegetable patch and that thing your mother once said to you about mint leaves? I wished this was the real world, because the energy of it bore no resemblance to the rest of life. The way people held their glasses casually, and gestured to people in their group to collude their story. The fact that they even had stories to tell, stories that were so banal that they had a perfect place here; they neither interrupted the flow of conversation nor worried the guests. The talk was easy.

A man bent down to tie his patent laced shoe; another clicked his fingers in the air at someone walking by to attract their attention. I saw Gwendolyn, Gloria's friend, her hair waved perfectly again, checking her lipstick in a small gold mirror, after asking the man next to her to hold her black sequinned bag. She wiped the edges of her lips with her index finger and opened her mouth wide, examining its shape and swell. Then she pressed her lips back together at herself in the small mirror, and in that movement, with a frown, made a decision. She fished in the bag she'd given to her partner and twisted the lipstick up until the bright pink stem emerged from its metal casing, perfectly straight-edged and vibrant. She traced the arc of her lips with it, boldly, pressing it over, making the pout flush and rounded, like the plump of a strawberry. She smacked her lips together, still holding the mirror tall with the other hand, before rolling the bullet of the pink lipstick down again with one hand, snapping the lid back on top, and placing it back in the bag. The man next to her didn't look up throughout this theatre.

I'd never seen a woman do a thing like that. The routine of it warmed me. I watched as she looked up from her bag, ready to have her partner's attention back, and him distracted, looking elsewhere. She smiled then, and reached around him, grabbing his behind with a full plump squeeze, which made him jump and shift in embarrassment.

'Gwen,' he said, harshly. 'Not with people around.'

'Oh, I couldn't give a flying fig,' she said, loudly, and laughed as she gave him another squeeze. She continued to laugh as Gloria passed by them, and she called over to her, 'Gloria, have you got any figs tonight?'

Gloria stopped, glass in hand, and called back, 'What, those little pruney things from the East? The devil's fruit aren't they?'

'Can't say I've ever had one,' Gwendolyn's partner said, straightening his jacket to regain his composure.

'Ghastly,' Gloria said. 'You'll know if we have figs in our delivery that something awful has happened.'

Gwendolyn laughed at this, looking greedily at her partner, and Gloria walked on. I tried to remember if I'd ever had a fig, and could only recall a certain false smell of a sweet, ripe fruit, which I wasn't sure belonged to it.

I turned back to George to tell him, to pat his arm and ask him if he'd ever had a fig, but he was lost in contemplation.

At these parties, his attention was always focused on discovering my inner life, and getting to know every part of it. He asked me things people were always too afraid to ask. It was a luxury of his, to be unafraid to talk about things that devastated other people. I touched his arm and his attention returned.

'Tell me about your mother,' he said. 'Did she ever leave the continent?'

'Why do you want to know about all that?' I said.

'Tell me.'

I tried to dismiss his morbid curiosity. 'Well, no she didn't, thank God.' I laughed it off, champagne in hand, like a winning anecdote, an answer I'd prepared in my head many times. 'She would've melted the moment she left France, so it's a blessing she never did.'

What was the true answer? She was severe, in her own way, which protected all of us against the rudeness of bank tellers and waiters and teachers who thought little of you. But her severity gave way to loveliness, the way her mouth would move in perfect amiable synchronicity with her eyes. The way she'd bite into a butter biscuit – *langues de chat* – with a snap and smile at you, like she'd tasted something new.

It's a devastation that she never had the chance to comment on the fall of France as we knew it. Whether we stayed in our blue apartment with the green shutters on Rue des Rosiers or not mattered little, because all the feeling of it left with her.

I suppose he knew this, and wanted a chance to empathise with me. He wanted a chance to say: I'm sorry, how awful, and imagine in a voyeuristically pleasing way, the collapse of his own country to rebel forces and civil war. The collapse of his language and family and the whole narrative of his life. I tried to explain some of it to him, in-between the champagne bubbles going up my nose, and my awkward pulling at the skirt of my dress.

'It's unimaginable,' he said.

'Yes, it is,' I said. I didn't say: So we don't ever bother to imagine it.

He held my hand at the buffet table with a solid intimacy, where laid out were the appetisers of the day, along with the drinks. There were neatly sliced carrots and celery and pots of dips and bowls of thick substances.

I wanted to place my hand in them and smear them around, like an infant, trying to identify taste with my hands. But instead, I picked up a small piece of peeled luminous carrot – what care had been taken over its appearance, what attention! – and bit into it.

'*Les carottes*,' he said, as a little joke.

'Yes, well done,' I said, and laughed, grateful that this was the extent of his knowledge.

He reached for a carrot himself and held it in-between his fingers. 'I learnt a little French once, at school. We used to complain about our test results, the way teenage boys do, adamant we'd done much better than our marks suggested, and our French teacher would always say: "*Les carottes sont cuites.*" It only fuelled our hysteria more, laughing about carrots and jumping about while she stamped her feet, telling us to be quiet.'

My smile slipped then, as I realised, after a few seconds detangling his unrecognisable accent, what he had said. My mother had said it, as a joke to herself, when the treatment was done and she lay in her bed in our apartment, knowing she'd never get out of it again, not to walk to the window and look at the sky, or run with us anywhere.

103

'What did it mean again? You're all useless turds?'

I looked down at the carrot in his hand and smiled briefly, before it left me. 'The carrots are cooked.' I said. 'It means: It's done.' I searched for the proper translation in my mind, but what was more difficult was trying to remember my mother tongue and its true meaning, rather than the English I used every day that swirled about my head. 'It means: The writing's on the wall.' I looked up at him and met his eyes. 'You're toast.'

I circled around the piano for most of the night. I watched Jaminder's face, her concentration. Also her distraction, when someone boomed something funny and the room laughed. She was not the wallpaper that Gloria had described. She was the only thing in the room. Even when George touched my hand and brought me more champagne, I kept turning back to the piano. He asked me if I liked the music, and I said yes. But I didn't say I'd never heard a piano being played before that first dinner party. Not in real life. It was better than the sound on any radio or recording, better than any broken stringed instrument someone might bring out in the village. A breathing, vibrating thing like that piano stole the room, only no one seemed to notice. Except, of course, Jaminder herself. Who – after Gloria put an old straining record on in the corner of the room – came straight towards me.

'I haven't seen you here before,' she said. 'You're drinking that champagne like it's petrol.'

'Not much of that about.'

'Maybe because they started putting it in drinks.'

I smiled at her. She looked at me warily. 'You came with George?'

'Yes.'

She nodded. 'I suppose he's told you about his little bee project.'

'His bees?'

'Oh, well, I better not. You know about bees? You've seen them?'

'We had honey sometimes.'

She raised her eyebrows. 'Stick around.' She downed her glass of champagne in one, spilling it down her throat, head tipped back. 'Stay. There'll be proper food later and you won't want to miss that.' She smacked her lips and twirled her glass, 'You know this didn't come from France. But better than all the tea in China.'

'There are no children here,' I said, carefully.

Jaminder laughed. 'Of course not, it's a party.' She tipped her glass towards figures across the room. 'Theirs are tucked up in bed; they didn't want any; she has four – ghastly – and me,' she tipped the glass back at herself, towards her chest. 'Had it all taken out, the whole factory.'

'You did?'

She nodded. 'Health reasons, of course. None for me. But plenty of—' she shook her glass at me and then eyed my own. 'And for you, too, I see. George's taken care of it?'

'Oh, no, I probably...' I stammered. I felt horrified, suddenly, to be drinking alcohol in front of people.

'He'll see to it, either way. Don't worry.' She nodded at me encouragingly, but I felt swamped without the noise of the piano. 'Must get another,' she said, and turned to go.

I grabbed her shoulder and pulled her back, a little too forcefully.

She looked at me, startled. 'What's your name?'

'Mathilde.'

105

'French?'

'Probably.' I shrugged my shoulders.

She smiled. 'Wonderful,' she said, 'wonderful.'

'And you?'

'I'm not sure,' she said, and winked at me. 'Are we ever?' She turned again to go.

'Wait,' I said. Jaminder turned back, smiled at me. 'What about the bees? What bees?'

'You'll see when the food arrives. You'll see the cake.' She looked me up and down, and nodded her head. 'This place is Versailles,' she said, and smiled. 'If I were you I wouldn't come back.' She said it so softly, I'm not sure if that's what she did say, or if I imagined it. But that's what I think she said, and what she'd say now, and what we'd conclude together. But if I'd never come back, I wouldn't have her in my life, and she was my good thing then, and my good thing now, my Jaminder.

It was imperceptible; no one heard, perhaps not even me. She raised her glass and skipped off, and shouted, into the boom of voices and the record swirling round, 'Let them eat cake!'

The room laughed.

The dress Gloria bought from my grandmother was a shiny slip of a thing; and if that was a fish, then this was the pond. I saw Gloria, wearing a different dress from the last dinner that my grandmother had painstakingly worked on. I had stitched the hem, and checked the beading, thinking each of these dresses were for an elaborate occasion no doubt in the presence of Mrs P. But they were for parties. They were there to make sure she fitted in with the other women, whose beading also resembled fish scales, whose slippery materials also shone like the glint in the pond. And there I was – in the

106

midst of it, everyone slipping past each other – the silt at the bottom.

But as the evening wore on and I stopped drinking champagne and everyone else carried on, I noticed the fish were garish, too. They left lipstick marks on all the glasses, they spilled red liquid on Gloria's rug, they sung out of tune to the discord of the record player, they even tore the linen tablecloth, starched white; the whitest thing I'd ever seen. I touched it; I watched as a woman tore through its edging with her stiletto heel. I saw her come off balance, laugh, and trot off to her partner, new glass in hand, with the beat of a cat.

Then there was George, who steadily continued to drink, his breath becoming denser, and his touches firmer. It was subtle, until the food came out and he grabbed my elbow and kissed me in front of the whole room. I heard a whistle from the corner and I tore my head away in embarrassment.

He laughed and kissed my forehead. 'This will be better than the fish paste from last time,' he said. 'I can't wait for you to try it. Gloria knows her stuff.'

I wondered how Gloria knowing food meant that she was in possession of it, but I didn't ask him. Everything was wheeled out on trolleys with big silver trays and pots, and as they were uncovered, one by one, I stared at the items. I waited for them to introduce themselves like they were guests at the party, but they lay there and people piled the food onto their plates and I only stood beside him, waiting.

He was distracted by someone calling him over to the other side of the room, and of all the things that overwhelmed me at the party, this was the most significant. I felt a childish sense of abandonment stood in front of the banquet, as people pushed past me.

I wanted to say, out loud, that I'd never seen so much colour and that it was almost unappetising. I wanted, desperately, to tell my mother: There's blue food! And yellow, and something that looks like the plush skin of a strawberry. I wanted to prick it, watch it ooze out of itself.

It was Jaminder in the end who dragged me forwards, as I remembered her talking about the cake. And I saw it, sticky and oozing. People were grabbing slices, their faces luxuriating under the weight of the tiny forks in their mouths. But she hadn't touched it.

I gathered a slice for myself and picked up a tiny fork, the likes of which didn't look very useful, and I stood next to her. She didn't notice me. I took a bite.

'Bees,' I said, prompting her to look at me.

She sighed. 'His idea of a little paradise. Mr Beekeeper.'

'It tastes like my childhood,' I said. 'Honey.'

'My grandmother used to put it in hot water for me with lemon. Lemon!' Her eyes searched the table. 'I'm sure I saw some lemon something here.'

The honey cake was even sweeter than the peaches. It was something else. It was my mother telling me to wash my hands before dinner, it was her laugh on the shady grass in the French countryside surrounded by lavender, it was the way she cut baguette into thick slices, it was her pulling her hair away from her face, it was her voice telling me not to worry, *tout est bien qui finit bien*, it was a teaspoon in summer to stave off hay fever. It was a time before.

'Don't be sad, sweet girl,' Jaminder said, but she was the one who looked sad, looking at my face.

'How did he get them? Where do they get all this stuff?'

'The bees?' she said, surprised. 'Well, where do you think? A little money can get you anything. They have contacts. If anyone can get things, they can.' She pointed across the room.

'They can?'

'Of course. You know what you're looking at, don't you?'

I looked. I didn't, I couldn't be sure. I hadn't wanted to know.

'You're looking at the wonderful Ministry of Environmental Affairs, amongst others. They're Mrs P's bloody cabinet, the lot of them. Most of them were tied up in the old way of things, and that still holds a certain sway behind closed doors. Of *course* he has bees, he can get everything. He's the secretary of state.'

'What old way of things?'

Her eyes narrowed as she assessed my face. 'A generation back. They were given sanctuary, paid off. The people had to be appeased but it couldn't have been a thing like France. All guillotines and storming of the Bastille.' She looked at me pointedly. 'Loose ties, you see. I don't mean, in line for the throne, apart from that one,' she pointed at a Minister across the room, 'he might have been number forty-three, or something. Apart from that, they were only loosely connected. But it all had to go, didn't it? So most of them were given a title or another that mattered, ushered into a place of power quietly. While the King and all his lot left for Norway or Denmark or whatever it was.'

'Oh,' I said. 'I didn't know.' But I did know something of that upheaval. Well underway by the time I was born, it took years for the transition from Constitutional Monarchy to Republic. The truth was, it scared us, even the French. It was always the thing people talked about. Evidence that something had really changed. When supplies started to dwindle and the crisis spread, just before the blackout, there was no place for a family, a whole network of people, to reside in palaces that were redecorated with money that could now be spent only on resources. The image of the King renouncing his throne before he was forcibly removed became the symbol of the new era. Opulence was gone along with luxury. Stability for its own sake, power. No King, no promise of history. We were equalised, and the French leapt from one broken Republic to another.

Jaminder laughed. 'They're going to save us all. Especially George with all his projects: the bees, the farming. They're going to bring food back, bring the bees back, reverse all the damage that's been done. Change our little climate. Change the moon and stars. Maybe after all that, one of them will be crowned.' She laughed and waved her fork in the air and looked towards the ceiling.

'Really?' I said.

'Of course bloody not,' she said. 'That's why they're all here, getting pissed off their heads and eating anything that's left. They know the state we're in.'

'But there must be a chance, with all this food? That must mean something?'

I found his face across the room, I looked in it. I saw something magical, the goodness of hope; the idea that he'd try to save our little spot on the world.

'It's done.' Jaminder said.

I looked back at him, the joy on his face. I couldn't see through it.

'He has his little projects. A hive off the coast, and the rest. Offshore investments. Fingers in all the pies.' She watched my reaction as she said the words, her eyes narrowed.

I imagined his large fingers with his thick nails, submerged through crust into sticky compote.

'And every country he finds useful,' she said, eyeing me up again. 'Maybe even France.'

'I doubt that. What use is France to anyone now?'

'Strategic, maybe. Were you here before the blackout, or still over there?' She shook her head, 'No, you look just about too young.'

'We came afterwards, as part of the recruitment drive by Mrs P.'

'Oh yes, one of Auntie's little schemes,' she said, sarcastically.

I stopped, looking at her face, wanting to ask, but never being sure that the English wanted to remember, just like we didn't. 'What was it like?'

Jaminder laughed. 'Your country was crushed by civil war, bombing, massacres, and drought. I heard Notre Dame was one of the first things to be blitzed.' She looked at my face for a reaction. 'And you're asking me what it was like?'

'Yes,' I said, quietly.

She looked away from me and out the window. 'My grandparents were killed in the protests. My grandmother left wearing a red scarf, and my grandfather gave me the keys to his car, and never came back,' she said, stopping to look at me, knowing I too remembered glimpses like these and held them to me when things were bad. 'We knew food was scarce, and the storms were everywhere. But you still had power didn't you? When the protests started, you could still turn on a light?'

'I don't really remember,' I said. 'We got out early. It happened later for us.'

'We were one of the first to go. One evening, bam,' she clicked her fingers. 'No power. Nothing. Only darkness.' She shook her head. 'There were no warnings. They said fuel was running out, but they didn't say it was going to

111

run out *today*. It's a bit like death isn't it? We knew it was coming, we just didn't think it would come so soon. We didn't think it would ever really arrive.' She looked at me, opening and closing her mouth, taking in a breath that lifted her shoulders. 'Months went by like that; protests, riots, famine. A whole mechanised industry ground to a halt. Eventually the energy companies stepped up the renewable stuff but it was only enough for the odd hour here and there. Only enough for the very rich. Not much different from now.'

'But it's better now,' I said. 'That's why we came here. Because of Mrs P.'

Jaminder smiled at me, but out of pity, rather than affection. '"England Isn't Eating", that's all we heard for months. I'd lost my family, you know. I knew the same as anyone that we were starving.'

'And now England Is Eating,' I said, looking at the cake.

'In a sense,' she said. 'But at what cost? You can't force farmers to give up crops for no money, and you can't force women to have children they don't want and can't feed because of warped family values.'

'But the farmers are the ones holding the country to ransom,' I said. 'You can't have a group of people making the country starve.'

She laughed at me, and I felt a fool, for repeating what I was told by other people. 'They're the ones who are starving. They're the ones with nothing. Look at us,' she said. 'It's like the last days of Rome in here.'

I looked across the room, I tried to find George in my eyeline, and search for some answer there. 'It's different here,' I said, 'Like the rules don't apply. Even to the women.'

'Maybe they don't.' Jaminder shrugged.

'I had a friend who died for that policy, you know.'

'We've all had someone like that. In a protest?'

'No, childbirth. She was eighteen and got sepsis. Nothing they could do.' I looked at her, and she gave me a nod.

'That's terrible,' she said.

'But they're helping aren't they? They're trying to make it better.' I gestured towards a group of men in the corner.

'Do you think if it was the other way round, that they'd put their necks on the line? That's not what they're doing.' She looked at me pityingly, almost held a hand out to my shoulder, and then retracted it. 'God, you're so young. But we're still in the dark. It's not like what they're doing will save all this.'

'Then why?' I put down my cake.

'What do you think? You wouldn't do the same?' She gestured to my plate. 'It's not some altruistic deed. He just wanted to taste honey again.' She tried to smile, but it seemed that she couldn't. She shrugged her shoulders, exasperated. 'That's all.'

'How did you make it through the blackout?' I said. 'You must have been very young.'

She looked at me, and down at the cake that I had left discarded on the table. 'I came back from the dead,' she said. 'Didn't everyone?'

People filtered out of the house as the evening of the party wore on, so drunk they smacked against the door frames and tripped over the gravel outside as they left. Gloria vomited in her guest toilet, and Gwendolyn stood outside, rapping on the door. 'Are you sick Gloria? Are you all right?'

Her voice moaned out from behind the solid wood. 'Quite fine, Wendy Darling. Fine. It just keeps happening, doesn't it.'

Gwendolyn turned around when she saw me, and

113

smiled at me. 'She eats too much. She's sick,' she made a swirling circular motion with her hand. 'She eats too much, she's sick.' Her pink pout was still perfectly intact, and I wondered if she'd had a drop of food or a drink the entire evening.

'Are you going to look after her?' I said, wondering if I should linger and help.

'Yes,' she said. 'I'm done with my date for the evening, I suppose.'

Gloria shouted from behind the door, in-between retching noises. 'Yes, Wendy Darling, stay. The Lost Boys can do without you for one night.'

She smiled at me and shrugged. 'She likes having me around I suppose, a friendly face at the end of the night.'

I smiled at her. 'You're a good friend,' I said, as I started to hear a tinkering of notes coming from the drawing room.

'And you?' she said, looking me up and down, 'How are you enjoying yourself here?'

I laughed in defence of myself. 'It's another world.'

'Yes,' she said. 'We get a free pass here. Away from all that population crap.'

'You don't have children?' I said, wondering if this was the wrong thing to be asking.

'God, no,' she said. 'What would I have one for? It's cruel isn't it? A very specific type of cruelty. To impose children on people who can't feed them.'

'They'll hear you!' Gloria shouted, a laughing gurgle coming through the door.

Gwendolyn looked towards it and laughed. 'Let them.'

'Do you know then,' I said, 'why they all think it's such a good idea?'

'I don't know,' she said, her hand pressed against the

114

closed door. 'It just wouldn't do to be another country that dwindles away to nothing. To run out of farmers, and food. It just wouldn't do.'

'Gwendolyn,' I said, taking a step towards her, wanting to say something to her but not able to find the words that would give it a form.

'Don't fly away!' Gloria shouted, and Gwendolyn laughed, turned towards the door, her hand on the handle, ready to turn.

'I'm coming in now, you fool,' she said.

I followed the noise back into the room, now a mess, stains littering the carpet, leftover food spilling out of corners. Jaminder was sitting at her piano and I went towards her. 'What will they do with it all? The leftovers?'

'Government waste,' she snorted. She passed her hand along its top and moved along the stool. She looked at me. 'Come sit with me.'

I went and placed myself beside her on the stool. 'Will you play?' I asked her.

She lit a cigarette and took a few drags, before setting it in her mouth. She started to play the keys. The panoply that emanated from the piano cut inside me. I wanted to remember it in times of isolation; that even though I may not always hear it, I will know it's there.

I watched her fingers move effortlessly across the black and white surface, as if each was their own person, their own identity, independent of each other. She touched the keys lightly at first, and then more firmly. The music grew melancholy, almost menacing, and I felt it reach out and touch me, warn me, tell me.

At least, that's how I remember it.

'It's wonderful,' I said as she stopped for a drag of her cigarette.

'It's a party trick.'

115

'No,' I said, to convince her. 'It's something. It's better than all that food, and all those people. It's really something.'

She smiled. 'Thank you, *Mademoiselle*.'

I touched the keys lightly, so they didn't make a sound. I fingered the black keys and their edges, pressing so softly no noise escaped them. 'I'm going to ask him about the bees.'

She shrugged. 'If you like.' She took another drag. 'Are you sleeping together?' She exhaled.

I put my hands in my lap. I didn't look at her. 'No.'

She started to play, quietly, a few notes, a twinkle. 'You can, you know. There are ways. To stop anything unwanted happening.'

I don't suppose someone like him would've thought about it, but I'd had other men. We all had, there were always ways, methods that were frowned upon, but they weren't illegal. They just didn't always work.

'I know,' I said. 'But it's risky.'

'No, there are real things.' A few more notes. 'Pills you can take. Injections. You wouldn't ever have to worry.'

'That's illegal,' I said. 'That is too risky.'

'Risk is a judgment,' she said, putting out her cigarette in a dish on the piano. 'Everyone does it. Me; Gwendolyn as much as she likes.'

'You?'

'Oh, I dabble. Geoffrey, the Minister for Transport. As you know, the underground is dying along with the rest of it, so you can imagine how glamorous a job that is. How glamorous he is.'

'Do you love him?' I willed her to start playing the keys again, but she only hovered over them.

She laughed. 'God, no. He's a way to scratch an itch. They're mostly awful, aren't they?'

'I don't know.'

116

'Yes, not your one,' she said, mocking me. I didn't know why, and I didn't care to ask. 'But why else come here then? If not for all that?'

'I don't know,' I said. But I did. To be free; for freedom. The funny thing about freedom is the many forms it takes. There was a freedom from one thing which may not give you a freedom from something else. Complete freedom is an absolute, and therefore imaginary. I didn't know that then. But I think Jaminder did, all the same, and I think that's why she chose hers so carefully.

'Go to bed with him,' she said, a lilt to her voice. Her hands started to play the melancholy music with sharp precision. Her cigarette lodged in the corner of her mouth. 'Just make sure you get what you want out of him. Don't tell yourself it's about love. Because it's not.'

I wondered about this: I pored over her words, for days afterwards. How could she be sure I wasn't in love? Wasn't I? The way he picked me, the way he pulled me out of myself and into something so new, wouldn't that prompt me into love? Whatever love meant, whatever love was, I thought I had it, I thought I could taste it. I thought if I kept going it might appear to me as a realisation or a dream, or an imagining. If I only carried on, it would surely take a solid form in front of me. I studied her words and my thoughts, I analysed every facet of my feelings. I worried about it.

I needn't have bothered. I didn't realise at the time that she was talking about his feelings, and not my own.

Jaminder carried on playing and I decided to find George. I walked out into the hallway again, hoping to check on Gloria on my way, and found her and Gwendolyn facing George, standing outside the toilet, gesturing towards him. I stopped by the drawing room door. Gloria was yellow and sickly looking, her hair a matted mess upon her head, and Gwendolyn was perfectly composed, arms crossed, levelling George's gaze. Gloria grasped Gwendolyn's hand in defiance, her usual cheerful disposition gone.

'I don't know what's the matter with you,' she said to George, not letting go of Gwendolyn's hand.

'Give over, Gloria, it's just a bit of friendly advice. To settle down, that's all,' he said.

Gwendolyn laughed mirthlessly. 'Am I a fallen woman?'

'It's a warning, that's all, a polite warning,' said George.

'Oh piss off, George,' Gwendolyn said, her pink mouth sweet and mocking. 'The lot of you can just sod off.'

Gloria tugged at her hand again and, not giving another look towards George, pulled her away from him and up her sweeping staircase. 'Come on, Wendy Darling,' she trilled, and they both laughed, head turned towards each other in glee.

George ran a hand through his hair and turned towards the door, spotting me for the first time. He shrugged, and I walked towards him.

'Sorry,' I said. 'I was just …'

'It's all right,' he said. 'Some people just can't take a hint. Ready to go?' He put his hand in mine.

'Yes,' I said. 'Ready.'

3

We took the underground back to his house, near St. James's Park. It was far from my own, but he told me I could call my grandmother from his telephone, tell her I'd been caught up, and would stay at Gloria's house, to return the next day. I did, and still remember my grandmother's small, worried voice, asking me if I was okay. Of course, I said, I'm very well. It's late. She told me she'd saved me dinner, cottage pie, *sans* lamb. She spoke to me in French, and I replied in English, as I always did. *Tout va bien?* She asked again, in her mother tongue, and I in my own kind, Yes, I'm fine, I'll see you in the morning. The thought of leaving her even for a night was desperate. But I did it. George said the watch would check on her, her neighbours would make sure she was okay. I didn't know if that worried me more.

We came out of the hot, empty mouth of the underground at Westminster. The four remaining lines ran all through the night, but shuttled along devoid of people, mostly. It was an eerie silence, and one forced by police presence. Whatever journey you took, there was always a group of armed forces, patrolling, weapons lodged in their belts, ready. The trains used to stop running. It used to be a place of sanctuary, filled with people on the platforms who needed shelter, wedged all the way between the Eastbound Circle line and the Westbound Jubilee. But Mrs P put a stop to it, eventually. Said it was too dangerous, that they spread disease like rats.

The fare was still expensive, but he paid for us both. I didn't take it very regularly, and rubbed my hands on the old carpeted seats, and held my hand against the worn-down pole by the doors. When it came to our stop he rammed his shoulder against the door to get it open, and out we came into the dark tunnel, with only a few electric lights in the labyrinth that lay beyond and above us. We walked up the four flights of stairs to the top, past two security guards, laughing, one arm on a banister, the other on a baton. We came out into the darkness of Whitehall. Even Big Ben wasn't illuminated. I'd never seen it at night, and always imagined it would be.

He took me to his house, made of pale Georgian brick, on Old Queen Street. It was bright, and neat, and I imagined what it would be like to live here, right next to the park with its large expanse of empty pond. It was still green from spring, and the summer hadn't wiped that out yet.

He offered me a drink as we stepped inside, but my mouth still tasted the vile tang of champagne and so I refused. He had few possessions, I noted, and attributed this to a sense of minimalism and charm. But he wasn't one to have his heart on his sleeve, or in his interiors. A man like him, who could gather together decorations for a house many of us could only dream of, decided to live an empty, solitary life. What truly decorated his life was on the inside, in the walls of his heart and his house, blocked away.

I noticed he had a radio and I leapt towards it. 'Does it work?' I said, looking at the buttons and wanting to press them, wanting to test them and get the frequency right and hear the lightness of music.

'Of course,' he said, and turned it on as though it was nothing. From that little box came a song as sweet as any I could remember. I leant against the counter, towards it, not knowing who was singing it or what the words were, but letting it block out any other noise from my mind. It was only when he put a hand on my back, softly, and laughed, that I realised where I was. I stood up and turned to him. He leant down and kissed me. 'You like your music don't you?' It seemed to please him, and he turned the volume up. It soared. I felt a stinging in my eyes as I looked up to him. I thought his house was magic.

'I have something to show you,' he said.

I thought it might be an excuse to take me upstairs, but he led me with such excitement, it betrayed a genuine interest. He took me to a room that was locked on the first floor. When he opened it, I saw it filled with rows of shelving, packed into the small space. The shelves were filled with dozens of jars of specimens. He picked them up and showed them to me.

'Honeycomb,' he said. 'From every kind of bee you could imagine. Honey bee, bumblebee, carpenter bee, hairy footed flower bee, Andrena fulva,' he laughed. 'Here it all is. Some of it.'

I stood in wonder at the pickled beings. A small horror came over me at these strange creatures: all legs; all antennae; all eyes and dead pupils and dead faces. But there was a lot of honeycomb. It was the most significant thing in the room.

'I've studied the honeycomb endlessly,' he said, looking at a jar of it, turning it about in his thick hand. 'It's fascinating. The structure of it. Its efficiency, the complexity of it. It's something Le Corbusier himself couldn't have thought of: a towering minimalist structure to house a thousand people, wonderfully productive. It's inspiring. And you know the only way they're capable of doing it? Because of the way they interact with each other on an individual level. They have no concept of the totality of the structure they've created. They just work by reacting to each other, with no central governance or system of organisation. They just do it because they're all doing it. And in these random interactions of production they end up making something a thousand times more intelligently built than the individual bee could conceive of making.' He looked at me, a coy expression on his face. 'Albert Einstein once said "look deep into nature, and you will understand everything better".' He put the jar back down on the shelf, very carefully, aligning it with the others. 'But I'll tell you about our bee project another time. You must be tired,' he said.

He took me to his bedroom and offered me one of his dressing gowns and a wash cloth. I used his bathroom; an expanse of marble with a sheen that I wanted to lick. I gazed at myself in the mirror for minutes, noting the shine to the surface, the corners that weren't cracked. The cleanliness of it all.

I would do as Jaminder said then, I had decided. I would be his, of my own choosing and decide afterwards what would come out of it. We would decide together. I would go to parties and maybe not drink, but I would eat, and I would listen to music, and one day I may even learn the piano, and play the keys as Jaminder had played them. I decided this, as I looked at my reflection, and decided I would need to ask Jaminder for a lipstick, and some powder. And maybe a comb for my hair, one that could pin it a certain way, and tame it. It was all possible, as I stood there. I would become.

He knocked on the bathroom door. 'Matilda,' he said. He had decided too, but decided differently, I imagine. I did wonder why he had decided on me, as I was so different from all of them, even Jaminder. But maybe that was exactly why. I didn't drag my heels through a tablecloth or rub lipstick on napkins. I was unspoiled; not like the ocean, or lakes or rivers or landscapes, unspoiled the way only a small person could be, not the sky or the earth or the moon. We'd touched even that.

I opened the door, I went towards him. He led me to the bed and I perched on its side. He sat next to me, and put his hand in my hair, traced the shape of my ear with his thumb. He held my head like that for a while. 'I went to Paris once, as a child,' he said.

'Tell me everything,' I said, I whispered it, luxuriously. 'Tell me every street you walked down.'

He liked this, these moments: feeding me with words and imaginings. He put on a silly faux accent and named the famous landmarks.

I grimaced. 'Not that. All the little places, the places that mattered.'

'Like what?'

'Like Rue des Rosiers, the little restaurant on Impasse Berthaud with the thick velvet curtains and the olive oil potatoes.'

He repeated the names back to me. 'You miss those places the most?'

'Yes, I miss the restaurants,' I said, my head leaning into his hands, and up to him. 'I miss the people. I miss my friend sitting across from me, our mothers letting us try a spoon of foie gras, joking about how one spoonful is enough to be lost forever. It's my friend's face I miss, and the look on it, when she tried something new for the first time.'

'I could try and find foie gras,' he said. He started to trace my mouth with his fingers, softly pushing on them, mesmerised by them.

'You'd try and find anything, wouldn't you.'

He smiled, he held my head closer. 'I would,' he said. 'I want to try it. I want to look that way. I want to be lost forever by a spoonful of something.'

He kissed me, his hands about my neck. 'I have something for you,' he said, and his face said it would be something good.

I sat patiently, like a child, waiting to be presented with it. 'What is it?' I said, trying to sound nonchalant, trying not to let the breath catch in my throat.

He opened a drawer of his clothes chest, and tucked

123

amongst his paired black socks was a fold of brown paper, a small slab of something, small enough to fit into his hand. He gave it to me and the paper was lovely and new, and crinkled at the edges in a satisfyingly crisp way. It was weighty and I felt what I wanted to feel, what I hoped it would be. A bar made up of squares.

'Open it,' he said, and I unfolded the paper which revealed another layer of thin worn out foil, but foil all the same. A thin silver slip of a thing I could remove, delicately.

'Here's the game,' he said, 'You can have one square for every one thing you tell me about your life. About your childhood, and the kind of person you are, and what you did before I was around and who you want to be. I want to know everything.'

I laughed, and my hands shook, because it meant I hadn't imagined it, but it was a bar of squares, and it was perfect. I held it up to my face, I smelt it, and I was back, next to the *pain au chocolat* and the *soufflé*, and the *moelleux au chocolat* and the milk bars and the *fondant* and the cocoa and the chunks of chocolate melting, coating the inside of my mouth.

'Tell me one thing first,' he said, pulling my hands down.

He held them clasped in his, and I did it without thinking, such a small exchange, never thinking of guarding my internal life from him, of protecting myself. The thick chocolate mixed with the lump in my throat and made me giddy. I held onto the brown paper all the time, never wanting to let it go. I folded it up afterwards and kept it in my pocket, to keep the smell and the feeling of it for as long as I could.

I laughed as I told him my sad little story, I laughed

with glee and he laughed back. One square for Rue des Rosiers; one for my school. One square for our old grey cat, and the drizzle in London. One square for my brown pair of shoes, and one square for thread.

One square for my mother, one square for my mother, one square for my mother.

He pushed off my dressing gown, his hand underneath the material by my shoulder. He peeled it off to reveal my nakedness, but touched instead my face, and held it to his own. I felt caught in an in-between place, where maybe I hadn't meant to stray, but where I'd wanted to. His hands were on me now, and I did want them on me, touching my waist, my breasts, between my legs. He was clothed, and remained so until my lips parted, and I asked him, 'Please.' Yes: I asked him. That first time, and other times. I asked him.

He laid me on the bed and, just as Jaminder had told me, had precautions to take. He didn't need asking, and he didn't tell me. He smiled as he looked at my body, and it looked back at him. I thought of Jaminder's words, *why come here if not for all that*, and I knew that he had come to the party for all that, alone. If he could have erased those hours with one bite, he would have, just to get to this moment. That was the difference between us.

He was careful with me, he hesitated. But I pulled him in. I wanted to feel the force of him. It had been years, hadn't it? I wanted to know. I thought of the clean marble and the mirror; the honey cake and the bees I hadn't asked him about. It didn't matter. I wanted to know only this. By doing this I would learn another life, where my body was not a burden, but a pleasure.

He moved inside me and I welcomed it. Anything that was different and out of the ordinary was life. Life was not stitch after stitch, potatoes at dinner, black mould on the ceiling, and cycling through the village. Collecting coupons; trying not to read the newspaper; trying not to read what Mrs P had said next; trying not to be prodded and poked.

I welcomed what I thought was its opposite: him, inside me. I didn't realise that he was so close to that other life: of parliament and Mrs P, and the strange order of things. He found me in my village I was desperate to leave. But he took me to the heart of it all: to Westminster, where my whole body was dominated.

He groaned and pulled out, at the end. I lay with my hands above my head, as he'd placed them. He kissed the inside of my elbow and I smiled over at him. I looked beyond him to the clean, bright windows in their white frames and imagined the park beyond the pale walls.

'You're so lucky to live in a place like this,' I said.

He snorted and sat up abruptly. 'Lucky? Is that what people say nowadays?' He looked down at me, arms crossed over his stomach. 'My family once had an apartment in Kensington Palace. I spent my childhood running around rooftop gardens, and we lost everything. Because of what, essentially? The weather?'

'I'm sorry. I didn't know.' I wasn't sure what I was apologising for.

He gestured around the room. 'This tiny thing was compensation for all that. But nothing can compensate for what happened.'

'Better off than most, still,' I said, quietly. He pretended not to hear me. 'Do you understand it? Does everything that happened make sense to you?'

He smiled at me, and kissed my arm again. 'Young people can't understand it. Can't conceive of it. People

126

don't believe that things happened gradually. That one thing slowly affects another. People only want to believe in the catalyst, the tipping point. People only thought it was real after the blackout. They didn't want to see that it was a million tiny things, for years, that brought us to a big mush.' He slapped his hands together to indicate what he meant, and I flinched. 'But Auntie saw it,' he said. 'She saw a way out. Still does.' He looked at me expectantly, his face flushed and smooth like an apple.

I nodded, 'You're right, I know.'

'What we don't know, though, is why it is so inhuman to see beyond the small, and the immediate. No one wants to see the big picture. There's no hope in that.'

I stroked his arm, my fingers passing over the soft hairs. I looked up at him. I hoped he would reach his arm over me so that I could thread through it. 'Do you believe in hope? Is that why you became an MP?'

He exhaled with a laugh. 'I knew it would be the best place to be. I wasn't about to let everything go, I still wanted a life. It made the most sense after the blackout. To be in the thick of it. Auntie made sure there was enough food for everyone, and that everyone got that hour of electricity that they wanted. But I was part of making sure that really happened.'

I wondered what he'd seen that I hadn't; what he knew that I didn't. But it worked both ways. He could never conceive of my own life being ripped apart, and how that destruction wasn't the same for all people.

'There's just us. That's we want to think, isn't it? There's only us.' He kissed me, lingering, and moved his arm away, before getting up to go to the bathroom.

I looked at the ceiling above me. I looked at the electric light, hanging from the socket. It was dark outside. He'd taken a candle up the stairs with us, saying he'd used his electricity already today. It flickered in the corner. I stood up, went to the light switch by the door. I tried it.

Everything illuminated.

PART 4

Jaminder
Piano lessons

1

We sit and eat oatmeal on our break at work. Mrs Campbell makes her usual comment about eating up and the devil making work for idle thumbs. We always laugh at the idea of the devil. But is that what the devil would do? I think he'd rather make work for people who are hungry.

We're mourning the last crop of potatoes. They were black and soft and oozing and I can't explain how horrifying a sight it was. It's as disturbing as if the potatoes were actually people's faces, all caved in and ulcered like that. They had to be discarded. We have oatmeal, the church has oatmeal, but other than that we have to scavenge for leaves surrounding the town. Our skin has become dry and red, and we're as lethargic as if we haven't slept in days. Mathilde insists we still crush down the nettles and chew on them, despite the fact they go no way towards making us full.

I pretend I am grateful for the oatmeal, but in my head all I can think about is the long smooth paper of a cigarette, pre-rolled and perfect, ready to light up and wash all my hunger away. I know those cigarettes end up making your lungs look like those potatoes – blackened and suffering – but even with this knowledge I'd still rather have one. Even with the knowledge of those last potatoes I still think about stuffing that mouldy mess in my mouth.

Mrs Campbell is especially positive today because she's worried. Maybe she's only worried about her own plate, and its lack of starch or chicken or plump ripe vegetables, but she's projecting a look of complete joy, to protect us. Ruby and Mathilde are grateful for the attempt, but I see straight through it. I think about the fat that coats her body and wonder where she got it and think about frying it on a griddle pan with onions and butter. I would happily sauté her.

She walks past us, her tread light and springing. She's wound around her fairly sizeable neck a thick woolly tartan scarf, made from that new squeaky yarn that tries to imitate the real stuff. She has looms too, and one day we might sit at them.

She strokes the scarf as she walks past us. She tells us it's her family tartan and she points to the colours and the different fuzzy stripes and we smile and nod. We don't challenge her on it, because there's no way we'd ever know if it was true or not, if her family tartan is five hundred years old or if she manufactured that pattern yesterday.

We let her have this little imaginary triumph of the tartan. We all need something. I try and imagine what the colours on my scarf would be like if I had a family tartan. I imagine they're wonderful.

'That'll keep the wolf from the door,' Mrs Campbell says, pointing at our oatmeal. We know she must eat more than oatmeal because of the way the skin on her fingers strains and folds about her rings. We think she collects things whenever she gets a delivery from one of those rarely seen trucks. If you have enough money, there's always a way, even up here. Even now, with the price of oatmeal shooting up, she must know she'll be fine. In the way that we don't.

But she runs the town. I have to remind myself where we'd be without her little factory.

'Are you worried?' I say to Ruby, scraping the inside of my bowl and praying it will miraculously fill up again in a steaming peat of oats.

'We've been through worse than this,' she shrugs. But I imagine in another time her face would've been fuller and her shoulders rounder, her eyes brighter. In London, she might have looked a little different. She might have been pretty, once.

I wonder what she'd think if I showed her an image of myself and Mathilde, from before we left, almost five and a half years ago. In another world, another time, five years would be nothing. But I look at us now and think we could have aged fifteen from the lines on our skin, our fatigue. People used to say: you are what you eat. I fear we are becoming nothing. What I wouldn't give to see a gleaming, plump, shining red pepper; slotting a knife through its core and eating it raw, feeling my face flush with its redness and my eyes brighten. What I wouldn't give for that.

'Have you?' I say. I want to ask her if she is lying to me. I want to ask her: Is the wolf really away from the door.

Because I can hear it, scratching, its paws matted and clinging to the wood, scraping indentations along its edges. I can see the wolf even though I am nowhere near a door.

I can see the thick saliva on its teeth and smell its breath hot and stinging on my face. I can feel its coarse coat as I push away the hunk of its shoulders.

Our whole lives are a way to placate us, slowly, with these meagre habits. And we placate each other. We tell each other when to eat our paltry rations and what to wash it down with. We tell each other to keep stitching.

133

We tell each other to chew on nettles and (imagine you could get some!) mint leaves. We tell each other to *imagine* chewing on mint leaves and smoking cigarettes, and sometimes we laugh, making the motions with our hands and then we tell each other how full we are. I couldn't eat another bite, I say, even as I am biting the air in my stupid pretend way and Mathilde laughs at me.

I think: that second she is laughing she is not thinking about being hungry, so I might have done my job for today.

The truth is, I am always thinking about it. It's such a basic thing, pushing at you. Pushing the line between the real and the wolves dancing about in your mind. But then I think, real wolves don't exist. Because if they did exist, if there were any left, by God I'd eat them.

People start sighing at the end of the day. That's when we get weak and tired and there is no way to satiate us, not with a joke or anecdote or that eternal oatmeal. We wander the streets and the fields and pick out anything that might be edible. There are still some vegetables, but not many. We gather nettles and crush them down, boiling them, squeezing them in our mouths in the hope of something. There is talk of people moving further, in search of supplies. But the journey alone might kill them. Father Anthony says he has called for emergency aid. We know this imaginary aid is supposed to come from London, but that is all we know.

We have enough, just, to live on. We always give more to Hugo than we give to ourselves, but we have enough. Once a day we feel that we are full; a new kind of full that we are used to. There is always the hope for more, and that is a feeling that we can bite on and feel stuck in our teeth: that the next crop of potatoes will be all right, that some unknown animals might wander close to the village. We might eat well again.

We lie together in our bed at night after Hugo's bath and he smiles between us. He is always happiest after bath time. After we've taken him to the old pink tub and warmed up the water over the fireplace, and poured it in, slowly. We're careful to save the rainwater in our storage tank for this, after what we need for cooking and drinking. He plays with the taps as we sit and watch him, like they're a toy. We realise he doesn't know what they're for, what they were once for. But he likes them all the same. He splashes the thin amount of water all around him and giggles. We wrap him in a towel and he becomes dopey after that, a satisfied tiredness that is pleasing.

We wait and watch him fall asleep while we talk over the top of him, in a whisper, our feet covered in stitched-up socks, not a draughty hole in sight, pushed towards the cinders in the fireplace, wiggling them above the heat.

We find new ways to entertain him. Now he is at school every day and is taught and shown new things, he has also become more restless, and craves more stimulation. It is not enough that we read him the same book, over and over again, or that we tell him that is all we have, that's the best we can do. 'But Jacob has a puzzle,' he says, 'and none of the pieces are missing. And he puts it together. Why don't we have a puzzle?'

Never one to be bettered, I've made him a puzzle out of the sheet of maths questions Father Anthony gave me. I shape them carefully with a knife and get him to bring home a couple of pencils that won't be missed from school. I draw an image on the paper and then cut it.

I think it's a pathetic looking thing and wouldn't fool anyone, but he wouldn't know any better and it certainly seems to fool him.

I lay it on the floorboards by the fire. I mix the pieces up. He's pleased. It entertains him for a long time, and Mathilde laughs at him. At first she says, 'You shouldn't be envious of what other people have,' and then she relents, watching him so content with such a silly thing.

'Maybe jealousy is what gives way to innovation,' I say.

She pats my shoulder. 'It's a puzzle. You didn't re-invent the internet.' She stops herself as soon as she's said it and watches my face. She's taught herself not to think of these things, but it's all wound up in our collective consciousness. You just don't forget a thing like that.

'What's internet?' Hugo says and she looks down at him, frowning, watching him crouching over his pieces of paper, distracted.

'It's nothing to worry about,' she says.

I try to distract him from this thought and reach over, fumbling, trying to hand him the next piece of the wonky puzzle that won't fit. But my hand slips and one of the pieces falls from the pile and down the floorboard.

Hugo wails as he sees me do it. 'No, Mummy, you threw the piece away! It's disappeared down the floor.'

'I'm sorry, I'm sorry,' I scramble about and try and stick my nails down the sides. I can see it, taunting me, lying on its side, stuck. I can't reach it and lament the price I've paid for trying to make something. I won't hear the end of this until he's twenty-five years old.

'Maman,' he cries to Mathilde, 'Mummy's lost a piece,

it's ruined.' He hits his hand across his head to indicate that I am a fool.

'Let's get it then,' she says, and bends down next to me, pushing her own fingernails down the edges of the floorboard. She pushes too hard and her finger slips through. The floorboard is loose, not fixed to the rest.

'Ha!' she says, in triumph, and pries the floorboard up, retrieving the lost piece.

'Well done,' Hugo says, looking at me, pointedly.

'Better now,' I say. I ruffle his hair, trying to assert my perceived authority at puzzle making again.

'Jams,' Mathilde says, her hand still down the floor, her hair falling over her face. I can sense she's agitated.

'What is it? Dead rat?' I think: how dead? Edible dead, or dead-dead?

'I can't believe it,' she says.

'*Mon dieu,*' I say, mockingly, and she ignores me. Hugo laughs. I almost start with the *haw-hee-haws* but then she reaches her hand up and replaces the floorboard, pressing it with her foot. As she stands up and her hand is lowered, I see what is placed within it.

I scream. Hugo screams, at my screaming. I crush her hand with mine, trying to grab at it. She laughs.

'Pineapple!' I yell, even though she is close enough to hear me. 'Tinned pineapple!'

We hug each other and Hugo jumps up to us and hugs our legs. He jumps about us in the excitement, his hair flapping like a bird, even though he doesn't know what it's for.

'Was that all there was?' And I grapple at the floorboard, pulling it back up, to reveal only dust underneath.

'Amazing,' Mathilde says, 'That's it. Someone must have hidden it, from before.'

137

'What is it?' Hugo says, reaching up to it, Mathilde holding it just out of reach.

'It's fruit,' she says. 'It's sweet.'

We sit by the table and I stick a knife in the can. I heave away at it, sawing, while Hugo waits patiently. I put a bowl out. I try not to cut my fingers. I pull back the lid as far as it will go. I slop the pineapple and the syrup from the can. Mathilde pushes the bowl towards me. I put my hand in the syrup and pass a piece to Hugo. He puts it in his mouth and his lips pucker and his eyes water from the sweetness. He closes them.

'It's nice,' he says, and reaches for more. 'Where did it come from?'

'We don't know,' Mathilde says.

'Is there more?' he says.

'No,' she says, 'Don't eat it all at once. That's the lot.'

'When will we have it again?' He says, pausing from shovelling the disintegrating pieces into his mouth.

'Maybe we won't,' she says. 'Maybe someday, later.'

I pick up a piece from the bowl and eat it, slowly. I think of all the pineapples Mama Boga had. And the mangoes. Her knock on our door and all the different kinds of fruit. I can see her face clearly, ripe and round just like the mango. I think of the intricate shape of the pineapple, its geometric pattern and the pride in its plumage, its beauty. And the things we did to it in London, picking it apart and putting it in cans. For what? Did we do it for days like this? Did we do it just in case? Knowing that it would keep, knowing one day that it might be found? Or did we do it to reduce it to anything other than a pineapple and anything other than what Mama Boga carried in her basket. To make us think of anything other than the red earth and the hot sun.

Even in the syrup, in the tin like that, it is just as I

138

remembered. It is everything. Mathilde rests her chin in her hand. She watches us.

'Aren't you going to have any?' I say. 'It's a miracle.' I waggle my hand in front of her to indicate the theatricality of this blessing.

'No,' she says, 'Miracles don't come in tins.'

I raise my eyebrows at her, syrup dripping down my chin. I don't wipe it away. 'They do now.'

When Hugo has fallen asleep and stopped complaining of his stomach ache I talk to Mathilde about all the things we ate in Kenya when I was a child. I talk of the plants and the smell of things and the carrots that were purple and the visits we took to the coast, and my grandfather and his suit. She doesn't say a word until I'm finished, until I'm giddy with it, and pleased for remembering such a thing, and knowing it was there.

When I'm done, she blinks, slowly, and looks down at Hugo, and strokes his hair. 'Do you ever wonder if you remember it right? I mean really, as it was?'

'Of course I do,' I say, indignant. I prod my temple. 'It's burned right in.'

'What about the bad stuff?' she says, 'What about the things that made you sad?'

I want to tell her nothing made me sad in Kenya; it was only England that did that. It was only when we arrived, my grandfather suited and booted, and we walked down the Kilburn High Road and it rained, endlessly, and no one else wore a suit, that we thought life was a disappointment. We'd never thought that before.

That is my remembering of it: my grandfather's heart being tested all over London. Coming home, telling me that someone asked him if he was a Muslim and shouldn't he go home. He pointed to his turban. Are they stupid, he said. I nodded. I told him how stupid they were. He made light of it but it hurt him, even if he didn't let it touch his pride.

His innate Britishness never stood up to the West London kind of Britishness he'd fallen into, and that was the thing that made me sad. He was more English than all his cousins who'd been born there, all the people that had that blue passport. He told them so; he told them how to make the right tea, and he taught them the rules of cricket, and he sat with me, night after night, and made me play that damn piano, because if I couldn't be as English as he was I had to be *something*.

'You don't want to be like some people here,' he said, tapping that old out of tune thing he'd bought in town for nothing but still couldn't afford. He was my metronome. 'You don't want to ride the train to sit at a computer and be a little desk monkey and ride home again. You have to decide to be good at something. And then you lean into it. That's what being good at something is all about. It's just about letting yourself be good.'

But it was about more than that. It was about late nights practicing Brahms and it was about his fingers tapping my knee. It was his face screeching into discontent when I missed a note and it was him shaking his head at my grandmother – not saying a word – when she asked us how long this would go on for.

It was only London that confused us, only London that messed us up. It was only that city that made me believe in not belonging somewhere, until you're there long enough that you have no choice. You end up leaning into it.

Now I'm older, can't I think of it another way? Can't I think that that's what my family went through with Kenya, which was a silken golden thread of paradise but also a gated enclosure. It was a segregated paradise where we were lucky enough to belong to the middle class. It was also refusing to eat our maid's food until she learnt how to make roti.

London wasn't always a place I despised. There are so many ways to remember the same thing. It was also a place where my grandfather came back from Kingsbury with a box of Alfonso mangoes which my grandmother peeled softly in her palm. Where we slipped the fragrant pieces from our fingers to our mouths and remembered something beautiful. Where I took the pieces to school in a Tupperware my grandmother prepared for me and I gave it to my friends to try. It's the best mango you'll ever have, I said, it's not like anything else. They'd roll their eyes at me but then they'd agree, it wasn't. They asked me every year when the mango season was, until it stopped coming. London was almost the real thing.

'Kenya was heaven,' I say, 'I'll remember it forever. If I remember nothing else, I'll remember the smell and taste of it forever.'

'I can't bear remembering,' Mathilde says, 'It breaks my heart, Jams. I can't think of it, any of it, it's so pointless to talk about. I won't wish for it.'

I shake my head. 'Isn't that all there is? The memory of it. That's all we have left. It's like believing in God, or something. You have to hold onto it, even when there's nothing there.' I say it, even though I'm not sure I believe it, not sure either of us believe in God, or believe in anything we can hold onto. I say it anyway, 'That's all there is.'

'Not for him,' she says. 'There's nothing like that for him.'

I watch his back and its rising and falling. I wish I could give him my memories. I wish I could give him something.

I hope he is asleep. I hope he is dreaming and that he cannot hear us speak.

141

2

We have arranged our hours at the factory so that we can drop Hugo off at school in the early morning and arrive at work a little late. Mrs Donald picks him up to occupy him in the afternoons. I look forward to the days when Mathilde is at the factory, and I take him on my own.

I tell him stories of my childhood, that Mathilde bristles at, and I tell him things about her own, too. I explain to him about France, as best I can. I try and think of small French things that he might understand, to better understand his own culture, if such a thing still exists. But I find I can only remember things that are of no consequence at all and are only snippets of things Mathilde once told me. Things like their attitude to bread; how it should be consumed as a side dish to every meal, which baffles Hugo, thinking it a meal in itself; that sugar was only taken in coffee in lumps, never granulated; that beef was bloody, tender, and not like our roast dinners (but when has he had one of those?); that lunches were hot, always, if you were doing it right; that there were different, polite ways, to address a stranger, or your superior, but oddly not God: *vous* not *tu*. There were a thousand intricate eccentricities that made up a whole people, his people.

But he can't understand. He can't even understand that the way he addresses Mathilde (Maman) is both a French word – not an English one – and a generic term, not particular to her. When I try to explain it to him, his hand in mine, I seem to have confused him more than enlightened him.

'Can we go there? It sounds good there,' he says.

'It's not like that anymore, Hugo. It's something else.' There is no word to describe what it is. There is no way in English, or French, to describe how it is not what it once was.

'Is it like here?'

'Yes,' I say. 'It's like here. Only, there's a war there. And we've all lost it, but it carries on.'

'How can it carry on if we've lost?' He scuffs his feet against the pavement as though he is angry.

'Because we might win it back one day. When we're stronger.'

I worry that he will repeat my words to Mathilde and she will be angry with me. I don't like to remind her. But I feel that he should know.

'Am I French like Maman or am I English like you?' he says. We are approaching the church and I want the conversation to be over before we reach the door. I don't want the other children to hear us, and wonder.

'You're both,' I say, 'And I'm Kenyan and Indian, too. So you are too. And you're French and you're English. You're everything. And so I suppose, you can choose what you want to be.'

'I just want to be normal,' he moans the words at me, as we near the door.

'No one's normal,' I say, and think that if humanity has learnt nothing, that would be the nothing they've learnt.

I take Hugo to the classroom, gleeful, as ever, to be left amongst the children. The worksheets are on the table but I look out for Father Anthony and find he's not there.

I walk out in my usual routine, holding a pocket of guilt inside me for leaving Hugo. I wait for the moment when he will cry (which he never does) or call for me. But I am met with a contented silence as I leave the classroom at the back of the church. The only noise I hear is the noise I let in, the noise I hear every time I come here and try and push away from my ears.

I hear it looking up at that crucifix, that alien symbol, meant to provoke feeling of the sort I do not feel. The pineapple has worn off by now, and I look at Jesus' ribs, arching and protruding, and think of my own hunger.

But then I turn, and continue my routine, and that is when a different sound enters my head, when I see it. It is the memory of the notes of the piano and it blocks out every word you ever said to me. It blocks out every word ever spoken to me, by anyone; any touch or feeling. It consumes me, without even playing a note.

I walk over to it, tucked away by the altar. I sit down and place my hands on the keys but I do not press down. I tap my feet on the pedals, and those I do press down but they make no noise. I play in my head all the songs I once played, that my grandfather made me play. I think of Ravel and Debussy, and my fingers stretch out, in agony, thinking of Clair de Lune, and how, long after my grandfather's hearing started to go, he still asked me to play it for him.

I played it at those parties though no one ever knew what it was. Especially not you. I never bothered myself to explain it. I never took the time. I just played it over and over and wondered why no one ever noticed that I played the same litany of songs every night. No one ever told me to play anything different. No one ever heard it, except Mathilde. She thought it was a melancholy song, and it was for me, because it was my grandfather's wish for me, all that money he spent on piano lessons when we came to England. It was his hands and the folds of his skin around his knuckles and the sound of them following my own. I used to fumble over it as he told me *pianissimo,* learning to read music along with me. I tried to make it beautiful for him. I tried to make it the saddest song in the world for him.

I haven't heard it for years, except in my head. And does that make it less real? Does that mean I don't hear it? Because I think I do. I played it, on a loop, when things were bad. It brought comfort to me, and reminded me of that disappointing Cornish beach in the summer. My grandfather's suit with his sleeves rolled up, our first experience of England, sitting with his shoes shined and his tie on, his feet pressing in the sand. It reminded me of walking around Wembley and my grandfather rubbing his forehead and looking down at me, confused. He asked me where all the beautiful British buildings were, the ones that had been promised to him. He asked me as though I should have an answer.

I sit like this for a long time and know I am late for work. I trace my fingertips over the notes – D flat major – and I hear them, even though no noise comes from them.

But do you see? How hard it is to make you hear it, how hard it is to explain it in words unless I play it to you? And I did play it to you, and you never listened. But I don't need to hear the actual sound, because it's in my fingers, and they remember without me even telling them, they remember on their own. And my throat remembers. It closes up and aches just at the memory of it.

The light from the window falls on a shape near me, and I turn and see that it is Father Anthony. I remove my hands from the keys.

'Sorry, Father,' I say, and put my hands in my lap. But I don't get up.

'Have you dropped Hugo off?' he says, moving towards me.

'Yes.'

'You can stay as long as you like, Jaminder. To pray, if you like.'

I look up at him, and smile. 'I'm a bit out of practice.'

'All the more reason to do so.' He's holding a book in his hands and as he moves closer to me I see that it's the Bible. I wonder if he reads it, if he turns its pages and believes it. He places it in front of me, his right hand lingering on its cover. 'There are always things to take comfort in, things to read, if you wanted.'

'Do I look like a Christian, Father?' I say. 'I just like the quiet here.'

He removes the Bible from my hands and takes it back into his own, standing over me. 'Do you believe in God, Jaminder?'

I don't look at him, and keep my hands crossed together. 'Would it make you feel better if I did?' I stay like that for a long time, with the both of us in silence. He stands there, unmoving, as though he is waiting for a better answer.

'I've seen you here, walking about the church. I wondered if there was something that brought you here, aside from Hugo.'

I lower my head away from him. I don't know what it will do to me if I say the words out loud, but I see them in my head.

'Should I repent for my sins?' I say, and there is a bitterness in my voice that I can't leave out.

'You can,' he says, earnestly. 'I will listen.'

I lift my head up. 'I did something terrible.' I look

146

towards him, but his face hasn't moved.

'You can ask for forgiveness. Jesus will forgive you.'

I think of my grandparents. What they would think, seeing me sitting in a church like this. I almost want to laugh as I imagine telling them: it's okay, Jesus will forgive me. 'Is that a promise?'

He shrugs his shoulders. 'If you want it to be.'

'I'd still like to come back,' I say, looking at the piano. 'If that's okay.'

'Of course,' he says, watching me. I stand up and thank him. I walk down the aisle of the church and look up at the windows. I think of London and the grey muddle of it, and how very far away it all now seems. I was six when we arrived, almost the age Hugo is now, but I didn't understand. I didn't really know we'd left. I waited for a long time to go back to Kenya. These places don't belong to me anymore.

I know his eyes follow me out the door. I don't look back. But I hear the music, still, of Clair de Lune. There's a sense of relief at the end, do you remember it? The notes open, and everything goes quiet, and that small noise is all that's left. It's those notes I would like to play again.

They remind me that somewhere, I have another home.

3

_____

It's Diwali soon. It passes by every year. Unnoticed, unmarked. So do many anniversaries. We mark Hugo's birthday, but not other things. Not the things we could mark, or think about. Not you, for instance. We don't mention you, George.

I don't even tell Mathilde that I think of you, and all the things you've done to her, to us. I know she thinks of you all the same, without me having to mention it, but I see her push it from her mind. I see her focus on Hugo instead, and the goodness of him. I see her enveloped in that gratefulness, more than any other feeling.

So why do I still want to think about it? Think about the way you held your drink and held onto her and held onto the piano. Why do I still see London, exactly as it was? Why do I still think of the way you held your cutlery, joking about polishing the silver knives and the silver forks, lording it over me? I see it as clearly as if it were here instead of these muddy streets. I see the pavement, I see the food on the tables, I see the lights on, welcoming us, begging us to stay. All that civilisation cannot be lost, even in my head. I know it's still there, as sure as I know I'm still a person, still in my own body. We might never hear from London again, but I know that it is there.

We never speak of the women, either, and where we know they go. Where we might have ended up. We do not speak of these things as we sit together by a fire, where we do have kindling, and we do have a son. We watch him fall asleep together, and I watch Mathilde's hair, falling over the arm with which she props herself up, leaning over him.

Her hair contains a whole world, and I watch it; each strand falling about her face and her arm and down towards her son. It comforts me, the many strands that I can't comprehend, the numerous, dense weight of it, as dark as the blue of the ocean (I remember the ocean). It comforts me because I can't understand the complexity

148

and the world of her hair as much as I can't understand the complexity and the world that we now live in, the world that we used to live in, that other women went to live in, and the world that we one day will live in: that other world.

The closeness of her hair reminds me of the closeness Gloria's hair once held over me. She welcomed me into that little London life and let me stay late, every night, sitting at her piano so I could practise. She sat next to me on that worn out black velvet stool, and laughed, her hair brushing against my bare shoulder, drink in one hand, cigarette in another. Her hair was so perfectly formed and so dense a colour, unlike any I'd ever known. Sometimes I would move it behind her ear just as a thing to do, and she'd smile and open her perfectly red mouth, just at my marvelling at it.

The thought jolts me awake at night, and sometimes it's because I've thought of you, and sometimes it's because I've thought of them, and sometimes it's from nothing at all, and just because I am hungry. But I always turn over and look across Hugo at Mathilde's long, dense, dark hair and am comforted by it. I am comforted by the sheer other-worldliness of it, something so human and so difficult to understand: its sheer molecular being, the fact that it exists, and stretches beyond what we see of it, stretches down into its small constituent parts and makes up this large thing that is as deep as the ground that we stand on.

Her hair is beautiful, and I don't think you ever knew.

These things trouble me, and I take them with me, every time I hold Hugo's hand and every time I go to work and focus on the stitches and remember all the things that Mathilde taught me, when we had a little time. They torment me, in a way that I can't see them bothering her. And I am grateful for it, and resentful of it, too.

So I happily go to church with Hugo, and although it is only ever to drop him off for school and never to attend the services, I take my time there. It is during that time that I sit at the piano and I think of something else. I think of London and Nairobi, I think of my grandparent's faces. I think of how hungry I am (and the limit of hunger, how hungry I could possibly be) and I wait for the food to come in. I watch Father Anthony every day, waiting for news that there is food coming in.

It is here, as I sit at the piano, my fingers touching the keys but never pressing down, that I think of my grandfather, insisting that he eat alone at dinner, being entirely misanthropic and solitary. I think of him tearing up his roti and throwing it in his dhal, scooping it all up with a spoon. And only afterwards, when he sat in the living room with his newspaper, would he lower it, and talk to me, and tell me about that cricket ball that hit him in the mouth and knocked his teeth out. It was only then that he made me forget my embarrassment at not taking to Punjabi and whispered to me in English about the cricket club, and all the things in his life that he wanted to tell me about. It is the same for Hugo, I suppose, never knowing his true mother tongue, and never needing to.

Because wasn't my mother tongue the kindness that my grandfather taught me, and the way to be alone, when you needed to? Wasn't that his way of teaching me how to speak, after all? Just like food is a language, and if it is, we don't have it anymore. I will always mourn that more than all the Punjabi I never learnt, that Hugo will never learn, all the French too. I will mourn the loss of all the dosas I cannot give him, and the jalebis, the syrupy, dripping, sugary jalebis he cannot taste, and the spaghetti, and butter, the kind I boiled in my flat every night after my grandparents had left me (and left the world) to my own devices. I mourn all the culture that is lost to him and all the things he will never know.

Perhaps music is the one thing that I can give him. Perhaps it is the one thing I have left, and my grandfather was right, and I should just let it take me. I should just lean into it, easily.

So one day, when I am not at work, and Mathilde is, I take a sheet of music home to him I found in the church. It is only the two of us, in quiet occupation, on the floor. I tell him to watch my hands and I move them in front of me, following the notes, and this is my way of talking to him, this is my speaking voice. I sing to him, along with my hands pretending to play the notes, and I know he's never heard my singing voice, and all the music in the world he's heard is limited. He laughs, hysterical, and hits my back in amazement. He stands up and tries to sing along to a song he's never heard. He pulls at my hair, and I tell him, Stop, you're hurting me. But he can't, because he doesn't understand his own feelings, and has no other way to express them.

'Mummy, why are you crying?'

'I don't know,' I say.

'Don't stop, keep singing.'

'I'm going to teach you. I'm going to teach you to play the piano for real, for yourself.'

'You can't!' he says, then, 'How?'

'I'll just teach you, like this.'

I promise him that there'll be something of his own to be good at. I promise him that he'll be happy, forever, because I'll have given him music, and it will always stay

151

with him, no matter where he finds himself. No matter how alone he is.

I promise him: the only thing I have to offer, I will give to him.

PART 5

Mathilde
Blackberries

1

We walked around St James's park the next morning. The heat had started to pick up; it wasn't long before summer would hit like a wall of clanging humidity. But in its beginnings, the heat was just a smell and a feeling. The warm air circulated, an ominous calling that the easy heat of early summer was coming to an end.

There was a little water left in the lake, a greying murky puddle that once housed pelicans and waterfowl. Now it housed our anxiety, as visitors came to watch the markers erected that showed how the lake had shrunk back from previous years. We stood by the marker that showed where it had stretched fifty years before. I dragged my feet across the dry, crumbling soil.

'It's still beautiful,' George said, 'It's still here.'

We crossed over the bridge and walked a figure of eight path through the centre of the park. We watched other people who strolled around it, some walking towards the allotments in Green Park, others wandering with strange curiosity to see what was left.

I wanted to see the palace and George indulged me, leading me up the Mall along the gravel, where I noticed some grass had begun to shoot through the stones underneath. Before the edge of the park I began to notice a wall of black. I felt like I was walking down the steps of the underground, being marked out and watched, and carefully trying to avoid eye contact with those men and those batons. This presence was not leisurely, but a rigid structure of interlaced people, as though they were waiting, and ready. They stood in front of a crumbling monument, a plinth of stone, and they circled the palace's gates, unmoving. I squinted to see if I could notice any movement from my vantage point, any gesture or speech. They were still.

George squeezed my hand and sighed. 'The bronze was melted down years ago, when the whole thing was emptied. A tragedy.'

I looked at him, so unmoved by the armed presence in front of us. I wanted to turn back, but I didn't want to appear fazed by something we should be so used to. His fingers didn't even twitch, nor his palms sweat, and his brow only raised in surprise when I was struck dumb, unable to speak until we were well away from the wall of intimidation that we were faced with.

He pressed on. 'Did you ever see it? The Victoria monument?' He gestured his arms up in the air to imitate the statue that no longer existed. He continued to walk forward and I stopped him, pulling him back towards the park. He laughed as we sloped back again towards the lake, further away from the palace gates.

'They won't bite,' he said, wrapping an arm around my shoulders. 'Not with me anyway.'

'Why are there so many of them?'

'Why not?' he said. 'We need to protect it, don't we? It belongs to us. Otherwise it'd be overrun with camps in no time. Like poor old Kenwood House. Filled with rot and disease. Auntie has to retain a sense of order somehow. There has to be some sense of control.'

'Oh,' I said, thinking of Kenwood and its sloping expanse of grass, not realising that the people there had been placed deliberately, and given shelter. Rather than what our neighbours said: that they'd broken the windows and boarded up the doors, taken it for themselves. Still, I wondered what the point of the dissolution of the monarchy was when the palace still remained as it ever was, more so: guarded, separate, drawn away from the reality of the city. 'I don't know,' I said, 'They need a place to go. Where do the people in the camps end up, eventually?'

He squeezed my shoulder, 'I wouldn't worry about all that,' he said. 'Somewhere better than here, no doubt.'

I looked back towards the palace. 'Is Mrs P in there?' I said, examining his face.

He laughed. 'Of course not,' he said. 'She just hasn't decided what to do with it yet. So it stays empty.' He reached up to a branch of an overhanging tree, plucked some foliage from it and dissolved it between his fingers, letting the last leaves fall to the ground.

'What do you think she should do with it?' We walked back to the bridge again, and he placed his hands on its railing.

'Divide it up,' he said. 'Give it back to the people. Back to the people who it was taken from.'

'The Royal Family?'

'And the rest.'

I wondered how many times he walked this path. The wall of armed police was supposed to deter him, but he most likely thought they were there for him: to guard a room or a wing he thought might belong to him one day. I slipped my hand out of his.

We continued to walk the figure of eight, and I almost suggested walking to Trafalgar Square and sitting at its empty steps, but as we approached that side we saw a group of people huddled just outside the park's railings.

157

'What's going on?' I said, as he took my hand again to circle us away and back in the direction of Westminster. There were placards scattered at the feet of five or so women, and they talked hurriedly between themselves.

'Come on,' he said, and tried to pull me back towards the bridge. Instead I stepped in their direction, feeling a pull towards the vulnerability of their sloped shoulders and long hair hanging together in a crouched huddle. Between them on the ground lay a prone body. At first I thought it was a fake plastic thing, an old mannequin, but I realised, by the way they were crowded round it, it was real; greying, clothed, rigid. I took another step.

'Matilda,' he said, but I barely heard him. It was a woman, her face bloodied and bruised, long drained of colour. The group of women around her didn't look up as I approached. I wanted to call out, but George was next to me, pulling me away. 'Leave them,' he said.

I tried to pull back, I tried to call out: what happened, but he started to drag me away.

'Leave them,' he said again, and squeezed the meat of my arm hard enough that I had to follow.

'What happened to her?' I said, trying to release my arm and comply by walking beside him.

'Don't worry about all that,' he said, looking across the park and away from me, as though I were just a thing to scramble after him. He led me over the bridge once again and back out towards Westminster, an indication our walk was coming to an end. I didn't ask him about their placards, I didn't tell him what I'd seen, strewn amongst the blood and the littered body, the concerned women. One was face-up and stretched towards me on the path, a makeshift sign made out of an old poster. People always talked about it, Mrs P's old slogan. But they'd turned it into a sign and painted on an extra word, slapped in black. England Still Isn't Eating, it read.

We ended up back at the tube and he left me with a firm kiss. I went down the stairs into the tunnel, too ashamed to ask anything from him, and too embarrassed to walk on, admitting I couldn't afford the fare.

My dress stuck to me, sweat dripping down my legs in the hot wind. I licked my top lip and thought expectantly of soaking myself in cold water when I got home, hoping my grandmother had left me some from the storage tank.

I turned back from the mouth of the tube, walking down the steps. I wanted to remember the look of the buildings from that vantage point: Westminster in bright daylight, the day after I'd been with him. I wanted to store it in my brain, not for sentimentality, but something else. I had a blank curiosity; I wanted to know things about him, but when I looked I found the starkness of it froze all the answers away.

Which is why I stole the papers I did. While he was asleep that morning, I walked around his hallway and opened doors, just as he said he'd dreamt, and laughed about. I opened the doors and peered inside and everything was blank. Especially the kitchen, which I imagined would be filled to the brim with all the illicit foods he'd given to me and that we'd tasted together. But the cupboards were almost empty. There was no trace anywhere of old bottles or remnants of the carcasses of forgotten vegetables.

I realised it was because that was the smart thing to do. The smart thing was not to bring it to your house and leave things lying around, as I had done, as he'd made me do. I saw a few papers in his kitchen drawer where the unused polished silver utensils also lay (giant serving forks and knifes for parties he didn't host) and I took a few sheets. The image of the first page struck me: a structured lattice, a beehive; the second was lists and lists of illicit ingredients, food you couldn't get here, food we dreamt of like children. All written down in ink with scrawled numbers next to them. There was more I didn't take and stapled packages I didn't touch.

I entered the heat of the tube and checked for the two leaves of paper I had hidden in my bag. I stood by the gates, watched by the guards, which made my hands shake and the coins rattle around, and scrambled together most of the money I had to take the tube home. I was alone in the carriage, when it arrived after ten minutes. I rode the line all the way to West Hampstead as I looked at the papers. They meant little to me, but they were plans for a future. As the train rattled on I hoped it was a plan to save us, a plan for something better. The carriage shook and wobbled, and I steadied myself, holding onto my seat. As the train bundled into the open air, nearing my stop, I held them until the edges crinkled. I knew I wouldn't ask him about them, but he'd notice their absence. I would lie to him, I decided then and there. But despite that, I hoped that there was hope, after all. They had plans and options. We knew the government's money was going somewhere. But I couldn't ask him.

I closed my eyes on the train and imagined it full of people, bodies sweating in the heat, people pushing against your back and treading on your feet. Obnoxiously refusing to lift their bag from the seat next to them, or leaning against the yellow pole and taking up space for people to grip onto. But London was starting to feel like a ghost town. Even in my memory it was dense with bodies, there was still the jostling and struggle in public spaces. The tipping point happened so quickly, for it to feel like a different city entirely. To stop seeing birds wheeling in the sky, to stop bumping into people in the street, to stop asking people how their parents were doing, to stop thinking things would be different.

A carriage door forced open with a whooshing sound and a guard slammed the door behind him. The carriage was empty. He came towards me, hand on his baton. I looked up at him, nodded to him. He opened his mouth to talk to me, releasing his hand. He had a patch of dark stubble on his cheek that he must have missed when shaving, and I was close enough to see his teeth yellow and shining. There were marks of sweat on his baton left from the indents of his fingers.

'Excuse me,' I said, standing up in front of him, the train nearing my stop. I kept my eyes focused on his hands as I brushed past him. He stepped towards the door.

'You be careful now, Miss,' he said, kicking the door until it slid open, gesturing for me to descend. I clutched my bag close to me, and didn't look back the whole way home.

I don't know why I feared the police as much as I did. It was just a feeling: a sick, panicked feeling in the way they held themselves. Because we'd all lost, hadn't we? After the blackout, and rations were brought in, none of us were exempt from the panic: cars stuck in the street, families separated, scavenging in supermarkets, draining the rivers and lakes for water. No one had won. Not in any country. But why did the police look like they had? How had they maintained a sense of decorum? I wondered what they had fought for, and how they had fought for it. Who they knew, and why it mattered. Why they walked around in that eerie way like they'd been given a gift. Like they couldn't be touched, but they knew that we could, in every small way. They knew they could be the ones to touch us.

161

I took what I wanted, too. But it was for something different than him; it was just for hope, for hope, for hope.

I carried the papers with me wherever I went. I was terrified. The idea of them being found on me was worse than the idea of the stolen ration card George offered me. But still I longed to know what they meant, and eagerly awaited another party to try and find out. He called regularly, and my grandmother answered the phone each time, her voice a high tone of joy, even though she spoke to me with a sort of melancholy. She encouraged me, and encouraged him no doubt, and every time he arrived at our house with produce it was reinforced in her mind that this was the only option I had. He invited the both of us to Gloria's house again, for a spot of dinner. He had a small sneer on his face when he asked my grandmother, knowing she would say no (*vous faites le fou!*), but doing it to win her favour.

He also began, in that time, to call me 'my dear', and he held my arm as he did so. I noted the air of possession. I enjoyed it with glee when it first began. But every time after he would hold my arm, I would think of his stark kitchen, and that one room that held strange possessions, and my poor smitten grandmother, and the blankness, and the papers, and there wasn't a word for my uneasiness that I could express. The way he held me like he held other things he owned, watching me with both delight and control. It was more than the usual melancholy with the world that pervaded everyone, the malaise that pierced me. I saw it in my grandmother as well, every time I left the house. Every time I left her sitting in her chair by the fireplace (untouched in the heat of summer, but still the focal point of the room), every time she murmured to me in French and I pretended she had spoken in English, and she dismissed my fake appropriation. Every time she pushed me out the door, saying the neighbours had been checking in on her more recently, so she was never alone. She encouraged me, but her encouragement was full of a sadness that didn't have a name, in any language, but that triggered her to talk about my mother more and more.

'Margot and I ate garlic potatoes together when she was a teenager and I imagined her children, just as you are now, just that look on your face, and the way you say Maman, just like that.' She laughed.

She could see I was leaving her every time I stepped from our house. But there was no other way.

I would lie in my bed on the nights I wasn't with him, and I would call to my mother, in a whisper. I would think of the years between us, and count them (thirteen). I would ask her to come to me, and tell her now is the time and I wasn't afraid, she could come and see me. I would blink in the darkness and imagine shapes and think that she might appear in-between them. That she might tell me an answer to a question. She never did.

I went to his house again before the dinner party. 'My dear, my dear,' he whispered, and he unbuttoned my shirt in the kitchen (an old workman's shirt – my late Uncle's? – blue, faded, too large for me). He switched the electric lights on now without a thought, without checking to see my reaction, without thinking about it. I watched him do it, and I watched his face in the stark bright light and kept my eyes open, always, in fascination that this was how he lived.

He placed a hand around my bare stomach and reached to my back, with a kind of intimacy accorded to those who know you very well. Where before the slightest touch was a crossing of huge gaping canyons, now the gap had been closed, there was no gap to be granted back. A rejection, a pushing away, would signify something greater than it would have only a few weeks before. Oh, I chose it all too, I conceded to his hands on me and welcomed it. But with that welcoming was a hesitancy that grew.

With the pulling of each faded button I was immobilised further. I did the same, I pulled at his buttons. He said to me, 'We'll go together to Gloria's, we'll go together.'

'You said you could help me.'

'I will help you,' he said. I said take me, I told him to, I could have said, even, possess me. He told me I was his little bird. 'I'll look after you.' He said it as his hands were on me, and he pushed me back a little, against the counter, and then up, on top of the stark clean surface. I looked towards the utensil drawer and he bit my neck. A sharp bite.

'Ouch,' I said, but it did make me hungry, and I pushed my knees towards him, around him.

Afterwards, we lay on the tiled floor. I looked underneath the counters, just in case, but there was nothing there.

'Matilda,' he said. 'If you need anything, you'll tell me.' He placed a hand on my stomach. 'Even this, I'd give to you. Whatever you need.'

I looked at him, I frowned, and placed a hand back across his stomach, wide and rising and falling with breath that was deep and piercing. 'I don't,' I said, 'I don't want that.'

He laughed. 'I didn't think so. Or you'd have it already.'

I waited. I tapped my fingers on his stomach, waiting

for him to say the other: that he could help me the other way. With money, bribery, anything.

He sighed. 'I don't want to say. But I helped Jaminder last year. Gave her the money. There's no chance of them ever getting hold of her now, no possibility she'll ever be made to, no physical option.'

'Oh,' I said. 'I didn't know.' Even though, of course, I did. She told me she'd had everything taken out at that second party, and I should have assumed it was him. I moved my hand away. I felt across the floor for my shirt and pulled away from him. I sat up and started to button it. Top to bottom. With each button I waited, I told myself, with the next button I'll know, I'll know what to say. Wait for the next one. I got to the last and smoothed down my shirt. He was looking up at me, he was smiling. I smiled back at him.

'What is it you want from me?' I said, kindly. 'Is there something that you want, other than this?'

'I just want you,' he said. He pulled me back down beside him. My thighs rubbed against the cold tiles as he pulled me towards him. I shivered, even with the heat burning outside the window. 'I want to know you. Your fingers and your toes,' he touched them, 'your body and your hair, and that look on your face. I want you, all of you.'

I crawled closer to the expanse of his body and wrapped my body around it. I knew then, that I could never ask him. That I couldn't take all that I wanted from him. Because it would mean, perhaps, owing him my fingers and my toes, and I still needed them. They were still my own.

I took the papers with me to Gloria's house and heard them crinkle – as she hugged me – as loud as an old train, but she didn't move or flinch or look at me strangely. I brought them to show to Jaminder, imagined laying them out in the bathroom and asking her. But, as it was, I couldn't find her.

I stayed by his side like a loyal dog that evening, looking up at him, always, to gauge his reaction to everything and watch the line of his sight and where it landed. In turn, he held my hand and patted it at various intervals, and I caught snippets of conversation. Domestic borders. Fever. Sugar imports. Sea levels. I imagined the expanse of the sea the way you might imagine a relative you know well in your blood but can't remember meeting. I feared I would never meet her again.

His friends talked to each other in an excited, doting way, of their various initiatives and projects, what their ministry had invested in. I listened and said nothing.

I noticed Gloria, unusually on her own, standing in the corner and eyeing everyone as though searching for something. As though waiting something out.

'I haven't seen Gwendolyn tonight?' I said, looking up at George, amongst his friends. They stopped talking then, and one of them coughed, eyes on his wine glass.

'Oh, she got sick of the lack of prawn in the prawn cocktail no doubt.' George said, without missing a beat. His friends laughed, and took another sip of their drinks, and went back to talking about closed borders and Scandinavia's record harvest.

Each conversation like this made me hopeful he was involved in something crucial, some life-giving force, and I waited expectantly for it to be revealed. But every time I alluded to it, he dismissed my questions.

They talked about many things I'd never seen. Lands I could only imagine, and the spaces between them, the significant space of the ocean that separated us from all of them. I thought of reaching the place in the world where the sea meets the sky and the blues bleeding into each other, a worldly mess. In that meeting I imagined inserting my fingers, one by one, feeling the tips of them turn blue. I could turn that blue of the earth and become it. I could die, that way, in that blue, a returning, and I wouldn't be afraid of it and I'd be happy to go back to the world and bleed into it the same way I arrived.

A strange kind of hope, but I waited for its permanence like the roads we have walked on for centuries, holed and re-filled, and gone back to, won over by plant-life and conquered back.

I imagined returning to the earth. In a thick, large, impenetrable box made with all the arrogance of man. I imagined, years after the end of my own consciousness, that shrubbery would grow, and take root. I imagined blackberries growing over my grave; I imagined their triumph, grasping back.

That was my only hope then, that the blackberries should outlive me, and us – and him. I imagined he'd help with that, I imagined he'd help the blackberries crawl over us, in the end.

I might even have said the word blackberry to him that night. Maybe that imagining was my secret too, why I clung the papers to me at all times, without asking him directly.

The lights burst brightly from the walls, and I real-ised that they were not flickering candles but flickering bulbs, above our heads. They were fitted to look old and dimmed and I thought this a strange fashion, to make something look less expensive than it was. I noticed them just as I'd looked at his lightbulbs before. They burned into my eyes and seemed to burn every object in the room for hours, well beyond what most people had. I worried after always dressing in the dark that this lighting would render me stark and childlike. I hid my face by his side. Being next to him was a kind of invisibility, as I had nothing to offer, nothing that anyone cared for.

There was one small gap of time that evening that was my own. We were interrupted by Frank, Gloria's husband, who had a kind face and thick-rimmed glasses. I expected him to ignore me just as the others did, but he had the same welcoming air as Gloria. He took my hand and shook it. 'Jolly good,' he said, when I told him my name. 'French, what a treat. I read some Baudrillard once, did you? Don't let anyone tell you it's a bore. It's magic.'

I didn't want to admit my ignorance. I adored the way he assumed I'd have read the things he'd read.

'I have a copy,' he said.

'Oh yes, they have it all, here,' George said, mockingly.

'Georgey doesn't like the philosophers. But that's no matter, it must be in your blood, with a name like that?' Frank smiled at me.

'Something's in there,' I said.

He nodded at me affectionately, before leading George away, wanting to discuss something with him. George turned from me with a pat of the hand and a gesture to the buffet table.

Alone, I approached it. I marvelled at all the pieces of untouched fruit. Even, the most elusive of all: the banana. I picked one up and held it in both hands. I hadn't tasted one for years.

'Fascinating, isn't it?' a voice beside me said. I dropped the banana, grasped out of my reverie. Jaminder caught it and handed it back. I looked up to a kind face with combed hair and small features. She was wearing a floor-length dress, which would have been out of place anywhere else in the world but in this room.

I thought her wonderfully handsome; her kind sloping nose and curious eyes and generous words an assault on the gross arrogance of luxury we had laid out in front of us. It was in these moments that I broke that imaginary barrier, between knowing her and not. She played a song on the piano and that was it. There was me before, and me after.

Jaminder looked at the piece of fruit I dropped with the same curiosity with which I looked at it. I noticed it. It warmed me.

I put the banana back on the table. 'The fruit is fascinating?'

'Well, yes,' she said, 'Don't you think so?'

I smiled, a kind of relief. 'Yes, yes I do.'

'Have you had a banana before?'

I said, 'Of course,' not to lie, because I didn't believe it was a lie, but I couldn't remember, not exactly, the taste and texture of such a thing, so it might as well have been. 'Have you?' I said, as though asking the obvious, but she looked at me with such kindness I thought we might be in the same situation.

'Yes,' she said, surprised. She placed the fruit I had dropped back in the overflowing bowl. I might have taken a step towards her, to hear her better. To elicit intimacy, maybe. Or maybe I had an idea that I could do it without thinking, to try and make it seem natural. Just one step and we're close confidants. One step and I'm happy, I thought. I'm glad she's still there.

I absent-mindedly felt for the papers in my jacket and felt them crinkle. I wanted to ask her about the bees. 'I know why I find the fruit fascinating, with all of London on ration.' I picked up the banana I'd dropped, and held it in front of me as though I'd mastered it and knew it well. It was nothing. 'But why do you?'

'We live in the same city don't we?' She snorted. 'I'm as much of an alien here as you are.'

Did that border have any meaning for her? People seemed to be fascinated by it, but to me it was arbitrary; a veil thin as that between life and death; of my mother living and then not; of being one thing or another.

'Do you speak French?' she asked me.

'No, but I listen to it sometimes.'

'That's more than most French people could say.' She gave herself a congratulatory smile.

'And who are the French people?' I mumbled it, caught in my throat. 'Who do you think the French people are?' These old distinctions hurt me, they weren't relevant any more. Everyone was everywhere, and no one was anywhere, and I don't have too much pride to say that I missed the distinctions as greatly as I missed my mother. She was the whole of France, and she was gone.

'I'm sorry, I didn't mean to offend you.' She frowned. 'I only meant to make you feel at ease. You looked uncomfortable.'

I bristled at that, hoping that I had been able to hide some of it well. 'As do you.'

She straightened up. She opened her mouth to say something and I looked at the O of it, forming a word, and my shoulders hitched up, waiting for what was next. What could that O be, O-range? O-rdinary? O-lives?

'George – being around him is like peeling back a terrifying onion, layer after layer, don't you think?' She laughed, heartily. 'No,' she said, gesturing to the banana in the bowl. 'I suppose I won't eat it.'

'Why not?'

She smiled. 'Guilt.' I didn't ask, guilt for what. 'I think my time at these parties is almost done, I'm not sure I'll come back again.' She stood, contemplating the food on the table.

'Oh, but you must,' I said, more desperately than I would have liked. 'The champagne is exquisite.'

She narrowed her eyes at me in curiosity. I didn't blink, I fixed my smile. I looked around the room at the sea of ministers and their wives, dressed so artificially and with such self-consciousness. And for what, each other? I felt the claustrophobia of this world push on me. Not just because I felt I was out of place, but because I felt *they* were. What did they know of the true world outside of this house, outside of this village? What did they know about what it meant to struggle? And if they didn't know, what could they be doing about it? Except of course, eating food most people couldn't dream of, and drinking drinks erased from the world's consciousness.

'We're just an island. It won't take long,' Jaminder said.

'What won't?' I said, and felt a fool.

'If I were you,' she said, 'I'd run.'

I frowned at her, I wanted to ask her. I reached out a hand (For what? To touch her?), and just as it lingered I heard Gloria from across the room, next to George and Frank. 'Where is she?' she was saying, loudly, having come out of her corner, standing close to George, facing him. 'You haven't, have you?' She pulled at his lapel, pulling his face close to hers. 'I know you know something. Tell me where she is.'

George shrugged, unmoved by her closeness. 'Neverland?'

She reeled backwards, and without a pause swiftly slammed her hand across his face. He didn't flinch as Frank grabbed her and held her back.

'Careful now, Gloria,' George said, moving a hand to his glowing face, embarrassed, looking about the room.

'Gloria,' Frank said, desperately. 'Come on, now.'

She shrugged Frank off without force and stormed away from them. She headed straight towards us with a look of fierce intention.

'Lord, Jams, what bores they all are,' she said to Jaminder, trying to smile, but her mouth juddered around her teeth.

'What's happened?' Jaminder said, holding out a hand to Gloria's shoulder.

'Don't let's talk about it now,' Gloria said. 'I can't get hold of Wendy, is all, and she promised me she'd be here.'

'I'm sure she's just holed up with someone for a few days,' Jaminder said, trying to laugh, trying to coax Gloria out of her distress.

Gloria shook her head, fumbling in her pocket for a cigarette. 'I'm afraid this is a rum do. Something's not right.'

'It'll be okay,' I said, my voice the sound of a child. 'I'm sure she's fine.'

Gloria clicked her lighter on and looked at me disparagingly over her cigarette.

'I have to go play,' Jaminder said, looking towards the piano. She reached into her pocket and handed me a scrap of paper, which she'd written her telephone number on. 'Just in case.' She looked between me and Gloria. I put it firmly in my jacket.

Gloria eyed the card that passed between us. 'We look out for each other, don't we?' Jaminder nodded her head, and went back to the piano.

I was left with Gloria, looking at me curiously, her fingers shaking around her cigarette. 'Please, Mathilde, let me take your coat.'

'I'm fine, thank you.'

'Well, have something to eat at least.'

'I'm not very hungry.'

'How bourgeois of you.' She laughed without humour, and her perfect hair moved with her head as she did so. 'Everyone's hungry.'

Gloria never meant to make anyone feel a certain way, but she did slide around like she knew the answers to certain burning questions. It was a great risk, but I knew if I didn't do it now, I never would.

'Gloria?' I said.

'Yes, kid?' She continued to look around the room, and took a forceful drag from her cigarette, wobbling between her pale lips.

'If I ask you a question would you give me a straight answer?'

'I can but try.' She picked up a glass of champagne from the table and raised it up to me. 'Ask away.'

'What else do you know about the bees?'

Her face grew even paler, her glass lowered.

'Where did he get them? How does he get everything?'

'He told you then?' she said, lowering her champagne glass from her mouth, sickeningly. 'Or, Jaminder didn't, did she?'

'No, I mean, I just want to know about the honey,' I said, to reassure her. 'I've seen something, I found some papers. I've got them, I can show you. A list of food. I don't want to ask him. I thought you would know, maybe Frank has told you something. I thought you might know.'

She whispered, 'I don't know anything more than you.' Her eyes scanned the room. 'You think I have any say in what goes on here? You think I have any power?' I felt for once a real viciousness in her demeanour.

'No, I just…I don't know.' I raised a palm to my chest. I tapped it. I searched her face for lucidity. 'I only wanted to know about the bees and how it might help. Help the planet, do you see?'

173

I mistook her anger and severity for too much champagne and confusion, and worry for her friend, who would no doubt be here, drink in hand, tomorrow.

She snorted, as though the word planet were a great joke. 'Whatever you think you know, un-know it. We don't ask questions.'

A chill went through me, not from her words but from the look on her face. I sensed she was trying to convince herself, and she seemed heavy under the weight of it. I had no concept of what I was asking.

'You must return those papers, quickly.' She let her empty glass fall gently on the table and it landed with a discarded thud. She stubbed out her cigarette on the table cloth and looked back to me. 'You've taken a great risk. You have to put them back.' She held my hand, tightly, crippling my fingers. 'Now.'

I looked at her, afraid. 'Should I not eat the honey?' I said, missing entirely the point.

Gloria laughed, her head back. She lifted her champagne up high again, as though she was toasting me. 'We're all just bodies in the end,' she said, smiling. 'That's all.' She said it with a cheerful smile on her face. No one heard her against the din of the room, full of people. She turned from me and made her way through them.

That's when I looked past the table of fruit and to the piano, searching for some reassurance, just to look at her face, and feel things might be all right. I hadn't noticed Jaminder had never started playing, and the record was still spinning around, filling the room with music. She was sitting at the stool, but the keys were untouched. And George had placed his glass on its polished black top, leaning forwards towards her. One of her hands was placed at the edge of the keyboard, and she was picking at the wood, looking down. But the rest of her body was leaning away, in quiet submission. I moved closer towards them, to hear what they were saying. George was smiling, fiddling with an olive in his glass.

'Shouldn't you be off polishing the silver cutlery or something, helping out in the kitchen?'

'I'm a pianist, George, why on earth would I do that?' But she didn't look up at him in her usual levelling way, and kept picking at the piano.

'Well, you're the help aren't you? What else do we pay you for?' He laughed, and I tried to decipher if his tone was jovial. It could have been construed that way, if only I didn't look at her face.

'To play music,' she said, quietly. She stopped picking the piano then, and looked up at him. She smiled a grim smile and placed her hands on the keys. They jumped, solidly, into position, and she slammed against them into a cheery, loud tune. Everyone cheered and someone slid the needle off the record, drowned out against the piano.

He stepped back, surprised, took his hands off the lid. His glass shook and he caught it. She carried on, cheerfully, wobbling her head with the tune, until he left her vicinity. She carried on playing, but her shoulders slackened. Neither of them saw me, but I saw what her eyes followed. They never left his direction as she watched him go.

2

I went home with George, my mouth thick with worry. I glanced across at him on the rattling tube home and he put a hand on mine. Even if he had been able to hear me over the noise of the train car, I wouldn't have known what to say. I was beginning to feel a great unease in his company. But I couldn't squeeze everything I'd heard and seen and thought back into my old life of sewing at the shop and sitting with my grandmother. I told myself I wanted to stay to find out the truth, but in reality I knew it had nothing to do with all of that. I was only curious, and I never thought about what I would do if I found something out. I never thought, not once, of the responsibility of knowing something.

We walked from the station in silence. I didn't need to telephone my grandmother to tell her I wouldn't be coming home. When I was at home she spoke to me less and less and watched the fireplace more and more. When we were in the shop together she focused only on her work. She handed material back to me, wordlessly, having unpicked my stitches, to make me work harder and neater.

We entered his home and went to the kitchen to get some water. George flicked on a light switch and smiled at me. 'Better?' He fussed around the cupboards of glasses and pulled two out to fill with water from the running tap. I turned on his radio automatically, as I did whenever I stayed there. I left it on as long as I could, and stayed in the kitchen listening to it for as long as I thought the sound wouldn't disturb him.

I stared intently at the drawer where I found the plans that were in my jacket. I tried to work out if it had been touched since I had opened it. I couldn't tell, and tried to move my eyes away.

'Do you want anything else before we go up?' he said.

I stepped forward, I opened up a cupboard, hoping to

find some illicit food. Only ration boxes and tins.

'You won't find anything too good in there,' he said. 'But I could get you something, if you like.'

'Where do you keep your honey?' I said, trying not to look at the drawer. Trying not to look anywhere.

He laughed. 'My, my, you are getting quite the sweet tooth, aren't you?' He stepped towards me and put his hands around my waist, a sign of delight. He pulled me towards him. 'All that sugar isn't good for you, you know. You have to be careful. I should make you an appointment with my dentist. Have you ever seen one?'

'Once or twice, maybe.' I said. The thought scared me.

'I'll send you to Dr Yang,' he grinned. 'He'll know what to do with you.'

'No, no, I'm fine, I've barely eaten anything.' More men in white coats. More hands on me, more prodding.

He squeezed my waist with a giggle. 'I beg to differ,' he said, 'Anyone would think I'm fattening you up.'

It was true, and what once would have delighted me, now only made me ashamed. He searched in my face for a similar delight, and there was none.

'Don't worry,' he said. 'I'm only doing what's best.'

I put my hands in my coat pockets. I felt Jaminder's scrap of paper there. 'I'm not sure we should see each other anymore.'

'What?' he said, releasing me.

I looked at the floor, I shrugged. 'I'm just not sure what the point is.'

He looked hurt. He ran his hands through his hair. 'What do you mean?'

I shrugged my shoulders, examining my shoes. 'I don't know if we're right for each other. I don't know if we belong together.'

He reached a hand out to me but I didn't take it. 'Where's this coming from? I thought things were going along well.'

I shrugged again and didn't look at him.

'So that's it then? Just like that. You're done?'

'Yes,' I said, and folded my arms.

'And you're not going to change your mind?'

'No,' I said, quietly, looking up at him.

'And you won't give me a better explanation than that?' He stepped towards me. I swallowed, and lowered my head again.

'There's nothing else to say.' I exhaled loudly, and my eyes started to smart despite myself. 'I should just go.' I looked up at him and he just stood there, unmoving. He watched me and smiled, this time with malice. I turned to walk towards the door, putting my hands in my coat pockets one more time.

He said, 'I saw you, don't think I didn't. Talking to Jaminder, to Gloria. What have they been filling your head with?'

'What do you mean?' I said, but it sounded nothing like a question. I turned back to face him. I tried to crumple the paper to nothing, then, in my hand. I'd already memorised the number.

'Give me the papers,' he said. I looked blankly at him. 'The papers you stole from me.'

'Where's Gwendolyn?' I said.

It happened just like that, and I can't say anything about it other than that I was surprised. If I had seen it all coming, unravelling before me like a spool of red satin ribbon in the shop, I would've left sooner. I wouldn't have let it begin. I suppose I should've realised. But I didn't.

All I remember is blinking and being on the floor, a

burning pain emanating from my head, so hot I thought I'd been scalded by an iron taken from the fireplace. The world in front of me was black, but I still had the sense to raise my hand to my head and feel the wetness there. I brought my hand back to the floor and leant on it. When my vision reappeared, I saw my fingers had been dipped in a pool of red, which I'd smeared on the kitchen tile. I looked up and saw George, with my coat in his hands. I wondered how long I'd been out for. He didn't notice me sitting up at first. I looked at his hands. I looked at what they were doing. I looked at the counter. There was a rolling pin there, but I couldn't even tell now if I was sure that's what he used.

I watched his hands, afraid. I saw them grasp at the papers that I thought I had kept so perfectly hidden.

He looked down at me, he lifted them towards me. 'If I explained them to you, you still wouldn't be able to understand.' he said. 'It's better you don't think of things that don't concern you.' George laughed, turned on the gas hob and lit the papers up before throwing them in the sink. He laid my jacket down on the work surface. He hadn't seen Jaminder's scrap of paper, then. It probably would have meant nothing to him if he'd found it. But I felt a small triumph that I had something that was still my own.

He lifted me and carried me up the stairs. I weakly felt for his lapel, for something to hold onto as the bannister spun around me and the floor merged into the wall. I felt my consciousness drifting, so out of my control, that blackness. It was as though someone was pouring warm oil over my head and all I could do was let it; the heaviness and pleasure of nothing.

I leant my head towards him, I tried to stop it. 'Why,' I think I said, or I thought, my mouth not opening.

He hitched me up again, to get a better grip on my body, before laying me on the bed. 'You're wrong, Matilda. We are right for each other. We are.'

My eyes closed.

3

I awoke the next morning propped up in bed, a spoon being forced into my mouth. Sweet, sickly, crystalline. I moaned.

'It's honey,' George said, as though to a child, dotingly. 'It'll help.'

'No,' I said, trying to move my head away, but I couldn't. I swallowed it.

'Are you upset with me?' He kissed my shoulder, sitting beside me. There was a tray on my lap of elaborate cakes made out of every colour that food wasn't. 'I brought you a bit of everything, to make you feel better.'

I opened my mouth to protest, but my tongue lay there, immovable, dead.

'I'm sorry,' he said, lowering the spoon. 'You can't imagine the kind of pressure I'm under. We're on a knife's edge.' He gestured to himself with the spoon, and it got stuck on his shirt, leaving a small, sticky honey stain, but he didn't look down. 'I'm on a knife's edge. And you – you're with me, you're helping me just by being here. I need someone like you, to keep me sane. I need you.'

I frowned, I still couldn't speak. I tried to move my fingers, one by one, and each time they relented. I couldn't lift my hand. I wanted to touch my head. But I could see on the nightstand that there was a curl of bandages, and he'd tried to patch me up. I felt pain everywhere, not just in my head. He clattered the spoon down on the tray and put the jar of honey down next to it. He took my face in both his hands, leaning across me.

'I know everything about you, Matilda. Didn't you think? I gave you that ration card, those fruits, the sugar, I gave you everything. You know what happens to people that steal? That try and cheat the system? Do you know where the women go that choose not to reproduce when they can perfectly well, who don't have someone like me to help them?' He squeezed my face. I could feel each finger's imprint on my cheekbones, in my jaw. 'I want to help you.' He let go, he leaned back. 'Don't be foolish.'

He moved my tray from across my lap and lay down on the bed next to me. Wetness pooled around my clavicle but I could barely move my head to look, I could barely move my eyes to look at him, to watch his hands all over me, and under the sheets. I thought it might be blood, running all down me, from my head, spoiling the sheets.

He moved up against me. 'Come on, now,' he said. 'You can't be angry with me. Don't you love me? Because I love you.' He felt his way around me, slid off my clothes. All I could do was close my eyes, which is when I realised it was not blood, after all, but wetness from my eyes. All I could do was lie there, remembering what Gloria had said, that we are just bodies.

And he kept saying things, over and over, things that were just words. Not words in the way that anyone else spoke them, words that had meaning or sentimentality, or anything that made them more than just air and dust. All I could do was lie there. All I could do was let him.

He brought the radio up, and tried to set it to my

181

favourite station. But the reception was terrible and the whole thing crackled. He didn't bother to turn it off as he was upon me. I held onto that sound; that white noise. I held onto it to try and drown everything else out.

Afterwards, I lay there, as dead in my mind as I'd ever known it to possibly be; only the black and yellow shapes of darkness and the searing wonder of pain beyond what I ever knew to exist. If in those minutes, I managed to form a word, or a thought, or an image resembling anything from my life, it was only to berate myself, to tell myself how stupid I'd been. I'd never even taken that ration card, had I? But I had deliberated, I had wanted to. And what I hadn't realised then, which weighed upon me now, in the night of my mind, was that it didn't matter if I'd taken it or not. I'd taken other things. I'd gone to those parties and eaten that food. I was complicit. Solely by his offering it, I already owed him something.

When I could feel for my head, and could stand, and George had left for work, I stood in the kitchen. I felt my scalp's solidity, guarding my inner life. And the sealed wound, still healing. I tried to comb my hair over it to hide the dressing. I lifted the telephone off the hook, and it released a dial tone. I turned on the kitchen light switch, just to check, and even in bright daylight it beamed on. I turned it off immediately.

I looked around the house to see if I could find (if I'd even recognise) anything that would be monitoring me. Did he have machines that did that? Were they in the walls? I laid my palm across every wall, feeling for anything different. I knocked at them, softly, to try and hear an echo. If honey made a noise through a wall, what would it be? I was sure everything was hidden behind them, I was sure if they could speak they would tell me.

I tried the handle of the locked room filled with jars. It was tightly shut. It took all my power just to try and open it.

The front door wasn't locked, neither were the windows. But there was an implicit understanding that I wouldn't leave. And why would I? Did I want my grandmother to suffer? Did I want my life smaller and more narrowed than it was? It was just like Gloria said, we say nothing. Is that all we say?

I lifted the phone. I dialled the number. I waited.

'Hullo?'

'Hello.'

'Mathilde, is that you? Where are you calling from?'

'Can we talk, Jaminder? Are we able to?'

Exhale. 'We're talking now.'

'But I mean, really talk.'

'No, don't. Put the phone down, Mathilde. Put it down.'

'But —'

'I'll see you later, at the party. You'll be there won't you?'

'Yes,' I said. 'But I need to talk to you now.'

There was a crackle as she exhaled. 'Meet me by Queen Anne's Gate, at the bottom of the steps, by the park. I'll be there in an hour.'

The dial tone droned. I stood there, the phone up to my ear for a long time, breathing into the receiver. It crackled again, and I thought about the people left who still made phones. People who sold them, if such people still existed. And what little electricity was needed for them, and how that was a miracle, because it meant that they were one of the few things that had survived. They'd endured centuries, relatively unchanged. The wiring was nearly all the same, and they worked just the same, and they still worked, and that was one of the few miracles we had left. When everything else went down, and people lamented the loss of everything they could remember (what was real or exaggerated, it was hard to tell), the telephone remained. The telephone still crackled.

I checked the gash on my head in the bathroom. It had crusted over. I tried to clean it again and re-dress it. I put my brown shoes on and left everything in the house untouched.

I left the house straight away to wait by the park's entrance, afraid that I'd miss Jaminder. She arrived after what felt like several hours, and I was sitting on the bottom step, away from the road, across from the park. She appeared beside me, barely stopping. She looked down at me swiftly, without a word, and I stood up and followed her.

I trotted alongside her. 'Where are we going?' I said.

'You look like hell.' She kept looking straight ahead, her tread swift.

'I know, I'm sorry,' I said, stroking the ends of my hair with my fingers. I looked down at her shoes, old and worn, crunching on the path. 'Did you walk here from your flat?'

She let out a small laugh at that. 'No, I arrived by chauffeur.' She pulled at my arm, as we turned down a side street and into a small pub on the corner.

The pub was crowded with people, dense with dark wood panelling. The room sat under a cloud of smoke that stung my eyes, and people at the bar sloshed golden liquid from mugs. I'd never been in a pub before.

'C'mon,' Jaminder said, pulling me down at a small sticky table in the corner, immediately grabbing a cigarette from her pocket and lighting up. 'Do you want one?' she said, the cigarette waggling from her mouth as she flicked the lighter on.

'No, thanks,' I said. 'Jaminder, I don't have any money,' I raised my hands palm up, afraid of being in a public house with no way to buy a drink.

'Oh,' she waved a hand to dismiss me. 'I know the guy,' she said, and then raised two fingers up at the bar and down to the table.

The man behind the bar brought us two tumblers of some kind of spirit, slapping them down with a cheerful, 'There you are Jam-jar.' He looked at me, leaning over the table so that I could see his red chapped skin beneath his stubbled face. 'Who's your friend?'

'Thanks, Tony,' she said, patting his arm and taking another drag. 'Just put it on my tab.'

He stood up and let out a laugh. 'Oh yeah, *that* tab. Shame your old man isn't around to pay it one of these days, huh.'

'That is a shame,' she said, smiling back at him. He laughed to himself and went back to the bar, slapping his hands together in amusement.

Her smile slipped as soon as he left and she turned back to me. 'It's safe here,' she said. 'No one who'd bother to listen to us talk.' She flicked her cigarette over the ash tray and sat forward, her thumb between her teeth. 'What did he do?' she said, quietly.

I felt my throat close up at her question, and my hands shake. 'I didn't know who else to call.'

She reached across the table and lifted a piece of my hair up, and then tucked it softly behind my ear. 'He hurt you.'

'It came out of nowhere,' I said, and clasped my hands together in my lap. 'I'm scared, Jaminder. I don't know what to do.'

Her face turned white and puckered, but she didn't look surprised. 'That bastard,' she said, before sliding the cigarette between her lips. Exhale. 'I should've dragged you from that party that first night,' she said.

'Maybe.' I felt my limbs ache at the weight of being inside my body, at the pressure of all my bad decisions.

'I've been trying to call Gloria all morning, but there's no answer. After you talked to her last night, I worried about you. I wondered what she'd said. I wondered what we could do, maybe,' she put a hand up to her face and dragged it across as though trying to reveal something in her mind, 'I don't know what I thought.'

'She wouldn't tell me anything, she wouldn't say.' I felt my vision start to blur and my breathing change in anxiety. 'Has Gwendolyn turned up yet?'

Jaminder shrugged her shoulders, looking down at the table. 'I don't know.'

'And George? Gloria thinks he's involved in something, doesn't she?'

Jaminder sighed. 'We have to talk to her.'

'I feel so alone in it, Jaminder, I'm at sea.' I put my hands up to cover my face, and was relieved when she didn't ask how I'd remember what being on any sea was like.

'I need to talk to Gloria first,' I heard her say. 'If the damn woman would just answer her phone. Anyone would think she's just vanished.'

I put my hands down and looked across at her, worried. She shook her head. She reached across for me then, over our tumblers, and squeezed my arm. It warmed me. She looked at me in a familial way, letting her cigarette burn through, and then remembered herself, pushed my tumbler towards me and tapped her cigarette. 'Well, with a face like that, of course you're in trouble.' She smiled.

'Drink your drink.' She knocked hers back in one go, and I watched the liquid slide easily down her throat. 'Better,' she said, as she waited for me to do the same.

After three bitter, salty gulps, my glass was emptied. I felt the liquid warm me. 'Better,' I agreed.

She promised me we'd talk, all three of us, at the party. She said she couldn't do a thing without Gloria, and I wondered what that meant. Mostly, I thought it meant that she was afraid too, and it was the only thing that she could say. She gestured for another round and I thanked her, while saying I couldn't stay long.

'No,' she said. 'Best to go back and pretend all's okay for now. And then later, we'll talk.'

I felt my throat twist sickeningly at the thought of going back to George, and seeing his face, and letting him lay even a hand on my shoulder.

'I don't know how this happened,' I said, after the second round was put away. 'I don't know how I got here.'

'The best of us do it,' she said, lighting another cigarette.

'Do what?'

'String ourselves up for love.'

I shook my head. 'I don't know if I did it for that.'

She took a drag of her cigarette, exhaled through pursed lips, nodded. She sat back in her chair, waved her hand at me, gesturing for me to continue.

'Sleeping with a man, it's sometimes…it can be awful, can't it?' I said.

'Excruciating.'

'Sometimes I feel that my body is a desert. And I can't believe that we were ever made for it. Because my body is so against it, and so unwilling, and it doesn't want another body anywhere near it, and it was never designed for that.

187

How men ever thought that our bodies, above all else that they could do, were primarily for *that*... If they could only feel the desert I felt, and the way I could do other things, how my legs could run and how my heart could feel and brain could think, they'd never even ask for it.'

Jaminder looked at me, unmoving. Her eyes narrowed, as though she were seeing me for the first time.

'Sometimes I feel like it's impossible we were ever designed for each other, in that way at least.'

She smiled. 'Completely,' she said in a non-committal way.

'Then other times, it's all you can think about. And your body changes. And the thought of it consumes you. And all you want and all you dream about and all you desire in the dead of night is another body pressed on top of your body, just for the weight of it, just for the smell of pure skin, and the plummy weight of it underneath your fingers.' I patted a hand to my chest. 'Sometimes the world won't do without the weight of a man.'

She looked away. 'I suppose so.' She took a drag of her cigarette, then patted it down in the ashtray. 'Have you ever been in love, Mathilde?' she said, seriously.

'With a man?'

'Sure,' she said, shrugging her shoulders.

'Not in the way I'm sure I'm supposed to.'

She nodded.

'But I have been in love, many times over. With cities, with the women in my life, my mother, my grandmother, the way they loved each other. With my friends.'

She smiled. 'You have a nice way about you, Mathilde. And I'm sorry about it. I'm sorry about this mess.'

Before we left, I went to use the toilet in the back. I rinsed my mouth out and washed my hands and face, trying

188

to make sure the smell of alcohol had left me before I returned to George's. I unlocked the bathroom door and stepped out into the small corridor behind the bar. Jaminder was waiting for me and I stepped aside to let her pass me to the toilet. She frowned, as though deciding something, and then stepped towards me and pushed me against the wall with a soft movement. She put her mouth on mine, and I felt her hot breath, and the smell of the dense spirit, and she moved her mouth with mine, and I didn't stop her. She put a hand up the back of my neck and through my hair, touching it carefully, avoiding the wound, and pressed her body on mine. My arms lay still beside me, and after a few seconds, I opened my eyes and she pulled away. She sighed, a sticky, dense sigh, and I looked at her, my face pleading.

'Please, Jaminder, I don't know what to do, I'm so afraid,' I reached my hands up to my face, and she grasped me in a solid hug, so that my head rested on her shoulder and she could squeeze me tightly.

'Oh God, oh Mathilde, I'm sorry. I'm so sorry. I only... this place is desperate, that's all. After a while, it just gets to you.' She stopped talking and stroked my hair, and although I didn't want her breath on mine, I was glad of the weight of her body and the way she held me, and how it washed everything else away.

When I returned home, just as I had left it, I picked up the phone again to call my grandmother.

'When will you come back to the shop?' she asked.

'Soon.'

'Will you come back for dinner tonight?'

'Not tonight, but tomorrow.'

'Things are going well then, with the MP?'

'Things are going on.'

189

She huffed and clattered things in the background. 'Well that makes me happy. I like to know you're taken care of, you're safe.'

'Yes, grandmother.'

'I know Margot would be pleased for it. *Ça me plait*.'

'Yes.' I said. I covered my mouth so she wouldn't hear the ragged noise of my breath over the receiver. My eyes widened and I stared at the drawer. I felt I was even deceiving myself.

'*Elle me manque*,' I said. That's all I could say. '*Elle manque à tout le monde*.' She's missing, I miss her, she is missed. She misses it all.

'Oh yes,' she said, 'Me too.' And then in a mumbled, tight voice, she whispered, '*Liberté, égalité, fraternité, laïcité*,' as though to remind herself, as though to remind me.

But I'd forgotten that piece of nationalism, and it had died many years before.

PART 6

Jaminder

The wolf, the door

1

The oatmeal is not enough. We have stood, all of us, in Mrs Campbell's office and asked her for help. We watched her frame and the waggle of her hips, the fullness of her waist. We watched as she said she had nothing to give. That our wages are enough, that we aren't *dying* – in an exasperated tone – and we need only sit tight.

But I am sitting tight. We all are. And it is achieving nothing. We are sitting tight as even our children are starting to complain about their hunger. Even they, who receive all we can afford, at the expense of our own food, because the price of oatmeal is too much for a whole family. Even they find their stomachs pierced.

The idea of Hugo experiencing hunger as great as the wolf scratching around in my mind is enough for me to beg Mathilde, to beg Ruby. We have to do something, I say, imploring, what can we do. Ruby says it might be fruitless, but we can search, we can try.

Yes, I say, and I say it to God, help me, and I say it to you: You can't be right about this. We have to win this one.

I go days only eating nettles, and a spoonful of Hugo's oatmeal. I feel the walls will start talking to me and I will let them. I have days when my head turns to black. And still I play the piano, as often as I can. And still I stitch and stitch and stitch.

Ruby tells us one morning at work: okay, let's go. I

look at her hands resting on her hips and I can see she's punctured an extra hole in her belt, wonky, not in line with the others, just so her jeans will stay up.

We travel with Ruby in search of food. We leave Hugo with Mrs Donald and tell him we will be back. He asks one of us to stay but we decided: we have to go together or not at all.

Ruby says there is a town five miles away. She lends us boots that she has and warmer clothes. She doesn't need to ask if we need them. Ruby says she's done it before and it helped, one winter years ago. She found a few things, and with more people, there might be more to find. We've been through towns like this before and know the state we might find it in. These towns in Scotland were left, mostly, as soon as it was clear there was nothing to stay for. We might be one of the only villages this far north but we can't be sure. We know people stayed because of Father Anthony, because he had something to give them. We stayed because we knew this was one of the last factory towns where we had skills to offer, where London was far from consciousness.

We've seen dereliction in London, of course, but this is different.

Our feet are covered properly, for the first time in a long time. We wrap our heads to shield us from the rain and walk on with our rucksacks that we pulled out from the cupboard, unused since we arrived. There's a road that is tarmacked and we stick to it. I hold a knife in my pocket. After a mile there is very little light. Even in the bright of day there is no bright. We sing songs together to pass the time, instead of talking about what we might find. We sing old songs from tapes and the radio. Sometimes we remember the same song and we laugh, all of us singing it in unison. This time we've all hit on the same one: she was a singer who wore high heels and sequinned outfits.

'Can you imagine it?' Ruby laughed. 'I wonder what she's doing now.'

No one answers her because there is no answer.

We walk on, humming something different. Mathilde stops and puts her hand in front of her face. 'What's that up there?' I think she is pointing to a large oak tree, split through the middle, presumably struck by lightning, but it is a large expansive thing and could be anything.

'We need to leave enough time,' Ruby says. 'Remember. Enough time to make it back before it's dark.'

We walk towards it, in a line of three. I grasp the knife in my pocket.

'There might be people in there,' I say. 'That would be a place wouldn't it, for people to be.'

I look at Mathilde and she knows what I am thinking of. It took us a long time to get this far north, and the further north, the worse it was. We found so many things we didn't want to find.

'We should go around it, then,' she says. 'Let's go around it.'

We walk into a field to the side of the road, waist high in grass and thrashing about in front of us.

'Is this superstitious?' Ruby says, looking at the tarmac road, and the tree we can see perfectly now, looming over us.

'No,' I say. 'It's not.'

We walk like this for a while, quietly, hidden by the grass, waiting to get back onto the road. When the tree is far behind us we veer back towards it. I look back at it, and see something move. My hands wobble and I scream, 'There!' and grasp onto Mathilde's arm. She grasps back, and looks at where I'm pointing. She squints and I blink several times.

'I don't see anything. There's nothing there, Jams.'

I blink again and see that she's right.

She strokes my hair. 'When did you last eat anything?'

When our feet are firmly on the potholed road, I think about singing again. I think of a song we all might know, and I imagine the singer in my head. I open my mouth to let out a note and then stop.

A shape moves in front of us. It moves, slowly, onto the road. We stop. But it's heard our feet. It stops. It turns its head towards us. We breathe, mouths open.

'I can't believe it,' Mathilde whispers.

It doesn't move.

'Deer. Can you see it?' I think I'm imagining it.

'Red deer,' Ruby says. 'It's a red deer.'

It's beautiful. Its antlers are curved and arching, half the size of its body. Its face is stern and scruffed. It doesn't look scared, it is unmoved by us. It knows this land better than we do. It's been here longer. We should be afraid of it.

It has long hair around its muzzle and spots on its back. I wonder that its head doesn't fall with the weight of its antlers. It's not a thing I've seen before. I thought they were made up for Christmas.

'What do we do?' I say, and I grasp at my knife, my fingers slipping about in my pocket.

'We kill it,' Mathilde says.

'With what?'

Ruby steps forward. She walks slowly, approaching it. I see she's holding something in her hand, 'Ruby,' I say, quietly. But it's no use.

She holds the knife by her side. The deer sees her. It flicks its head, but doesn't move. She makes a decision because there is no time. She runs at it, she screams, her hand is up, knife above her. It reacts, in a second, its long legs scuttle. In a movement, it is gone.

There is nothing before us but long grass and the shape of Ruby, screaming furiously, hitting her knees.

'How are you still alive?' She screams in front of her, at nothing. 'How are you still here?'

I look back at the oak tree, and it looks like nothing now, having passed it. It looks like nothing to be afraid of at all.

We make it into the town a couple of hours later, following the dim light from the clouds and the long road that soon turns to rubble. Out of nothing, buildings appear. Some are half-formed, from where they have burnt down, from where people burnt them. Others stand, exactly as they were. We walk down the main street, and Ruby guides us. We look out for other people, but there are none. There are still shopfronts; pharmacies with the green cross extending from the awning. There are still displays with bottles inside. 'We'll come back for those,' Ruby says.

We're making our way towards the supermarket, to see if anything has been left from years before. There are houses too, just off this main road. We enter a few, the ones in the best condition, to see if anything is in their cupboards. We swing open the doors, and dust and dirt covers everything. But you can see what's there, underneath. A paisley sofa and a rug, a cabinet with china. We go into the kitchen, and there's a table there, with three places set: plates, knives, forks, spoons, cups. And a tablecloth. I pick up a fork and examine it.

'They must have left in a hurry,' I say.

'Didn't they all?' Ruby says.

Yes, it happened like that up here, just like London. One night, people were at their tables having dinner. There was little power left. Then all their lights went out.

I wince, thinking that Hugo has seen all of this. He has seen so many towns like this, all his life, and this is all he knows. He asks us what happened, and Mathilde won't say a word. She doesn't know what to say. She feels guilty for taking him away. All I can say is: We broke it. We were given the world and we took everything, and then one day, there was nothing left of it.

'I found something,' Mathilde says, and her arm is reaching far underneath the counters, she is lying on the floor, stretching around. She retracts her arm and it is covered in dirt, but she doesn't seem to notice. 'It must have rolled underneath,' she says, 'Peas.'

She hands the tin to me and I look at it. The whole house smells, so I don't notice it so much at first, but then I see the piercing.

'No,' I say, 'It must have punctured when it fell. It's spoiled inside.' I hold the can up to her face and she contorts.

'That's vile,' she says, and takes the can from my hand and rolls it back under the counter. 'For someone else to find.'

The cupboards are empty, and it's clear that people have been here before. The beds upstairs are overturned; objects have been removed from drawers and litter the floor. I walk along the corridor and cough in the dust. I turn to one room and open the door. A small bed is in the corner, mattress taken away, springs broken. To the side of it is a rocking horse. It's small and wooden, and the horse still has hair. I touch it, its thick wiry strands. My hand is covered in dust. I wipe it against my jeans. I push the horse's head and it moves. It rocks, slowly, back and forth. I wish we could take it back with us. I wish Hugo could see it. But it's solid and heavy and we'd never be able to make the trip back.

I think of this tiny child and wonder where it is now. Or where it is not.

'Let's go,' Ruby says, from downstairs. 'We can't hang around. There's nothing here.'

We leave the house, deflated. 'It's all been gone over a hundred times before,' Mathilde says. 'I don't think there's anything here.'

Her face is drawn and her hands muddied, and as she brings them to her face to rub her eyes I stop her. I spit on my sleeve and wipe them for her. I try to clean them as best I can. 'Be careful,' I say, 'Who knows what you'll catch here.' When you catch something, you can't un-catch it.

We make our way down towards the supermarket. I look at the staircases of buildings through the windows that have collapsed in on themselves, roofs that have been torn down. But there are still pictures in their frames on the wall, serving no useful purpose. I look at them, anyway. There are sunscapes and pictures of other worlds. Pictures of worlds that might still exist somewhere, but we can't be sure.

The supermarket stands largely intact. The sliding doors have been wedged open and the glass is broken. We slip through and it is dark inside. Ruby has brought a lamp with her and she lights it. 'I'm low on matches,' she says. 'If you see any, shout.'

We follow her, with the lamp, going through each aisle of the supermarket. It is mostly food that has spoiled and disintegrated. Stained and sticky surfaces and old fridges, empty and warm. There's a stand of school supplies with paper and sticks of glue. I put them into my rucksack. The shelves have been cleared, completely, and with Ruby's lamp we stick our hands underneath them and behind anything we can find. We climb up on top of them, we rattle the old rusty trolleys and look underneath the tills, that once were lit and beeping. We go through the back of the supermarket to the old warehouse, through the bakery. There is wrapping and machinery and parts, but nothing to eat. There is nothing, nothing, nothing.

'Christ!' Ruby says, 'Last time there was a lot of stuff we could carry back. I had no idea it had been got at like this. Who would even come here?'

We go through the offices and check the cupboards and the units, but it has all been toppled over, it has all been searched. There is a computer there, huge and imposing. Mathilde goes over to it, and sits down in the chair in front of it.

'I barely remember this stuff.' She taps the keyboard and it crunches with the weight of the dust. She taps the screen with her fingers and presses the buttons. 'Just in case.' She laughs and looks at me.

'I suppose I was a bit older than you were,' I say. 'When everything went down. The blackout.'

'Did you use it then? Do you remember the internet?'

'Of course,' I say. 'People lived their lives on there, that was all people were.'

'How about now?' Ruby says, smiling, moving old paperwork aside to lean on one of the desks.

'Now? I don't know. Maybe we're invisible? Maybe we don't exist?'

We laugh, under the light of the lamp, in the dark, dingy office. We laugh because that's exactly what we've hoped for all these years. That's exactly what we've wanted.

2

We make our way back before dark and our rucksacks are heavy with odd things we've picked up: crockery, books, lotions left in the pharmacy – but no food.

'This has happened before,' Ruby says. 'But we're lucky, because we have oatmeal, and as long as we can produce that we'll be fine. And we're working on the rest. Father is always working on the rest.'

We nod and don't question it. We've been through so many towns that have hoped for more and had very little, but they always had some small way to survive, they'd always found some part of their village to draw on, and gain something from. We had faith we'd be able to stay a little while, unnoticed, but we didn't count on being this hungry.

We hug Ruby goodbye as we return to the village, and we walk back towards our flat. I look at Mathilde's face. 'We'll need a wash tonight.'

'We've got some water collected, we should have enough for a bath.'

It's a treat, and I look forward to filling the old tub with water warmed on the fire at the end of a long week. I look forward to Hugo turning the taps on and playing with them and pretending water is spilling out from them.

'I've missed him today,' I say. 'So stupid, isn't it? How you can miss him after only a day?'

Mathilde takes my hand in her own. 'Oh, Jams. I know what you mean. We got so lucky with him.' She strokes my hand with her fingers.

'We got lucky with each other, too,' I say. 'I don't know where I'd be without you now. Without my strange friend.'

We climb the stairs to Mrs Donald's flat above us. We knock on the door and there's no answer. We knock again. Mathilde looks at me. We wait. There's a scrambling sound from indoors and then footsteps. The door swings open and Mrs Donald is behind it, red and flushed. Her cheeks are shining with sweat, which is strange in this cold weather.

'Everything okay?' Mathilde says, and moves forward to enter the flat.

Mrs Donald shakes her head. Her glistening cheeks wobble.

'What is it?' I say. Every molecule in my body stops with that beat. That horrible, sickening beat of silence.

'It's Hugo,' she says, and her voice comes out as a wail. 'There's something wrong. He has a temperature.'

Mathilde pushes past her and I follow without thinking, calling out his name. Mrs Donald tells us he's in her room.

He lies under the covers in her bed, shivering and sweaty. He's as pale as I've ever seen him and his dark hair is stuck to his forehead, clinging to him. He blinks at us as we enter.

Mrs Donald rushes behind us. 'He just suddenly got worse this afternoon,' she says. 'He said he wasn't feeling well and I thought he was hot but not like this. Then we were trying to have some lunch and he wouldn't eat, he was sick. I don't know what to do.'

There's a bowl of steaming water by his bedside and a

bucket with vomit dripping in it, stuck to the sides of the plastic and green, bright green.

'He's been sick?' Mathilde says, to Mrs Donald, wiping the sweat away from his forehead. 'Are you okay baby Hugo?' she says to him. She used to say this to him, every day, until he decided he was too old. The sound of it makes me desperate.

He tries to nod at her, and holds out his hand for us.

'He's so hot,' Mathilde says, and looks at the bowl of water. 'Why is there hot water here?'

'I thought that helped,' Mrs Donald says. 'Steaming it out. I didn't know what to do.'

Mathilde doesn't say anything. I go through our rucksacks, burrowing through, trying to find anything we picked up from the pharmacy.

'Don't you have any paracetamol?' I say, to Mrs Donald, 'Don't you have anything to give him?'

'No,' Mrs Donald says, her face crumpled, her hands around her neck, 'We don't have any of that now, it's all gone. Father Anthony always says he will bring us these things, we just have to wait for Father. Maybe he has something already?' She starts to wail and I pat her arm.

'I know you've done everything you can,' I say.

Mathilde gives me a sharp look.

'Should I ask him? Should I make sure?' I pass Mathilde everything we've already gathered from the pharmacy, but it is only soothing creams and chamomile lotion, and gel for mouth ulcers. Still, I tell her to slather what she can on him, in hopes of cooling him and making him better. I go downstairs to our flat and check every cupboard and there is nothing, we haven't had painkillers in a long time.

I go back upstairs.

203

'Nothing else,' I say, 'I'm going to go see Father. Call the doctor,' I say to Mrs Donald, and she looks at me blankly. 'Call the local doctor?'

'Well,' she says. 'That's Father Anthony, too, isn't it?'

'What do you mean?' I say, 'He's a priest.'

'He's a healer,' she says. 'There's no doctor up here. He's the healer.'

'Fuck,' Mathilde says. '*Putain.*'

I bring my hand up to my face. 'We never checked. We never thought about it. There's always a doctor, in every village. There's always someone who has some drugs, or something, who's hoarded things, who knows things.' I start shaking Mrs Donald by the arms, 'It can't be true, even in the worst places, even in places worse than this, there was always a nurse, there was always someone.'

Mrs Donald shakes her head. 'God will help him,' she says, 'God will heal him.'

I stare at her. My mouth is open. I say, 'I don't understand.'

'Go,' Mathilde says, crouching by his side. 'Go now, quickly.'

I leave the flat as fast as I can, and see the path beneath my feet disappear in a blur. I break into a run, slipping on the mud, my clothes drowning in the rain. I think of how people used to do this for fun. They'd never run for anything real in all their life. And with every step the pain in my throat grows louder until I let out a noise which might be a scream, on the way to the church, gasping for air. I am watching his face in my mind, telling him I was going to teach him chopsticks on the piano, just like every normal child always did. I was going to make him feel normal, like he wanted, and not like an afterthought. I was going to give him something that wasn't left behind, or wasn't used before, or wasn't leftover. I was going to give him something that was his, like we never had done before. I was going to give him something brand new.

I enter the church and it is dark. I push open the heavy door and it's cold and there is a draught coming from the corners of the building. I shout Father Anthony's name. I stand at the bottom of the aisle and put my hand against a pew. I call his name again. I call it until a match is struck and a lamp moves down the aisle towards me.

'Jaminder?' he says, and his face is opposite mine. In the dark I barely recognise it.

'Father, Hugo is sick. We need help, we need medication. There's no doctor here,' I say, as though he doesn't already know.

'What's wrong with him?' he says, and he doesn't move, holding the lamp in front of him.

'He has a fever, he's been sick,' I look up at the stained glass and I can't see it in this light, there's no colour. It's not there. 'Please, hurry.'

'I can't,' he says, and still his arm doesn't move from in front of him. And his face doesn't change. 'I'm sorry he's unwell. I can give you some of my oatmeal, and water. I can offer you prayer, I can offer to heal in this way, but I have nothing material to give you.'

'What do you mean?' I say, calling out to him, 'You're the priest, you own this town, you must have something. You must have medicine, you must help us.'

'Oh, my child,' he says, lowering the lamp. 'I've tried. I've called out, I've asked for help, but none has come. I've failed.'

I shake my head, 'Why can't anyone help us?' I reach out to his arm and grab it, pressing down, and he steps back from me, a look of horror on his face.

'Because there is nothing left.'

'There's something,' I shout, pleading with him, 'They still have things in London. They have so much. They said you might have something. There is still something.'

'Not here,' he says, 'Not now.'

'What should I do?' I gasp out, up to those high bright windows. 'He has a fever. We have nothing to give him.'

'You'll take care of him, it will pass.'

'People don't survive these things any more, people don't make it like they used to.'

'You must pray, Jaminder, you must pray to God.'

I, in turn, step back from him. 'That won't save him. We'll die here. If we stay here, we'll all die. I don't know why we came here.' I turn to walk away, thinking about how I haven't needed God and he hasn't needed me. To talk to nothing now would be akin to madness, futility in its worse sense, selfishness and entitlement. It would be fraudulent of my own thoughts; words called into the air, addressed to no one. 'After everything I did, why would I pray to him only now?'

'What do you feel guilty about, Jaminder?'

I stop before the door, with my back to him. I look up at the ceiling, and my eyes blink in the darkness. 'I thought it would be difficult, I thought it would hurt me, and I'd be afraid. But it didn't and I'm not.' A sickly lump catches in my throat. 'I'm not sorry for what I've done. I don't feel guilt.' I turn to him, and he is unmoved, holding the lamp up above him. 'I'm more afraid of this place, of what there is for us. I'm more afraid of this darkness than of the things I've done. I'm more afraid of the idea of God than of my own sins.'

'You shouldn't fear him,' he says.

'I'll never be sorry,' I say. 'I'll never repent. I'll never feel bad about it.'

206

'Then why do you continue to search for something? Why are you here?'

'I don't think you have to believe in God to look for something. I don't think you have to believe in God to be kind.'

I turn away from him. I push the door open into the wet night air. I walk home with nothing to offer upon my return.

We sit around Hugo and stay with him through the night. We have candles lit, of course, so Mathilde remarks that we are taking vigil. We leave the fire unlit, so we are huddled and cold, as we try and lower his fever. We bathe cloths in cold water meant for our bath and place them on his forehead, but it only makes him shiver. He is asleep, but in a fitful state, and I grasp Mathilde's hand. We wait.

'Do you think parents always worried about their children like this?' she says to me, her palm sweating beneath mine, despite the cold.

'I think they did,' I say, 'I think my grandparents worried about me. I think they sat with me and worried.'

She places her head on the side of his bed, forehead to sheet. She exhales. 'I keep thinking about how old I thought my mother was. Not just when she died, but when I was a child. She always seemed so old. But she was only in her thirties, and now I'm approaching it, and I feel in many ways older than she ever was. These five years have been a lifetime, haven't they?'

I forget that she's younger than me. I forget that I've entered a new decade without her. It doesn't really matter, up here. We're as old as each other, because of Hugo, because of the life we've lived. I look over at him.

'It's been a lifetime for him,' I say. 'This is all he's ever known. London, Mrs P, the lot of them, it all seems so far away.'

'Do you think we've done something terrible?' she says. 'Do you think, if we'd stayed in London, or further south, there'd be more for him? Is this because of us?'

'What, *Auntie Knows Best*?' I say and grasp her hand firmer in mine. 'I don't know. We didn't have the privilege of choice. We knew when we had him that it would be nothing like London, that it would be hard.'

She looks at me like I've insulted her, and pulls her hand away. 'You think we made the wrong choice having him? You think we shouldn't have wanted him? You think I should've wanted to get rid of him, like you did?'

'You know I didn't want that,' I whisper. 'You know that.'

We never speak of the decisions we made to bring us here. So I hate her for it, when she brings it up, when she reminds me of the person I was almost six years ago, the person who is different from now and separate, who exists in a separate world. I hate her unkind face that is only unkind because it is scared. She raises her eyebrows at me to say: I am right and you are wrong. I think she might be misremembering in her unhappiness, I think she wants to say that she loves Hugo more than me, and she wanted him more than me, but it's not true.

'I know what you really thought,' she says. 'That it wasn't right for a child, this world. But I knew,' she pushes her hand against her chest in self-righteousness. 'I knew he was worth it.'

I shake my head. 'I always wanted him! I just didn't know, *we* didn't know how we could do it. If it was worth living like that. You know that, we both thought that. It was a valid choice, either way, in that situation, wasn't it?'

'And now you're saying it's not worth it? You think we should never have had him? He's our son, too, he's our son, and you don't want him?'

I hate her, in this instant; I hate her for the things she's made me do. I hate her for attempting to love you, even if it was only for a moment. I hate her for assuming that because I considered not wanting Hugo, I don't love him now.

'I've been teaching Hugo about France,' I say, because I know this will hurt her, I know this will upset her more.

'In secret?' she says, 'Why would you do that?' Her mouth is tight like her words.

'I thought he should know where he's from.'

She snorts, a vicious snort. 'He's not from anywhere.'

'Well, that's a stupid thing to say.' The accusation hurts me. 'You should've spoken to him in French. You should've spoken French, sometimes. Just a few words. You should've taught him something.'

'I can't,' she says, in that same forced way. 'I don't think I even could if I tried. It's gone.'

'Where has it gone?' I wave my arms around, gesturing about the room. 'Your first language can't just vanish.'

'It can,' she says, quietly. 'English words come first now. It's been so long. I've forgotten the French for so many things, or maybe I never knew to begin with. If I had to have a conversation like that now it would be stilted. My brain blocks me from retrieving the words.' She looks up at me, pained. 'I'm a foreigner in my own mind.' She prods at her temple, a little too forcefully, and I want to take her hand in mine. 'So how could I teach him? What do I have to teach him? And what about the words I can't describe in French or English? The things that don't have a name?'

'That's not right,' I say. 'Some words have to be spoken.'

209

'I can't help it,' she says. 'That's just how I feel. It's not your right to tell me what I should or shouldn't do. It's not your right to teach him about where I came from. Whatever sense of culture we have left, whatever history there is, it's gone now. What do you know of it anyway? What does it mean to you?'

'I only do it because he should know. He should know where you're from, who you really are.' I want to hurt her. 'Do I even know who you are?'

Now her mouth is open and wide and pulled back from her teeth. She is not trying to restrain it. 'You know nothing!' she says, screaming in every way apart from the volume of her voice, lowered for Hugo's sake. It is a rasp, forced out. 'You left somewhere that wasn't even your home, voluntarily, when you were a child. My whole life was obliterated. You can't know what that does to a person.'

We're playing that game people sometimes play: who has it worse, who has suffered more. There's no answer, and no sense of being right, there is only its antidote: empathy. But it's hardest to come by with people who know you the best.

'It was obliterated,' I say, slowly, 'and now you obliterate it faster, farther – you didn't try to keep anything of it, you just lost it, you let it slip away.'

'Because I'm not like you,' her voice is a hiss of a sound and her body is straining forwards as though under a weight, 'I can't bear it.'

'And I can?' I jab at my own chest now. 'Did I not take a bullet for the both of us once?'

We don't like to think of it this way: she did one thing, I did another. We like to think of it as though we were both complicit in every action the other took. But that only works half the time. The other half we blame each other, we resent each other, we are jealous of the other.

'I never asked you to do it.'

'You never stopped me.'

'All right,' she says, her arms are up, her face is wet. 'I'd be nothing without you.' Her tone is mocking and cruel. 'I'd be nothing without you.' But as she repeats it she meets my eyes, her face is sincere. She says it slowly: 'I'd be nothing without you.'

I shake my head. 'I wish I could've done more.'

She leans closer, she strokes my hair. 'We're doing all right, aren't we? We're okay.' She looks at me guiltily. '*Jusqu'ici, tout va bien.*'

'What does that mean?'

Her eyes are large and brown and brilliant, like she's a child, like she's apologising. 'So far, so good.'

I want to tell her, I want to explain: that she's hard to get at, that she doesn't always let me in. That I wanted to be around her, always, and her presence at those parties helped me in ways she can't know. That her presence took me here, and as much as I might protest it, I couldn't have done it on my own.

But she is also a wall, and I don't always like the way she does things. I don't like what she hides from Hugo, and I hate what she hides from me. I wish she'd embrace herself, and maybe I hate it in her because it's the worst part of me, too.

I might hate the way she holds her fork and the way she says that affected 'dig in' when it should be '*bon appetit*', but I also love her. She's an incomparable beauty, in every sense, down to the creases of her knuckles and the freckles on her ear lobes, and she is just one of those people – in the way that some people are – that you want to possess. And that might have got her into trouble before, but it's got me into trouble too because I don't know how to reconcile it. I don't know how to want her and save her and hold her and help her and also hate her, let her upset me, for always wanting things for her, and never being able to rescue that feeling, never being able to make it better.

I know she wants that for me, too. But it's different. The responsibility of feeling and decision of feeling has always lain with me.

I never told her what they did to people like me. How they changed us if they found us, took away the parts of us that made us human. I was never able to tell her. I never knew how to tell myself, even after Gloria. I didn't want to hurt her. I didn't want to explain to her the myriad of things they took from me, my own sense of self. I wanted it to remain invisible. But things that are pushed to invisibility have a way of coming out through the cracks. And she is one of those cracks in a dark wall, where all the light forces its way through, and I see it as clearly as anything. Although I hide it from her, she knows what I've given up. I want to embrace her, I want to be near her, always. I want to touch her, I want to make her happy. But I know the only way to do this is to keep what little distance we have left between us. So I keep it. I keep myself from her.

So I hate her, too, in these moments, but I also understand her. We're the only two in this world that could understand the other. Because of how our bodies are woven with fear, and how that gets to you, after a while. How living a life that is only a memory of other things makes you something else. And how you try, despite this, every day, in the tiny ways you can do it, to stitch it all back up.

I know her so well, every line of her, every space. I see through her, in its most privileged sense. That is why I take her hand and tell her, 'He's going to be all right, Mathilde. He's going to be fine.'

'We're going to lose him,' she whispers to me, head turned towards me, leaning against his bed, her hand limp in mine. 'We're going to lose him to the flu. Can you imagine a thing more stupid than that?'

'No,' I say. 'I can't.'

We listen to him breathing all through the night, watching as the candles burn down. Mathilde falls in and out of sleep, her head resting against his sheets, and I sit cross-legged, her hand in mine. I look at the candles and at his feverish face. I think back to when I was a child, and all the lights I left on. All the switches I clicked and bulbs I left burning. All the streets I walked down lit up for no reason other than so people might see the way.

I think of Diwali, and that comforting ritual we had, so like this one, where we turned off all the lights in our house and lit candles. We covered the rooms in candles.

We filled brown sandwich bags with sand and stuck red candles in them and lined them up the driveway to our house. We boiled milk and strained mixtures through cotton and added sugar and laid it out and cut them into sweets. And we lit so many candles.

Diwali is warm and surrounded by people, not like this. I swallow a sickening taste in my throat, thinking this is now my Diwali, the only one I'll get. Lighting candles because we have to, around my ill son (yes, mine, too), sitting with all the family I have. It is nothing like it once was. I feel guilty at the thought that I have let my grandparents down, how sad they'd be if they could see me, and see what we have got ourselves into. How they might be ashamed of me for being like this. How I am ashamed of myself, that Hugo will never know the farcical exchange of identical gifts, and my grandmother's false surprise at

213

receiving the same sweets each year. I imagine their fudgy softness on my tongue, but I cannot dream of a thing like that anymore. And he will never know that kind of sweetness for its own sake.

But he will know candles. There is no temple for him, only a church. And maybe one is not better than the other, but one is more foreign than the other. I long for it: to push back against all those years and sit on the floor with the crowd of women, our hair long and covered and our feet bare, and praying for something, whether we knew what it was or not, praying to something.

If I could push back on those years and be in Kenya, and be with my family, and show Hugo to them, I would. If I could tell my grandfather about my son, and tell him the idea I have that he might play cricket, or at least play a ball game, that he might play the piano; that he might taste roti, one day, and tear it up, and roll it about his tongue, just like he did, and continue on, like us; if I could tell him that and it was true, in this instant, I would wipe away everything else. Looking at him, lying in this pathetic cold flat, surrounded by this hopeless dream we had for him, I realise I would rather take back the past, in all its sincerity and splendour. I would rather take back the past in my imagining of it, than have anything we have now.

I watch Mathilde and wish I could show my wish to her. I wish she could see what I can only dream of. And I wish I could see hers, too. I wish she'd spoken French to Hugo because then I could hear her say the words, I could imagine another life for her. I could re-learn her, and all that she is. I could meet her for the first time, and all the magic of it. I could watch her as though I was only now just meeting her, a beautiful stranger to me, once more.

214

The candles burn down and the others stay asleep. I watch their breathing, checking their movements, carefully, making sure. I look at the candles, and the dripping wax, and how wasteful that might be. But I still light them. When they go out, one by one, I still strike our last matches, and light them.

PART 7

Mathilde
Matilda

1

George arrived back to his house without a word spoken about what had passed. I was sitting in the kitchen, dressed for later, looking at my hands, with the radio turned on, loudly.

I had picked up the telephone again several times, after I got back from the pub, and listened. I tried to decipher the pattern of noise it emitted, and I spoke words into it, to no one. George entered the kitchen jangling a set of keys in his hand. He put them down as soon as he saw me.

'Why are you just sitting there like that?' he said, a frown on his face. 'You look miserable.'

'I was just waiting for you,' I said, and tried to smile.

He looked at me fiercely, then to the radio. He marched towards it and pushed the button forcefully to turn it off. 'It's this damn radio, isn't it. This damn violin music you listen to incessantly. Honestly, Matilda. It's driving me insane.'

He gestured with that word – accompanied by a high screeching sound to exclaim *insane!* – and hit the radio with his hand, so that it fell from the counter and onto the cold, hard floor. My face crumbled, and I held my hands up to it.

He looked at my reaction, grimly satisfied. Then he stamped on the radio until he drowned the music from my world.

*

'I've got something for you,' he said. I tore my hands away from my face and I looked up. He looked happy.

'Oh?' I said.

'You have to come outside and see.' He gestured towards the front door and I followed him. He opened it and I stood on the threshold. I hadn't put my shoes on. I didn't need to step out any further; it was bright and possessed, unapologetic.

'It's a car,' I said, trying to hide the horror in my voice.

'Yes,' he said, laughing and tugging at my arm in childish delight. 'Can you believe it? I finally found one. I've charged it up, it's ready to go.'

'Go where?' I said, scared of getting in such a thing controlled by him, alone, facing forward, cramped, so near the front window and so close to smashing through onto the streets. 'Are you allowed?'

He shrugged his shoulders, 'Of course, they're not illegal.' He gave me a look, perturbed by my lack of enthusiasm. 'You should be pleased that you're with someone who can afford the power for such a thing.'

'I am,' I said, looking up at him, trying to show some willing. He pulled my arm and I stepped forward onto the street. The pavement was burning underneath my feet. I lifted them up, one after the other, to try and cool them.

'Look at the seats!' he said. 'The interior.'

I looked. I didn't know what I was looking at. Grey upholstery with buttons. Dials and switches and glass, glass everywhere. Seatbelts, I checked. Everything looked new. Plump tires with deep grooves, for grip. Grip along these paved Westminster roads? You could go somewhere in that car, you could really go somewhere. If you could afford to charge it up. If you could find somewhere that still did that kind of thing. 'It's marvellous,' I said. 'I'm impressed.'

220

'Exactly.' He held my hand. My fingers twitched. 'Are you ready for Gloria's later?'

'Yes, I'm ready.'

'Good. I need to change my tie.' He looked down at my feet. 'What on earth are you doing with no shoes on? You'll burn your feet to cinders.'

I padded them up and down on the hot stone.

The door was open when we arrived at Gloria's, and no one responded to our knocking. We walked up the staircase alone, ourselves. I spent the whole ride over gripping the window ledge of the car, and looking out of the glass. I stared at the traffic lights and watched them change, usually indicating to no one in particular. It was a smooth ride, even though George had to keep braking along the city streets, remembering the speed limit. Around the city centre, the car crawled past a few pedestrians. Their heads flicked around as the car went slowly by. We went driving around the streets before heading north to Hampstead, so he could show me what the car could do, how it could drive.

'I wish there were fewer people around so we could really get this thing going,' he said, before turning out over Waterloo Bridge.

I looked onto the roads and wondered how you could want that, in this desolate place.

From the bridge you could see where the city was lit. Hospitals, schools. Some lights still emanated at night. The lamps on the bridge were turned off. A few people lined its edge. One woman stood on the first rung of the railing, and as we passed and our headlights lit her up, she turned. Her face was a black smudge against the river, her eyes widened. She didn't step off.

As the car headed north and the roads emptied and

widened, George sped up. He laughed, jumping a meaningless red light.

'Isn't it wonderful?' he said, turning his head towards me, unafraid.

I didn't say anything. I felt smothered by the car. What I didn't say was I was embarrassed. I hoped no one saw me, even if they were strangers and I never saw them again. I didn't want to be in anyone's memory as a person in a car. I didn't want to be remembered in any form, even a blink, a tiny accumulation of molecules for one millisecond, as someone using electricity to drive from Westminster to Hampstead.

I hoped no one would see us as we pulled into Gloria's drive, greeted by two other cars. I hoped Jaminder had come. I hoped she hadn't touched another piece of fruit, not even to hold it. I hoped she'd never ridden in a car, not even as a child. I hoped she had nothing to be ashamed of.

As we reached the room at the top of the stairs the mood was ashen. People milled about, quietly, but my heart lifted as I heard the piano. But Jaminder's playing was slow and deliberate, not even close to the energetic, jolly tune I had heard once before.

I looked at the food on the tables. Some of the fruit had turned. The plates were laid out just as yesterday, half-full. The bottles were depleted.

'No delivery today then,' George mumbled.

I didn't ask from where. The electric lights were off, and this time there truly were only candles lit, held in black candelabras all around the room.

Gloria was sitting by the large sash windows, facing towards the glass with her hand extended from her, cigarette in place. I was relieved to see her, even like that.

'Smoking indoors are we?' George said, with great

amusement in his voice. He dropped my hand and walked towards her, but her head didn't turn. No one addressed him. I looked to Jaminder, and her head turned to me; a slight shrug of the shoulders, *I don't know*, her movement said.

Gloria's hair hadn't been brushed and she was wearing old blue jeans, the kind that fit tightly all the way down the leg. She didn't have shoes on. Her hand flicked the cigarette ash onto her lap. Her fingernails were painted in Affair in Red Square, or I imagine they were because I think she would've liked that. It would have pleased her to have that again in my telling of it.

Gloria didn't move for a long time to talk to her guests or look towards them. She stayed, contemplative, peering past her reflection in the window out onto the street below, one leg tucked over the other, cigarette after cigarette greeting her fingers. The party was quieter than normal, and discussion quickly turned amongst the groups of people to the lack of care taken over the night's proceedings. Glasses hadn't been washed, floors hadn't been swept, food or drink hadn't been ordered. Frank had obviously tried, in haste, to fix the neglect of his wife, but it was noticeably different. It was discussed among guests if she was ill. Why then did she sit at the window? People tried to talk to her directly and they were ignored; one woman went to touch her and Gloria only flinched, but didn't look towards them. Frank walked around, apologising, laughing, filling glasses and taking care to address each person in turn. But the atmosphere was lost.

Frank came towards me, pressing his glasses up his nose with one hand, and holding a bottle of something with the other.

'Is Gloria okay?' I asked him.

'Oh, yes,' he said. 'She's just having a quiet moment.

Don't we all need that, sometimes? I'm sure Proust had many of them, didn't he?'

'Who?'

He frowned at me. 'Gosh, you're as English as tea, aren't you?' he said, before patting me on the shoulder and wandering off. I waited patiently for a break in Jaminder's playing, and time seemed to slow to a pulpy thickness I couldn't get to as I watched George working the room, I watched Jaminder hit the keys, mechanically, and I watched Gloria, unmoving.

I thought she might never leave the window. I imagined her for all eternity sitting there, as the buildings crumbled around her and the world flooded. I suppose that is how I imagine her, in my eternity, now.

When Jaminder stopped, and left her stool, I released an intake of breath and followed her to the food table. She glanced up at me. I touched her arm, 'Jaminder?'

'Slim pickings today,' she said, as though she were talking to anyone.

I whispered to her. 'Do you know what's happened?'

She looked up, taking a bite out of a cracker. Her eyes scanned the room in one quick sweep.

'No,' she said, 'I don't. But I think I need your help.'

That was the first time she asked me for anything. I remember that feeling of inclusion. She touched my arm, the arm that touched hers, and we were one linked body like that. It made me feel strong. I would have done anything for her then.

'Follow me,' she said, 'once I have Gloria. Follow us.' I didn't ask why, but she told me anyway. 'I'm afraid I can't do it on my own.'

I wonder if she suspected, then, what might have happened. The inevitability of it. She might not have known at all (and this is what she claimed later), but she knew that anything could have happened; that it was all possible; and it scared her.

She released my arm and stuffed another cracker into her mouth before pouring a tumbler of gin and gulping it whole. She nodded at me and then left my side. My eyes followed her, as she walked over to Gloria at the window. She said her name gently. Gloria's head moved and lifted towards Jaminder. Her eyes were glassy and vacant, but they gradually focused on Jaminder in front of her. She stubbed out her cigarette onto the windowsill and followed Jaminder from the room.

A noticeable ease took hold of the party then, a great exhale of breath. The awkward presence had been removed and the jollity continued. Someone put on a record. Someone screeched a laugh.

I saw George's stern face across the room, and before he could look for me, I slipped out the double doors and circled back to the exit Jaminder and Gloria had taken.

I heard them before I saw them. A small wail from upstairs. I followed the noise and it led me to the upstairs bathroom. I had been in it once before; large antique bath on feet, porcelain sink, tiled floor. Plush towels and bottles. Cupboards and cupboards of bottles. I tapped lightly on the wooden door. A bolt slid across and it opened. Jaminder stood behind it, and ushered me through quickly. Gloria was sitting beside the sink, leant against the wall facing the bath. Her mouth lay open, her eyes followed mine as I sat opposite her. I hitched my knees up as she had done and Jaminder sat beside us, the circle complete. We were like schoolchildren then, gathered on the floor of the bathroom.

Gloria looked at Jaminder. 'What's she doing here?'

'She can help, she knows things.'

'She'll talk to George.'

'I won't tell him a thing,' I said.

She looked at me, at Jaminder. Jaminder nodded.

Gloria's face relented. 'I got this today, with our food delivery.' She handed me a folded piece of brown paper. I took it, looking at Jaminder to gauge what kind of reaction I should have.

The paper had a dark, uneven surface. It was an invoice, a list of food, in some kind of Nordic scrawl, with the English translation next to it.

'Your food delivery?' I said.

'Look at the last item,' Gloria said, her face a contortion of worry.

My eyes ran down the list in swirling black pen; a list of all the usual items that arrived nightly and were laid out on the buffet table. All the bananas and apples, and small tins of fish and dairy too: six eggs, and a small pot of cream. At the bottom lay an additional item, written in dark pencil, different from the rest, rendered by a strange hand. It read, with soft, cramped markings: *FIGS*

'Figs?' I said, not understanding.

Jaminder gave me a sharp look.

Gloria lit a cigarette. 'Figs,' she said, slowly. 'Don't you remember? They were always the fruit I was glad to see the back of, the wrinkled things I hated the most. Wendy used to tease me about them, and I said,' she took a drag, her hands shaking. 'If figs ever appeared on my list, something terrible must've happened.' She shook her head. 'We always joked about it being our code word for the death of all good things. It was the only way to get a message to me. Inconspicuous, perfectly unnoticeable amongst the rest. Means nothing, to anyone else.'

'Where is she?' I said, quietly. 'Where is she now?'

Jaminder released Gloria's hand. Gloria's cigarette butt hung from her fingers, burning through. The ash slowly drifted down to her jeans. She didn't wipe it away. Gloria lifted her head up towards me, a sickening expression on her face. 'The little hive George has by the coast, that was his first foray into foreign investment. He imported these bees and tried to breed them. And people liked it. They liked tasting what they hadn't had in years. They're obsessed by this idea, George in particular, that now we've fucked nature up we can own her. That we can create this little utopia in London where we can have whatever we want, while everyone else starves.'

Jaminder was shaking her head and I frowned. 'Where do they get it all from?'

'George organised it all. There were still close ties to Northern European royal families after ours was lost. And they fared best, didn't they? They avoided the worst of it all, and so production carried on well for them. Until the influx of people in Norway brought yellow fever. Then they were desperate for people. They can grow everything there, better than here, but not people.'

'We're not animals, can't they see that?' Jaminder said, sickeningly.

'They know we're screwed,' Gloria said. 'Why not save the privileged few that can be saved, why not live in the lap of luxury for your remaining years, if there are ways to do it.'

'What ways?'

'They struck a deal that worked well for them both,' Gloria said. 'We get the produce that still grows in that milder part of the world, and they get our best women. Our most fertile. The ones who won't be missed. The ones who don't play by the rules. The ones who don't do their duty, they're the easiest to give up.'

'But – Gwendolyn,' I said. 'What do they do with them?'

'I don't know,' Gloria said, 'Probably kept somewhere to fulfil their duty of adding to the population. They're just traded, like they're pieces of fruit. I can't think of it, can you?' She looked down to her knees. 'Oh, my dear girl. I never thought it would touch us. I should've protected her.'

'You couldn't have done anything,' Jaminder said, a hand on her arm. 'It's not your fault.'

'George warned us, didn't he? He said Wendy was a trollop. He used to think it was funny, but he wanted her to settle down like the rest of us. Set an example, have a child. But she wouldn't do a thing like that. And we just laughed at him.' Gloria stamped out her cigarette on the bathroom floor, lit another. 'The list was just on top of our strawberries. Can you imagine it? She's in transit, already, crossing paths with our deliveries. In a van filled with strawberries. After the delivery turned up, and I saw it, I ran three miles down the road to chase after the car. Frank had to pick me up in Camden Town and I told him I'd die if he didn't bring her back. He said there's nothing he could do, it wasn't his decision. She's gone.' Gloria let out a wail, and put her face in her hands.

'What do we do?' Jaminder said, desperately.

Gloria let her hands fall from her face. 'I've been here, and I've known, and I've done nothing. I've drank myself stupid and hosted these parties every night. I've eaten that food and I've taken it all, just as he did. I'm complicit. If it wasn't for me, she'd still be here.'

'No,' Jaminder said, 'It's not true, it's not your fault.'

I handed the piece of paper back to Gloria. She folded it up without looking at it and put it into her pocket.

'Frank helped me, you know.' Gloria said. 'A man in a position like that. I was so grateful to him, so I married him. We just wanted to live our own lives, and we thought it cruel to bring a child into this mess. And I was terrified of dying in childbirth like my mother, or being forced to marry a fool just to have a child who dies at the age of three from a goddam cold. So we agreed. He could do what he wanted and he'd sort that out for me. We were friends, mostly.' She reached in her jeans pocket, her hands shaking, she pulled out another cigarette. 'You know what they do with people who don't like the opposite sex. You know what they make them do.'

'No,' I said, 'I don't know.'

'It wouldn't warm your heart.' She held her lighter up and lit the cigarette, inhaled, slowly, her fingers shaking delicately. 'I might as well not have bothered,' she said. 'He changed. Stick around here, and you change. The pressure of it got to him. He cracked like an egg. I love him, you see, as best I can. And he loves me. But in this place, it doesn't mean anything. So I said nothing about what was going on. I couldn't say anything.' She looked at the cigarette intently, letting the paper burn through without flicking the ash away. She inhaled as she nodded her head. 'I got it wrong, all these years. I got it wrong.'

Jaminder moved towards her, took hold of her knees. She wrapped herself around them and placed her head on top of them. 'Oh, Gloria,' she said, and she sounded as desperate as ever I've heard her.

'Were you with Gwendolyn?' I said, afraid of my own question.

Gloria looked at me. 'What does all that matter now?' She let out an amused sigh. 'What does it matter to you? What I wanted, what she didn't? She was still my family. I still treated her like my sister, I treated her like a husband treats a wife; better, even, than that.' She swallowed, sickeningly. 'What does it matter? Now that she's gone, I feel I'm already dead.'

Jaminder lifted her head up. 'No, Gloria, don't say that. Please, don't.'

'All of us,' Gloria said, her eyes glassy and vacant. 'We all are. We're sitting ducks. Ready to be traded like government waste. Oh, Gwen, you damn fool, you should've run.'

I shook my head. 'I tried.' I said, in a small voice. 'I tried to leave. I can't now.'

'No,' she said. 'You can't.'

The sickness returned and travelled up my stomach and into my throat, burning me like acid. Jaminder didn't release Gloria's knees or look at me. But I knew her silence meant agreement.

I watched the bath and its slippery texture, the shiny porcelain and the smoothness of its surface. I imagined it filling with water and slipping inside of it. Submerging. I know they imagined it, too.

We heard the drum of the party downstairs. And the noise became gradually louder and penetrated my senses more and more. I worried they would come and call for us.

'Oh, God, Gloria.'

We sat in silence after that for a long time.

Gloria was the one who eventually spoke. 'I imagine the world,' she said. 'Like it's not a thing that is dying, that it's not a thing that was born out of a bang or matter or stars or explosions. That it's just a thing that manifested because the conditions were perfect, and all that's happening now is the conditions aren't right, and it's manifesting itself out of existence, as it perfectly well should. I imagine it's the same for us. Time isn't linear. We just choose to live in this moment as a comfort to ourselves. Everything that's already happened, and everything that will happen, is already contained in this moment. There's no birth and there's no death. There's only the right conditions to appear, and then the conditions gradually cease, and we leave.' She looked at us. 'There's no sadness to it. We are both everywhere and nowhere. And everything and nothing. We exist and don't exist. We have been born and we will die. Just like the world.'

Jaminder put her head in her hands. I leant over the edge of the bath and put my hand in it. But there was no water there. It stayed empty all that time I'd imagined it otherwise.

'We can help her. We can help each other.' I said desperately, urgently. But even as I said it I knew we couldn't. And still, Jaminder smiled at me while Gloria looked down and wiped the ash from her jeans.

She sighed. 'Wouldn't that be a thing,' she said. She lifted her head up to the ceiling. 'Can you imagine a thing like that.'

Gloria tapped her fingertips to her lips, one by one. Afterwards, I tried desperately to remember if her nails had been painted. I asked Jaminder, who hadn't known. But I wanted to know. I wanted to know if she'd bought the acetone, for no other reason than for swallowing it. Or did she have it in her cupboard all along, and it had been waiting for her for months, years, waiting for her to get to it. And she used it to remove her nail varnish and she'd re-apply it, leisurely, afterwards. It was such an unimportant detail that meant so much to me.

I like to imagine her as the wonder that she was. I think she'd have preferred her nails to be red, even if she'd never had red nail varnish. It would have laid itself on top of the life that she was leading as a reminder of how things used to be. A reminder of how human we all were, after all.

I think about Gloria's idea of manifesting sometimes. It makes me think we could be a substance as liquid as

231

water. That our molecules could just appear and dissolve, and succumb to the earth, be beaten by the blackberries. I found the idea of the tangle of shining beads taking our place a reassurance, that we all have our hour in the day. I wonder if she meant it to be as comforting as I found it. Jaminder and I left the bathroom, and Gloria stubbed out her last cigarette and said she'd be down in a minute. We re-joined the party and the minutes passed. When Jaminder went to go and check on Gloria she said she found her unconscious on the floor of the bathroom, blood pouring from her mouth. What we heard downstairs, above the record player, were Jaminder's delayed screams. We all froze, watered-down champagne in hand, and Frank bolted from the room, startled like an animal.

George came to stand beside me, took my hand. In a last, desperate attempt, I looked around for Jaminder. I tried not to feel the moist closeness of George's hand in mine, the lines in his palm sticking to my own, the grooves of each finger and their individual animal-like form. I counted them in my palm, tried to decide which was the worst finger, which finger held the power, which finger caused the trouble. Had his hands done it, themselves? Had they been the ones, physically, to do it? I spent this time waiting to know what the screams were, thinking only of his extremities, and nothing of my friend.

An ambulance was called, on the shiny black plastic phone in the hall, and Frank's voice could be heard throughout the drawing room. 'I don't know what's wrong, there's blood everywhere, come soon.' And their reply, which surely would have been, There's only one ambulance available, it might be twenty minutes. Twenty minutes! And the phone slammed down.

That's when I prised my fingers apart from George's and followed Jaminder's wailing, which was now outside the bathroom and up the stairs. She was being held away from the closed bathroom door by a large man, arms wrapped around her waist, her legs kicking. Frank looked up to her from the phone with a grimace and I followed that look. She looked like something terrible had been dropped inside her head, her legs kicking at the closed wooden door, arms pressing down upon the arms that pressed her.

'What did you do?' Frank shouted at her. 'What did you tell her? What did you make her do?'

She didn't respond with words but noises, a word straining to get through, her mouth a wide orange O, her lips stretched apart and over her teeth.

Eventually her wail did turn into words, and those words snapped Frank's head towards her. They lead him to mount the stairs towards her, and take her off the man holding her, as though she were a small thing, a plate of fruit, something inanimate and portable. He threw her down the stairs like that, slid her down them, not even forcefully, carelessly. She landed in a heap near me. Her eyes were closed, her mouth open in that horrible O. Her dress had slunk above her knees and revealed her stockings; worn and repaired and laddered, faded through, so that the skin of her legs could be seen. No one was there to cover them back up for her.

Before I could fall to my knees in front of her, hands fell all over me and I was ushered into the drawing room again.

George took my face in his hands. 'We should go.'

'I want to know that they're all right,' I said.

He told me we were going home. I looked up at Frank, standing at the top of the stairs, hands over his face. 'Where's that bloody ambulance,' he said, smacking the top of the banister.

'I want to go home, home,' I said, and I repeated the word in the hope that it made sense to him, and I said it over and over: home, home, home, and I said it underneath my breath when we were back in that car, until I was dropped at my grandmother's house and he had left me there.

I said it as my grandmother stroked my back and I looked at the car reversing from our house with unease, and fear. I said it as I listened to the words in my head Jaminder had said, had screamed them down the stairs at Frank: You killed her, you killed her, you all killed her.

I worried for her life, both of theirs. I sat on my bed in that old garden flat and didn't sleep. I went downstairs to the kitchen and watched the old phone, that one remaining thing. I worried about who would call, and I worried about trying to call someone myself, and thought only of hearing that drone, and not being able to get through.

2

I was taken ill, then, and developed a high fever, and told my grandmother to relay this information to anyone that called. She intercepted several calls from George, and none from Jaminder. I didn't dare ask after anyone, and couldn't read a word of anything, or look at a piece of food on a plate, and so I spent several days in a dreamlike state, staring at the walls and the stitches of my duvet.

I was aware that during this time my grandmother still brought me hot soup to my side, and seemed delighted to have me back, ill health or not.

She sat next to me, with her piles of sewing, and lit torches and candles for me in the evenings, even though I needed the light for nothing. She read to me, too, and we listened together to the words of old books, which she'd pause over and muse, out loud: I wonder what that was, I don't remember that. She read to me in English, and she talked to me about my mother in French, and laughed to herself, even when her voice strangled around the words. My fever shook my limbs and hands, and I held them out in front of me and watched them reverberate, as though they were a sail on a boat on the high seas. I thought it might be Dengue, but didn't have the words to ask. I slept for hours at a time, and sometimes I would wake up and find myself calling for Jaminder.

After two days I began to talk again. 'What does George ask when he calls, grandmother?' I said. She sat next to me, working on the hem of a blue garment, delicate and careful work.

'He just wants to know how you're doing. I told him not to come round.'

'Good,' I said. 'That's good.'

'How are you feeling?' she said. 'George sent round some medication, you should feel better soon.'

It wasn't grave then, I would recover. I didn't want to tell her I wasn't relieved. I couldn't go back to him and he wouldn't leave me here. I knew too much. I began to eat a little soup, and my grandmother watched me carefully.

'How did you get that mark on your head?'

I rested the spoon back in the bowl and lifted my hand to my head. 'I don't know.'

'George sent the doctor round yesterday, he said you should be careful.'

'Maybe I fell down the stairs,' I said emotionlessly. I thought of Jaminder and her body crumpled next to mine, and my whole world fell down the stairs in an endless jumble of images.

'You would tell me, wouldn't you? If something was wrong? If you needed help,' my grandmother said.

I turned my face from her. 'Have you heard from Jaminder? Have you heard from Gloria?'

'No,' she said, 'I'm sorry. Are they your friends?' She put her sewing down on the floor and came to stand beside me. 'I'm worried,' she whispered. 'I'm worried for you. What can we do?'

I turned my face towards her. I felt that my eyes were stretched thin and peculiar, and sight was a drain on my whole head. I closed them, for her sake. 'There's nothing to do. I think I will have to have a child.'

My grandmother grabbed my shoulder, her fingers gripping like the claws of a bird. I didn't open my eyes. 'No,' she whispered. 'Not with him.'

'It's for us.'

'It can't be.'

'I'm sure of it.'

'He told me not to tell you. But I have to.' Her hand shook against my arm. 'Oh, Mathilde.'

I opened my eyes and her face was a blur of worry and pain. 'What is it?'

'Your friend, Jaminder. She was arrested for possession of contraceptives. He's working on getting her out.'

'Who is?'

'Well, George, of course.'

I shook my head. If it wasn't such trouble to stretch my mouth over my teeth I would have laughed. 'Oh, no,

236

grandmother,' I said. 'He is the one that put her there.'

I lay in bed for several hours, without speaking. I counted the cracks in the ceiling, one by one. I named them after Jaminder and all her family, who I imagined, and who she'd never spoken of. I imagined the cracks to be her ancestors and her children, which she'd never have, and I named them, one by one, girls and boys and men and women and I counted up the cracks of her life, as a way to search for an answer. At the thirty-second crack and the thirty-second name, I came upon one.

I sat up in bed in one smooth motion. My grandmother yelped, having thought me asleep. 'My jacket,' I said, a cry in my voice. 'Is it here?'

My grandmother stood up, 'Oh, yes,' she said. She ran from the room to retrieve it, and in all my life I'd never loved her more. She came back, and I told her to look in every pocket, to find a piece of paper with a number on it.

'There's nothing here,' she said, and she looked at me worriedly.

'Where is it,' I said, 'How will I find her.'

'The doctor said you're improving. Your fever is going.'

I raised my hands to my temples, 'I memorised it. Can you take down this number?' I sat there for a good ten minutes, trying out the combination of numbers, to find the right one that fitted inside my brain. I haven't forgotten it since.

'Call it,' I said, and I told her to dial the number, and to find Jaminder on the other end of the line, and to tell her I would come and get her, would bring her out of there in any way possible.

I waited for hours. I stared at the ceiling in the darkness and counted the cracks again. I looked at the black ceiling and imagined it a sea; and Jaminder and I were sailing along it, getting lost amongst the waves. We kept losing and finding each other and our hair was damp with wetness, and our bodies were soaked too, but we swam for miles. We became blue whales, the kind you see in old colouring books, with their fat tails and large, round bodies. We were whales, those animals that don't exist, but we existed. We called them into being.

The phone rang. It was in my room this time. My grandmother must have brought it up there after I asked her so often who called. She wasn't around to pick it up. I leant across in the darkness to answer it.

'Hello,' I said.

'Hullo,' she said.

I grasped the phone with both hands. 'Oh God, Jaminder.'

'I'm sorry if I scared you, I'm out now.'

'You're safe?'

'Of sorts. I'm safe for now.'

'Oh, thank God.'

'What are you thanking God for?' I could hear the click of a lighter and the intake of her breath, and it was the most blessed sound.

'I'm not sure.'

'You sound strange, are you all right in bed like this?'

'I have a fever, I've gone funny in the head. But I'm better now I know you're safe. You are safe aren't you?'

'For now, for a few hours. I need to leave.'

'Oh, Jaminder,' I said. 'You can't leave me. You're my dearest friend.'

'I have to, Mathilde. We know what the other option is.'

'Have you heard anything about Gloria? What have they done with her?'

238

'She's in the hospital. She pulled through, despite all the sores in her mouth and her stomach. She should've used a razor and a hot bath.'

'There's no sense to any of it.'

'I have to go, Mathilde.'

I cried through the phone, shaking the receiver. 'You can't, Jaminder, you can't. Let me come with you. I love you, Jaminder, what would I do without you?'

A hand extended towards me and I realised it wasn't my hand, and I wasn't holding a phone. It was the middle of the night, and not a candle was lit, but I could just make out Jaminder's face, and she was looking at mine. She sat in my grandmother's chair, and was reaching out her hands to calm my own. She was as beautiful as she'd ever been like that, in the darkness, the only light coming from the embers of her cigarette. She took another drag. She coughed slightly.

'Oh, Mathilde,' she said, exhaling. 'I lied to you.' I looked at her face in the dark, I grasped her hand that laid itself on mine. 'I'm nothing.'

'Jaminder, no,' and I was desperate now, clinging to her hand like that, desperate for her to be all right. 'I love you, Jaminder, I love you.'

I tried to move towards her, to reach out to her. I wanted to tell her that she was something to me. But my hands padded the air and felt nothing, and she moved away from me, retreating into the darkness.

'I'm pregnant,' she said, stubbing out her cigarette on my grandmother's painted chair. The image of her face extinguished with it. 'And George is the father.'

It was dark, and I tried to make out the lines of her face, or at least the remnants of embers on the chair, or where the cigarette butt had fallen. These were the trivial things that travelled through my mind, instead

239

of what should have registered. I felt as though my arm had been severed but it was still feeling its way for her fingers.

I heard her clear her throat, swallow. 'Will you look into my eyes and tell me that you love me now?'

3

I lay still in the darkness and I listened to the sound of Jaminder's breathing, making sure she was still there. I reached my arm out to her, and it caught her hand, but she retracted it.

'No,' she said, 'It's no use now.'

'Oh, please light a candle, I need to look at you.' I tried to sit myself up but I was weak, and I felt my stomach couldn't support the small movements in my upper body to try and lift myself. I laid my head back down on my pillow and turned desperately towards her. I wished she was closer to me and I could touch her. She clattered on the table next to me and with a small hush a candle was lit. She held it in her hand, and I saw for the first time that her eyes were hollows and her face was a small tear of worry.

'It's too late for me,' she placed the candle in its holder back down on my bedside table. 'But not for you. I just wanted to say goodbye.'

'It's not true is it?' I said to her, and wondered what I looked like in the foggy candle light, my face a blur of itself.

'I wanted to tell you before,' she said, and fiddled again in her pocket for a cigarette. 'But there was no right time.' She struck another match and held it up to her cigarette, inhaling slowly, giving herself time. 'I didn't know how to warn you, I didn't know how to get you away. Then I realised I simply couldn't – because if he got wind of the fact I'd told you, I'd told anyone, I'd be done for and so would you. So long as you didn't know, and George held you next to him, I thought he wouldn't do the same to you. I thought it meant you were safe. As a woman with no children, you were safer being close to him than with anyone else, than your doctor or your grocer or your grandmother or anyone walking down the street and knowing you didn't have children and that the act of them giving you children would be applauded. With him you'd sort it out and you'd never have to worry. I didn't think he'd hurt you if he wanted to be with you. If he thought more of you than he thought of me.'

'He did hurt me,' I said. My sheets felt slick and moist underneath my body, and I tried to count the days I'd been lying in them, and when I'd walk again. I wondered if my grandmother had let Jaminder in, or if she'd slipped through the unlocked front door, and if it was still unlocked. I opened my mouth to suggest we lock the door and as Jaminder spoke again I realised I'd forgotten what she was telling me, and I wish it had just been isolated to me. I wish it had just been me.

'I know,' she said. 'That's when I realised that none of us were safe. And then with Gwendolyn, and Gloria – but there was no time to do anything. It all happened so quickly.' She reached a hand up to her head, as though quelling a deep-set headache, as though squeezing it between her fingers would release it and it would leave her.

'What happened at the police station?'

241

'It was only two nights. After they'd beaten me over the head a couple of times, I had to tell them. They took me to the hospital and checked and the doctor told them I was telling the truth and the baby was healthy. That was all they needed to know; they let me out straight away. But it's only a matter of time before George finds out. Of course he won't think it's his, they never do, but he'll assume we've spoken. He won't let me get rid of it. If you're lucky he'll let you stay to have your child, when you have one.'

There was a draft coming through the window and the flame of the candle wobbled in response. I shivered and my wet sheets made me feel even cooler. I wanted to tell her I needed to move, or be wrapped up, or bathed. But I knew that first I had to listen. 'How did it happen? When did it happen?'

'I'd known for a while that George had taken it upon himself as a personal mission to procreate, and to send women away. The women he has he lulls into a sense that he can help them, but it's not true. He knows that Mrs P and the rest will thank him personally if he sets an example like that. He's been doing it for years.'

I imagined the multitude of women discarded, but found a number like that too large to comprehend or visualise; I tried to count them but it was useless. I thought only of Gwendolyn, and people like us; the rest didn't have faces and they didn't have hair and they weren't women or people, they were just things: piles and piles of things. They were the soil that was tilled and the individual grains of matter that made up the soil and the individual molecules that made up the grains. They were ground down to dust and were so small and so huge in number that they became nothing in my mind. The thought terrified me like nothing else and I still remember this thought as though it

242

had been an actual horrifying event in my life, as though Jaminder had slapped me across the face and cut off my arm. Nothing had happened to me here, only elsewhere and to other people; but to imagine it in such a way chilled me, and to imagine someone you know, or yourself, as one of them was too much to imagine at all.

'I thought it might happen,' Jaminder was still talking. 'But like you, I thought that I was safer as part of that group than being outside of it, and they'd get me in the end. He told me he'd helped me, years ago, taken everything out and my periods were just memories of ovaries and eggs. I didn't know the difference. They just put me under and scraped around and left me bruised and unchanged. I used contraception for the most part, anyway, because I didn't want all those men knowing what I'd asked George to do for me. But he knew, of course, and so I suppose for him it was only a matter of time before he took what was his, knowing that there was a chance I would fall pregnant by him easily. That's why I didn't believe it for months, I thought it wasn't physically possible. I felt different, I suppose, but I didn't believe it. I'm still deciding how to end it.'

Her voice started to shake at that, and I'm sure she was imagining knitting needles and coat hangers and whatever else women found, and the doctors who helped them and were sent away, and became dust like that. She put her face in her hands after stubbing out her last cigarette. I could make out the ashen marks they'd made on my grandmother's painted blue chair and I hoped that if we vanished into thin air, as you could in dreams, that people would one day come into this room and just by looking at those marks they might understand what had happened between us and how desperate we were, and the things we told each other. I hoped they'd understand our foolishness. The smokescreen George and the others had put in front of us, the sweet, sweet smokescreen that looked so much like something we used to see, moving about the flowers in our gardens.

'I tried to stop him,' she said. 'There was no reason for it and it hadn't happened before. It was just a party and you weren't there and he'd had champagne and honey cakes, and the honey cakes I could taste in his mouth, and even then I knew about everything, I've always known, and it sickened me, more than the actual act. It was just one of Gloria's rooms and maybe I'd laughed too much with him that evening or been too afraid not to laugh with everyone who was there. Playing the piano was the only time I was allowed to not laugh with the men when they said something to me. They didn't expect me to laugh, and I could be as macabre and melancholy as I liked playing the piano like that. Maybe that was one of the reasons I kept coming back, apart from that I knew too much. I don't think I said no. I didn't think there was a point to saying no or trying to stop it. The honey got in my mouth and it was like tasting someone's blood. And I did bite his lip, until it bled, but I think he only liked it. I was thankful he didn't come near me again after that, and I tried to warn you in some way, only I couldn't, not really. I racked my brains for days about how to get out of this situation and what to do, and in a way you might be the answer to all of that. You're the only answer I have left, if there's ever an answer to anything at all, it might just be you, Mathilde, it might be you.'

I wiped the cold moisture from my forehead and looked at her. She took her hands away from her face and guided them towards mine in the candlelight. My mouth was open.

'There are only a few ways out of this, and that car

might be one of them. Your proximity to him might be one of them.' She stopped, and looked at me, waiting patiently for my reply.

'I'll do anything for you, Jaminder, you know that,' I said, swallowing amongst my words and lying back, turning my head away from her. 'But I'm coming with you. I'll do anything for you, as long as I can come along with you.'

'No. We could die. We will die.'

'Is this place not a kind of death?'

She didn't respond and when I turned my head back towards her she was nodding, 'All right,' she said, 'All right.'

I began shivering again. It had grown colder and we'd lapsed into silence. 'I think you should keep it,' I said.

'I'm not a mother,' she said. 'I'll never be a mother.'

I thought of my own mother, and all she'd done for me; how we'd looked after her when she was sick, how I'd ended up mothering her. 'I could be,' I said. 'Or I could try.'

'Why would you want to do that?'

'I don't know,' I said. 'I think we might be able to make something good out of this world. I think we could do it, I think we could try. We might be able to make something beautiful.'

'I'm scared, Mathilde. I don't want to die.'

'I'll be there, you won't die. We only need to cross the Scottish border, and then none of this will matter. We need a way to get that far. And then a man will never touch you for the reasons we are touched here.'

'What would we tell the child?'

'That we are its parents.'

'I don't understand,' Jaminder said. 'Why would you want a child? Why would you want his child?'

245

'It wouldn't be his,' I said, and I stretched out to her again and took her hands. 'It wouldn't be his at all.'

I couldn't explain it, but I'd never been surer of anything in my life. I knew we had to do it. I just knew.

'Will we love it?' Jaminder said. 'Will I love it? How will I love it?'

'Of course you will, because we'll love each other, because that feeling isn't dead yet. There's still something magical left, there's still something new, there's still a feeling they can't crush out of us, don't you feel it?'

'No,' she said. 'Not anymore.'

I kissed her hands, and they were colder than my own. Her breathing became ragged and as I looked up at her, her face crumpled like a sheet of paper, the lines of her skin bleeding into each other. I wanted to reach up my hand to her and smooth them out, and make it better for her.

'Do you really think we could do it? The two of us?'

'Yes,' I said, and I kissed her hands again. 'We belong together, the three of us. We could be a family.'

She watched my face, she touched my skin. 'I don't know, Mathilde.'

'You do, you do, there has to be something good. There just has to be.'

She studied me for a long time, my breath panting out of me, my mouth open, waiting for her answer. Then she smiled. 'All right. I'll do it.'

'Do you mean it?' I said, desperately.

'Yes,' she said. 'If we stay together. If you want it, I'll keep it for you.'

'Oh, Jaminder, thank God, thank God for you.'

She took her hands away from my face. She noticed the ash on the chair and wiped it away. 'We don't have long. And you need to get better.'

'I feel better,' I said.

'We need to make a plan. Tomorrow night. We need to get that car. And until then, you have to act to everyone like everything's normal. Do you see? Everything is the same. Just act normal.'

'Yes, I can do that.'

'You need to go to him, can you do that? You need to distract him, so he doesn't notice the car disappear. So he stays inside and doesn't leave. When the time is right, you leave, and you meet me on Piccadilly. Do you know where the old Ritz hotel is? They kept it open for politicians. It's one of those places where there are cars, so it won't look odd, parked up there. We'll hide in plain sight. Be there at six. And then we'll get as far as we can with whatever's in that battery. I have family in the Midlands, we'll go there first, for a night maybe. Then we need to cross the border.'

'What if he doesn't let me go? I'm scared, Jams.'

'He will. Just say you're going to the park for your constitutional. You'll be back soon.'

'How do we cross the border? In a car?'

'If we're lucky and the battery hasn't run out. No one goes that far. It's madness to leave the city, the electricity and the food just to try find a pocket of civilisation up there. They don't need to monitor it, because who would go that far?' She looked at me, her eyes still and round, like a wild animal in the dark. 'You still have a choice,' she said. 'You don't have to come. If you can't leave her.'

'No,' I said, thinking of my grandmother, alone in that house. She'd saved us from France and found a way for us to live, and I had obliterated it. I thought of her muddling through on her own, having to let me go the way we let my mother go. But the alternative: my life, crushed, in his hands. 'I never had a choice.'

247

Her eyes closed, softened. 'Do you know where he keeps the car keys?'

I thought about the night driving over Westminster Bridge, his pride, my fear. 'It doesn't have keys, you just need the code.'

'Do you know it?'

I nodded. 'It's his birthday.' I told her the date. 'He told me when we went driving. He said it was safe with just a code because no one knows how to drive a car anyway.'

'Be at his at five, meet me at six o'clock,' she said, 'Thereabouts. Six.'

I paused. 'You do know how to drive, don't you, Jams?'

'My grandfather taught me more than just the piano,' she said. She moved away into the dark and I didn't ask where she was going. I was afraid by everything she had told me, but the idea of something that was hers and could be ours and was growing inside her electrified me. I felt like I could blow every fuse in London.

4

Gloria didn't die. There were no more parties after that, of course, and I'm sure there were none after we left. She did live with a limp, and had a walking stick when she left the hospital.

We found a London newspaper months after we left, in a solitary town. It was lying on a table in someone's home, two months old, and when we opened it, starved for news, there was a picture of her, walking stick in hand, with Frank. The incident was described as an 'accident at home'. We tore the page out and kept it. We never saw a newspaper like that again.

I think of Gloria often. I worry after her, as I worry after all the living people I can't touch or hold, or care for. But I imagine her as gathering herself up and towering above all of them, still. I like to imagine her like that, as the force she was. After everything, it might seem strange, but I do like to imagine it.

I spent the next day preparing to leave while my grandmother was at work. I packed a small bag that I hid in St James's Park on the way to George's and would collect on my way out. I put small things in it: a book my mother had given me with her inscription; a recipe she had written for tarte tatin; a hairbrush; a toothbrush; all the money I owned.

I thought of my mother, dying slowly and us waiting for her to go so we could leave, too. The drought and famine that prompted the riots, that tipped her illness over the edge. The rebel forces trying to take control. She told both of us to go. But we couldn't, not until we'd been with her, not until we knew she wasn't alone. I thought of the civil war and foreign bombing we narrowly avoided, our country obliterated while it boiled. My mother was French for as many generations as there had been generations. And what was I? In England since the age of nine. Was I to be blamed? I wanted to be. Did we call people French after that? Can you be French if there is no France?

All our people, the ones who stayed. All of culture, all of memory, all of food, the idea of belonging to a place, an arbitrary piece of land. A language. All of it, my mother: gone. All those years, I hadn't changed my name. It was one of the few things I had left.

These were the things I would take, things that mattered above all else. The things that reminded me of home.

I thought about leaving and what that would mean. How long we'd be on the road. My fever had subsided but my head still burned. And it had left with it a solid ache in my jaw. I went into the bathroom and took the rest of the drugs George had given us and put them into my bag. I looked into the greyed and murky mirror and pulled my top lip back over my teeth, trying to see where the dull ache was coming from. One of my front molars had a distinctly grey colour, and when I lifted my head I could just about see that the middle crevice was black. Shit, I said to myself. I thought about where we might end up. How long we'd be away. I wondered if we'd come back, or what there might be out there. What there might not be. I thought about the ways you could die on the road, and I thought about how this could be one of them.

I went through my grandmother's sewing basket and retrieved some thick thread and her nail cutters, in case. I went back up to the bathroom. I tied my hair up. I tied the thread tightly knotted to the door handle, and the other end, taut, to my blackened tooth. I looked at myself in the mirror, with the thread pulling out of my mouth like that and I let out a low moan. I breathed out, one, two, three. I held the door handle in my hand. I swung it gently back and forth. One, two, three. One, two –

I slammed it as hard as it would go. I heard a crack, and my whole body convulsed. A loud noise of horror came from inside me and I heard it as though it were coming from another body. I held my mouth open, wailing, and felt inside. It had cracked, but was still partially attached. I continued to wail, grabbing the nail clippers and feeling for what was left of the tooth. I reached inside and with all my strength, pulled. One, two, three twists. I felt it fly from my gum and my body fall. Everything went black.

I awoke in a small pool of blood. My mouth was encrusted and metallic, and my throat tasted strongly of that dense iron taste. I didn't know how long I'd been on the floor but the two parts of my tooth still lay next to me. I got up, slowly, and took a couple of the pills that George had given us. I washed my mouth out with water, and tried not to feel the gaping hole with my tongue. It was cavernous and weeping, but it was out at least, I could tell. I looked at the grey remnants of it, the solid roots, the way I'd had to twist it out. I vomited in the sink, a pale stream of bile. I washed my mouth again and tidied the bathroom just as I'd left it. I kept my bedroom neat, made my bed, even as my hands trembled.

I went into the living room and sat by the disused fireplace. I looked into the old cinders and felt the surface of my grandmother's chair. I laid my head down, but my eyes clicked open, as though I'd forgotten something. I checked my bedroom one more time, and waited for my grandmother to come home.

I couldn't tell my grandmother I was leaving; that I knew without Jaminder having to tell me. I didn't know if she'd understand either way or if she'd ever figure it out. The idea of her alone in this house threatened my strength to leave, but I knew they had no reason to hurt her. Not like me. Not like Jaminder. When she came home she went straight to her sewing. I came into the kitchen, holding my small bag in my hands.

'I'm going for a night,' I told her. 'I'll be back tomorrow afternoon.'

She looked up from her stitching. 'Oh, Mathilde. Do you have to go back?'

251

'Just for a night,' I said. 'And then it'll be over.'

She had laid out silk patterns on the table and was trying to keep them smooth with one hand and cut with scissors with the other. 'It's a slippery fish,' she muttered, trying to keep the animal of cloth still underneath her hands. It was expensive, and with one wrong movement, she could ruin it. I looked at her like that, and wondered at the futility of making expensive clothing for rich people when she could knit and could prepare plenty for people to live out the winter. But this is what paid her way for today.

'If you hold it down like this,' I showed her, 'It will be still for you. There, now cut it.' She cut with her scissors along the lines she made.

'How did you know that?' She smiled at me.

'I learnt from the best.'

She put her scissors down to begin the pinning. 'Did you hear about Kenwood House?'

'What about it?' I said, and felt my resolve weaken.

'It's been cleared out, apparently,' she said, without looking up from her pinning. 'Empty again. Police came round last night and cleared the lot of them out.'

'Where did they go?' I said, but I knew, didn't I? It was only a matter of time.

'I'm not sure,' she said, quietly. She looked out the window. 'They're always watching, aren't they? They always know where we are, and what we're doing.'

I hoped for my sake that wasn't true.

I hugged her around her back, and laid my head on her shoulder. She had three pins hovering in her mouth, and couldn't speak so she took the pins from her mouth and laughed. 'You remind me of Margot sometimes,' she said. 'You'll do something and it will make me think of her, just as she was.'

I released her and looked at my small bag and thought

of its contents. 'Do you need reminding? Don't you think of her?'

'Every day,' she said.

'Me too,' I said. 'And I think: I'm glad she died with France. I'm glad she never saw it burn. She would've hated it here, wouldn't she? Pretending to be English, in some way or another.'

My grandmother laughed. 'Yes, Margot would have hated it here. She would've hated it just like you.'

Act normal. I parked my bike outside George's house at five o'clock, and didn't bother to lock it up because no one was around. I knocked on the door, and he opened it. He wasn't wearing a suit, for once, and had on an old t-shirt that hung loose around him. I could tell from the fabric it was years old, and from the design too. Nothing was manufactured like that now. It was the first time I'd seen him off guard, and it frightened me.

'Great,' he said. 'I've got something for you.' His face said anything but great. His skin was ashen and he looked distracted. Just act normal. But he was supposed to act normal too.

'Okay,' I said and followed him inside. He led me into the kitchen and then took my hands in his.

'Are you feeling better?' he said.

'Almost,' I said. I directed my mouth towards the ceiling, hoping the malice would end up there, and would dissolve by the time it reached his eardrums. He held my hands and shook them as though I wasn't the one who had just spoken, as though I wasn't listening.

'Thanks to the drugs you got for me. It could've been worse, I suppose.' I said, and I felt again his hands in mine and wondered about where his fingers had been and what they had touched.

253

'I only ever try and do what's best,' he said.

Maybe in his head that's what he really did think, and he did imagine it was all the best out of what we had.

'I'm glad anyway,' he said, 'you need to stay healthy. You're young. You've got a lot of life to live yet. A lot of life to give to others.' He smiled at me.

'I don't know if I'll ever have children,' I said.

'What you're saying,' he said, earnest again, but faintly amused, 'you know how illegal that is.'

'Why would I want a child when we can barely feed ourselves?'

He let go of my hands and rubbed his face, as though he was smothering a laugh. 'You might change your mind, you can't know. But I respect you for it. For considering it.'

I couldn't determine whether his tone was threatening or sincere, but I followed him, my eyes glued. After all this time, his movements weighed on me; I still followed them. He gestured at the counter. 'By way of an apology, for the last one.' There sat a brand new radio just the same as the last. As though nothing had happened. My hands shook as I willed for the noise to drown out my fear. I went over to it and turned it on. I smiled at him. I meant it. He had cemented the distraction I needed.

The music blared and the old tunes beat up at us, and I wanted to laugh, thinking about how I could listen to music one last time, then tell him I wanted some fresh air and I would be gone. He took my hands in his again. I thought he might want to dance with me, and I thought, as I was so close to freedom, I didn't mind. He had a broad smile on that didn't match his t-shirt and he looked at me expectantly.

He turned and gestured towards the kitchen table. 'Look,' he said, over the music. There, like a photograph of what life should look like, was a chocolate cake. Glossy and thick and perfectly built. I shuddered, wondering where it had all come from. How he got it.

'Chocolate,' I said. Dirty word.

'I know you like your chocolate. I made it myself,' he said, 'on my own.' He sounded like a child, like I was his mother and should respond appropriately with a well done or a congratulations or a how sweet of you.

'I can't eat it,' I said. 'My teeth hurt. I have toothache.'

'You can,' he said. 'It's the least you can do. You should be grateful.'

'I feel ashamed of all the food we eat, when everyone else has nothing.'

He snorted. 'That's new. This isn't shameful. This is pleasure.' He said pleasure as though he could feel pleasure just as he said the word, that the *p* of pleasure was something dropped on his tongue, and maybe the *l* and the *e* and so on had a different sort of taste that was: pleasurable.

'I don't want it, George.' I tried to sound kind. I counted the seconds in my head, as though I was saying them to Jaminder. Ten more seconds and I can try and leave? Twenty and I've acted normal, I promise. Thirty and maybe he can't see the hatred in my eyes, pure and red, glossy like the cake.

'I'm telling you,' he said. 'I want to watch you eat it.' He took my hand again and pulled me to sit at the table. I sat down with a thud. I felt the hole in my mouth, still weeping.

'My teeth hurt,' I said. 'I can't, please, George.'

'Think of all I've done for you,' he said. 'You have to eat it all. Every last bite. I put everything into it.' As he said that he pulled up a chair next to me and tapped my knee and handed me a fork and tapped that too, on the table.

If I didn't eat it, would he know? Would he know that it didn't matter whether I ate it or not, because I would be gone by the morning? If I didn't eat, he'd know that I didn't have to eat it, and if I didn't have to eat it, then he'd know I was gone, and he would undo it like a line of knitting gone wrong. One pull and he'd unravel the whole thing to a curly cable threaded mess, like cotton brains. That's how I'd end up, and no one would ask. He'd say I'd gone anywhere. He could say anything and no one would ask him ever again.

Would she do it? Would Jaminder eat it, with no complaint? I thought, what's worse, what's already happened, or this? What happened to Jaminder or this?

I wondered how much time I needed, if the car was gone yet. I had to hold his gaze, like she'd said, for as long as possible. But my hands shook at the thought of it. I had to keep my eyes on it. I had to not look towards the window, as though I were waiting for something. I glanced at his watch: five fifteen. Not yet. I couldn't leave yet.

I thought of all the times I had been desperate to eat chocolate and dreamt of it, tried to taste it in my mouth and taste with it the smell of my mother and her stirring chocolate and the care she took not to let the water in and turn it to mush. Her taking the chocolate's temperature like it had a fever and making sure it was perfect, and then spreading and smoothing it out and caring for it like it was another child of hers, like it was me. I strained my ears but I couldn't hear her voice in my head telling me what she'd do or if I should be ashamed or if I should be grateful. I couldn't hear anything. It didn't matter, anyway, because I didn't have a choice. And it was better to do this than it was to die.

I picked up the fork and he nodded. He bit his lip in

anticipation and I wondered what it was he wanted from me, what he was waiting for, what he wanted to see. I sunk the prongs in to the cake, moist and slippery. I spooled it out and watched the crumbs fall on the table. I didn't watch his face watching me. The sound of the radio blared over us but I couldn't hear it. I couldn't hear it because the cake became a noise and it soared in my ears. The chocolate melted and spread around my teeth and I swallowed. As the first piece of cake went down, the first piece of my childhood came up: all the times I'd stood with my mother and waited with her as she mixed and poured and I pressed my forehead to the oven door and licked the spoon. I thought of the bag I'd left hidden in the park under the old rickety decking of what once was a café. I thought of the recipe of tarte tatin and the way the first line started: *commencer par préparer tous les ingrédients* and the double m of *commencer* curled up and into each other with her perfectly familiar and reliable lilt. The first taste of cake made me miss all those things. Life as we knew it.

'Keep going,' he said. He began to press on my wrist like I was a peach and he was testing me for ripeness. It was his way of saying: you're not ready yet. Every moment I wanted to get up and leave the table, and shut off the radio and tell him I'm done, was a moment I thought of Jaminder, and what she would do. The faster I eat it, the faster I can get to her.

I ate half of it, slowly, each fork becoming more tasteless and claggy than the last. I slowed to a sickly halt. My belly had swollen to a hard mound and my knees shook from the sugar. Moisture escaped my eyes as though my face were being squeezed and pressed, too. I felt outside of my body and not part of it. I felt it revolt. I felt its disgust with me, and the pressure on my insides. I felt the bitter coating

257

of bile warming up my throat and I dug my fingernails into the kitchen table. I wanted to ask him if this is what he wanted, but I didn't want to look at his face.

I put the fork down. I could feel the weight of my body pressing up on me. I bent forward. He raised a hand to press on my wrist and then the feeling became bitter and urgent. I screeched back my chair and made it to the kitchen sink and that's where it all came up, piece by bloody piece.

With every retch I heard him laugh. He clicked the radio off to hear me better. He laughed, in the silence, with genuine mirth. I didn't turn to look at him. I kept my face swung over the porcelain sink, clutching its cool edges. He said my name, or some version of it: Matilda, Matilda, Matilda. The anglicisation which once warmed me now felt like possession, a stripping of self. He said that name and then he laughed, like I was a great joke I myself didn't understand.

I felt he'd fled his body, and all that was left was the laugh.

5

The feeling of sickness left me as quickly as the vomit. I wiped my mouth. I turned to him.

'Why are you doing this?' I said.

He stopped laughing. 'No kindnesses were ever afforded to me. Don't you see how lucky you are?'

I was given sanctuary. I was taken in, on this arbitrary

plot of land. I was lucky where so many were not. Because we got out just in time, because Mrs P let us in. Because we had the right words on the right papers. Because we were able to work, because we had something to give. I felt guilty for it every day.

We had no religion, we never had; we were taught not to have. Because of this, when I imagined God, I imagined him as a human man, a fatherly figure I had never had. I imagined him talking to me and sometimes I talked back to him.

I spoke French to my mother in my head, and sometimes out loud to this God-like man. I rarely spoke it to the concrete, to anything real. My God belonged to no temple or church or any man-made structure, except the one that I made in my head.

I implored him, then, for something. I asked him for forgiveness. I asked him to make sure an answer would be brought to me, in some form. I asked him for this small kindness, and I promised him I wouldn't wish for anything else. I promised him I'd never wish for chocolate, or any superficial, material thing ever again. I promised him I'd never wish for pastry, or bread, or butter, or wine, or the sweet crackling of sugar in my teeth or the weight of a fruit in my hand. I promised him, if he granted me the kindness of our plan working. If he granted me the kindness of letting me go. I promised him I'd never wish for things that weren't there, I'd only be happy for the things that were. If he could save our lives, if he could free us, I would sacrifice this liberty.

'I know everything about you,' George said. 'I know what you know. And I'm not sure I want you around anymore.'

Perhaps his dressed-down attire was an indication that he wasn't sure of his decision to send me away. He might have arranged it already, and intended to follow through with it, but maybe he wasn't sure. Maybe he tore at the decision; maybe he tore, for a second, at the idea of owning someone like that. Or maybe that was attributing too much humanity to him.

I glanced at his watch and could see the hand had passed six o'clock long before. I wouldn't be able to leave, not like this. I thought of Jaminder outside that hotel. Every minute she waited was a minute lost. A minute granted to them.

'I want to see the jars again,' I said. 'I want to see them one more time.'

He smiled at me, grateful for this suggestion. He ran his hand through his disordered greying hair. 'I'm glad you've shown an interest,' he said.

I followed him up the stairs. He took a key out of his pocket. I watched it. He unlocked the door, slowly, and looked over his shoulder to check I was still there. We both entered the cramped room, amongst the yellowed creatures. I hadn't noticed the first time, but there was a wall of birds: suspended in the bubbled liquid, feathers textured and bright, wings askew, eyes bright and dewy. Several species and variations, things I'd never seen. I wasn't grateful to see them then, because they still weren't real to me. Perhaps I would've been overwhelmed if I'd seen them as they were meant to be seen: in amongst the leaves of a tree or high in the sky, a fleeting blurred moment of aviation, a jolly soaring. They could've been anything here. He couldn't bottle up what they truly were; he couldn't fit that into a jar. I wanted to set them free, I imagined that I could.

'This is my little paradise,' George said, fingering the lids of the jars. 'This little collection. The answer is always in nature, don't you think?'

He looked at me, waiting for a response. That's when

I heard it: a soft, solid, electric purring. Unmistakably foreign in the new stillness of the house. I swallowed, I pretended I hadn't heard it. I pretended I wasn't watching an electric car in my mind's eye that was theirs; that I couldn't see myself being dragged into it, being bundled across the whole of London, hidden.

It wouldn't be long then. I listened for the click of solid doors, I listened for footsteps. My heart caught in my chest. For once I wished it wasn't there at all. I wished I couldn't feel anything. I wished I could wash it all away.

I watched the key on a shelf by the door. If I could just get to it, with his back turned, I could lock him in. I could get out.

'You can't bring the world back to how it once was,' I said.

'No,' he said, and shrugged. 'But you can try. Isn't there some honour in that?'

I looked around at the insects suspended in their liquids. I didn't say anything.

'We have so much to learn from them.' He gestured to the creatures with the dead eyes. He smiled at me. He was pleased with this idea of preserving nature, of finding something in it. But he'd found the value in it too late.

I listened out for that electric noise, for the door to go. He must have been waiting to give the signal. And if he was the one to give it, I just needed more time.

'Is it working?' I said. 'Are you happy about it all?'

'I suppose it wouldn't affect things to tell you my anxiety about it,' he said, taking a step towards me. 'To tell you what worries me.'

'Oh.'

'It's harder than I thought.'

He put a hand on my shoulder as though he was confiding in me. 'I just wanted a way for us to thrive, in

261

our own small way.' He rubbed his forehead, he squeezed my shoulder. 'I've always helped Auntie to find the best solution, to do what's right. But it never seems enough for anyone. No matter what we've gained, it's never enough. I suppose it took me a while to realise what it was I really missed, what I wanted back.'

'What was that?' I said, feeling a small burn in my shoulder. Trying not to breathe in his breath that was so close to mine.

'We had tradition once, didn't we? It all means nothing now. Once, my ancestor sat on the throne. Chosen by God. It's all been stripped away.' His eyes glazed over. I wanted to ask him who it was, I wanted to imagine a King or a Queen that looked like him. I wanted to ask him if any of it was true or if it was only what he imagined he deserved. I said the name of a monarch and he smiled at me. 'Maybe you understand me a little better, now.'

'I don't know.'

He nodded. 'Can you even imagine how hard it is to do the jobs we do, without all that? Without relying on processes and traditions and order? Without technology, without anything,' he raised his hand in a sweeping motion, 'Obliterated. Do you remember the internet?'

'Not really.'

'It enabled us to do things that would be inconceivable now. It enabled us to live like Gods of our little world.' He released my shoulder. He smiled at me, 'If only you'd seen it. Everything is more difficult now without it. We need something good to hope for. We need those supplies to feel like civilised people. We need those supplies to save our spot on the world. Nostalgia is the real killer, isn't it? Remembering is what brings the fog rolling in in the afternoon, is what brings the black dog.'

I listened again: there it was. The sound of the front door going. I opened my mouth, afraid. 'But what about the others, what about them?' I stepped away from him. My back hit a shelf behind me and the jars wobbled. My hands searched behind me. Something. Anything. A knife. A heavy container. 'We're still human don't you see? I'm still a person, too. I had a life once, too.'

I could hear the tread of feet on steps. I could hear the crack of floorboards. The creak of a shoe. I knew the house well enough to know. I knew the sound of a human.

'I'm trying to save people like you, I always have. I've always wanted to do what's best for people like you.' He stepped towards me, and my eyes widened. 'There's no going back now.'

I looked at him and nodded. '*Les carottes sont cuites*,' I said.

His face was pleased and rose up in a smile. He opened his mouth to say something, but out came only a gurgle. A bubbling, gurgle noise, as though he was the one contained in a jar.

Jaminder's breath came heavy and thick behind him. He dropped to his knees and flapped at his neck. A long, sharp serving fork protruded from it, stately and polished silver. His eyes widened in horror. He pulled it out, but it only made things worse. She'd known then, she'd made sure. It had got him in the right place.

'We have to go,' she said, calmly.

'You came back,' I said.

His hands still grasping, I stepped over him. My foot slipped on a pool of blood, my hands tried not to touch the splattered walls. I regained my balance. With his body behind me, it was as though he wasn't there.

'We have to go,' she said again.

I took the key from where he had placed it on one of the shelves, next to the jars of insects. We stepped out of the room and I closed the door behind me. I locked it, and put the key in my pocket.

PART 8

Jaminder

Another home

1

We wait by Hugo's side. There are two of us, so we never leave him on his own. On the third day of his fever, he starts to take a little food. We give him everything we can. Mrs Donald brings us her oatmeal, but even this supply is dwindling. We still go to work, and do our hours, one by one, for the money for what little food we can buy. And at night, we sit next to him, and it is on these nights that we wonder, and apologise to each other and try and think of an answer. It is on these nights that I think of you, George, and talk to you in my head.

I ask you what you would think of your son if you could see him. I ask you if he is your son at all, if you feel that he is, if you feel anything. I ask you if you're still alive. I ask you if you feel that you are dead, if you can hear me. I describe to you what it felt like to push that fork into your throat and twist it, and see the blood oozing from it. I ask you if you felt pain.

I do not ask for forgiveness. I tell you I am not sorry.

We don't talk about you. We don't talk about you being dead or alive. The likelihood is that you are dead. But the word 'dead' does not describe the things that you are now and the things that you are not. 'Dead' does not describe the person that you once were and the things that you did. 'Dead' does not describe how you fooled me and fooled us all; how you took us for yourself. 'Dead' does not explain the taste of your breath in my mouth and the way I tried to push the texture of your face away with my hand. 'Dead' does not describe the insignificance you attributed to me. 'Dead' does not describe how you are everywhere and in everything.

Nor does it explain my fear, my unrivalled terror, as I look at Hugo and wonder which parts of you might linger there. These parts, we hope, are washed away by myself and Mathilde.

Dead is not one thing or another, dead can be quantified, I think: and so you are more dead to Hugo than you are to us, because he's never known you, and never will; but we remember you, we still think of you, and so you are less dead to us. And that is maybe how you're not dead, after all.

Maybe this thought should horrify me, and maybe I should be worried about the place where you exist in my mind, in that gap between the imaginary and the real. But if you exist there, then maybe other corners of existence are alive there, too. Maybe Kenya exists there, and our back garden with cacti and palm trees. Maybe my grandmother exists there, icing my birthday cake. Maybe the heat exists, and my grandfather, sitting on the veranda with his newspaper in the sunshine with his suit on. Maybe my Canadian friend, Alice, exists there with her blonde hair. Maybe my grandfather is taking us to school there, when the bus broke down, and I am turning around in my seat to look at my friends and smile at them, and tell them I am proud of him. Maybe the ugali exists there, and the chicken curry, and the bananas, the ones that tasted nothing like bananas we had in England.

If your body pressed upon me has given me hatred, your existence in my mind has also given me hope. For if hate can be as strong as that, other feelings can be too.

I didn't get to choose what was important to me,

or why, but hatred was. After you, and your death, it became so obvious how you don't get to choose anything in this life, even the things you want to choose, and could choose, but decide against for reasons that are not your own. It has nothing to do with being right. Hatred opens a gap in you that is infinite. It makes you want to do terrible things you've never even thought of. I wanted to pull your hair from their roots and break your neck, I wanted to smash your windows and steal your life from you. I wanted to be hated. I wanted you to know. But I didn't, of course, and instead I stood behind you as I did it, and you never turned around, you never saw the look on my face. I left that night as cowardly as I've lived the rest of my life.

Hatred is possession. When you have been offered nothing else to possess you can possess that feeling for as long as you like, as much as you like. You can own hatred and you can be proud of it. We had so very little; it was the one thing I could hold onto.

But it wouldn't be true to explain to you that all you gave me was hatred. Because Mathilde convinced me, in that way that she does, her long dark hair around her shoulders and her hands always grasping and loving, that there was something else to be had, even when we couldn't see it. We fled, and still I couldn't see it. My belly swelled, and still I couldn't see it. My body seized with pain and collapsed with the weight of itself, crushing itself out of itself and still I couldn't see it. We took him for our own and only then, when Mathilde held him, and placed him onto my body, could I see this other thing, this other thing you gave me that was so different from hate.

Perhaps knowing you will never understand it is why I talk to you at night. Perhaps knowing that kindness is as foreign as chocolate to you is the reason I try to explain it:

269

that love in your terms is something wildly different and painstaking and debilitating and selfish as compared with how we love. Family is something you never understood, and that's why you ripped Gwendolyn from Gloria, and the women went where they went, and why you thought a policy to increase the population was admirable, and why you misunderstood the fundamental nature of all humans; why you will never understand that family is not something that you can force people into or buy. Why you will never understand how we need our little packs, and our groups, how they are essential to survival; and how family is something that is born from love.

I talk to you to tell you that you gave me Hugo but he is not yours. He is not your family and never has been, never will be. Mathilde and Hugo are my family. And the families we had before still belong to us too. I think about my grandparents as taking up a box in my mind, like the boxes in Mrs Darling's mind from the book we read to Hugo, one laid within another like Russian dolls. I see it in Mathilde's mind too: that box where she keeps her grandmother, and goes to her. The way she lifts the lid on her, and remembers her, and looks after her there.

You didn't trick me into having a family, you see; I made a family for myself. And if I hadn't wanted one, I wouldn't have had one, because family is also a choice. Of the so few choices we have in this world, in this life, how we love our family and how we make our family is a choice we can have.

When people say blood is thicker than water, what does that mean, do people ever wonder about it? How water is the thickest, most life-giving, deepest, heaviest of all things? How much water is in blood? I bet it's a lot but not enough to explain how much that phrase misses the point.

I wasn't sure about a child. And you know that, everyone did. Mathilde wasn't sure about it either. Could you blame us? What did having children mean when there was nothing to give them?

Maybe we were just selfish. It was something we could do on our own, having Hugo. It was something we could control, in a small way. Just in the way Gloria had taken control.

We hoped for more for Hugo. We wanted so much more for him. Sitting by his side through these nights, I wonder what more I could give for him to be all right. I wonder if this is what the future looks like, after all. There is only this. This world is what we've given to him. This is all that's left. And I am sorry for it. And if his future is lost, and therefore ours too, what legacy have we left, other than this muddy chalk earth and the grey smudge of the sky, and this oatmeal, this incessant, relentless oatmeal.

'I prayed for him,' Mathilde says, her pale face illuminated by the fire, as we sit by the end of our bed. 'I prayed for us, too, that we'd be all right. Can you imagine that? I prayed.'

I'm surprised. She reaches out her hand for mine and I let her take it.

'Have you prayed too?' she says, squeezing it.

'Sometimes,' I say. 'I'm not sure if that'll improve our chances.'

She laughs. 'Maybe not. But do you remember? On our way up here, when we first left? When you told me about your family for the first time? You told me religion was important to them, that it mattered. It could matter to us too.'

'It's not the same,' I say. 'Not now.'

Mathilde nods her head. 'Do you think we'll ever see Gloria again?'

271

I look down. I want to let go of her hand. 'No, I don't think we'll ever see her again.'

'Don't you think,' she says, looking up at Hugo asleep, 'We're all just orphans? We're a nation of orphans? Like in the fairy tales.'

'We're too old to be orphans.'

'But we weren't, once. We're all so alone, all of us. When the blackout came, and the floods, the heat. The rationing. All it did was make us so alone.'

'He's getting better,' I say, 'He's really getting better.'

'Until you, all I ever felt was alone. After my mother, there was just you, and then Hugo. I know you felt the same.'

'Yes,' I say. 'I was lonely. It's easier like that.'

She grasps my hand again. 'I don't know what to do.'

'He's getting better,' I say again, and the repetition of it makes me want to scream, the futility of my own words. I slept next to my grandmother once, when I was ill and had a fever. But it was warm in our house, and there was so much of everything, no one thought about it for a minute.

Mathilde shuffles towards me, and puts her arms around me. She lays her head on my chest and her head rocks back and forth. She's shivering, even though we're near the embers of the fire. She muffles the sound of her voice by pushing her face into my clothes. But I know she wants to scream, I know she is afraid.

'We're all orphans,' she says again, and there is wetness pooling around her mouth, and it is open, like a question, a desperate, confused question. 'All those women that we never saw. The women like Gwendolyn. All those women sent away, they're orphans too. They're all alone too.'

I stroke her back and try to quieten her, but Hugo sleeps soundly. It is torturous, that we are the ones left with these images, that we are the ones who struggle with it. And you are the one who built it, you are the one who helped build the way of things, and the image of it never burned in your mind, and it never mattered to you at all.

2

Father Anthony is sitting at the back of his own church, as though he is part of the congregation. But there is no congregation. He is the only one here.

'Father,' I say.

He's looking up at that ill, stricken Jesus. I wonder what he is saying. He turns around, to look at me.

'Jaminder,' he says. 'How is Hugo?'

'The same.'

He turns away from me and slumps forward. 'I'm sorry,' he says. 'I've been praying for him.'

He doesn't get up or come towards me. He has lit a few candles inside but not enough to read a passage from a book or see very far in front of him. I walk towards him and sit beside him in the pew. 'Mathilde is with him now,' I say.

He nods, but doesn't look at me. 'I'm sorry for the way I spoke to you when you were last here. I'm sorry you thought I had more to give you.' He wrings his hands together in his lap.

'Why do you tell people you have something? Why do you lie to the people here?'

He looks at me, surprised. 'It's not a lie,' he says. 'I used to have things. We used to be sent aid.'

'They think they'll be saved by you. They stay because of you.'

'Is that a terrible thing? That I give them hope?'

'It is when it's a lie.' I look up to that Jesus again.

'It's not a lie, Jaminder.'

'Sikhs believe that people are equal. That we are all equal. Our Jesus is just a mere mortal, he is not a God. And we were told it didn't matter what gender, race, class or sexuality you were, because all humans are the same.'

'It's an admirable sentiment.'

'Life hasn't been like that. None of this is like that. And we're scared all the time. We wake up with pain in our shoulders and hands. We work for something but we don't know what it is. We're afraid for our children. It's not what my grandparents wanted for me. It's not what they imagined for me.'

'There is much to be gained from a humble life, Jaminder. People thought they couldn't live without electricity, but there is much to live for.'

'It's not the electricity. It's knowing that we are afraid, but we're lucky. There are so many more people who aren't.' How will we ever be free from that thought?

'Your grandparents were smart people. You found us here, from nowhere. Where were you planning to walk to with your son? The end of the world? But you found us here.'

I look at him, and he is still looking at the man on the cross.

'There is always hope. There is always innovation. The Stone Age didn't end because we ran out of stones, Jaminder. There are many freedoms that lie ahead.'

'I can't see them,' I say. 'I can't see that they are there.'

'*Sous les pavés, la plage,*' he says, 'You may not always see it, but it doesn't mean that it isn't there. That there isn't an escape. There will be a new form of energy. The lights will turn back on.'

'French?' I say, frowning at him.

'I was an educated man once,' he says, resigned.

I stand up, and move away from the pew. I look down at him, and understand that he is a world in and of himself; that he had a past life, just like the rest of us. That he wishes for a future, too. 'I'm leaving,' I say. 'I want to go and find help. I can't stay here, with the food the way it is.'

'I'm sorry to hear that,' he says.

'I just wanted to play the piano one last time. That's why I'm here.'

'The piano? What do you mean?'

'I just want to play it one more time. Hear the music. You'll grant me that last blessing, won't you?'

He gets up and stands next to me. He rests a hand on my shoulder. 'There's no piano here, Jaminder. It broke my heart, but we burnt it, two winters ago. It was so cold.' His brow furrows, he doesn't release his hand. 'I didn't take it lightly. It broke my heart.'

I look to the corner where the piano was always sitting, where the piano always waited for me. Every church has a piano. And I can hear the notes, can't I? I hear the music, in my mind, without even touching the keys, I can hear it.

'But I played it,' I say to him, my voice as small as a child.

He looks at me, his face contorts. I want to step away from him and his pity. 'When did you last eat, Jaminder?'

I look again, and in the dark, imagine that he is right. I imagine that there never was a piano. Not in the solid, man-made, structural way that we once knew, not in the physical sense. I imagine it, but that doesn't mean it isn't there.

'There are still so many things to be grateful for,' he says. 'There is still so much that grants us freedom.'

I walk up the aisle. I hear the notes before I reach it, before I sit down in front of it, before I put my feet to the pedals, before I press my fingers to the keys. I hear its melancholy tune. I hear the notes before I sit down, before I begin. I feel the song in my stomach.

I look above the piano, and up to the hanging Jesus. 'Funny,' I say, 'that God never had a daughter.'

3

Mathilde is sitting by Hugo, sewing. She reminds me of the way she used to look in London, and it warms me.

'You've told Father?' she says, looking up from her stitching, pins in her mouth.

'Yes.'

'We should be going together.'

'No, you have to stay with him,' I say. 'This time, you have to stay.'

She continues to sew, rhythmically, and doesn't look up. I go over to where Hugo is lying in bed. He opens his eyes, slowly. I feel his forehead. He is still warm, but he has more colour now.

'Mummy,' he says, stirring. 'When will I be better?'

'Soon,' I say. 'So soon. I'm going to get help and then I'll come back for you. I'll be back soon.'

'Don't leave.' He coughs, and I prepare the bucket for him to be sick. But he isn't, and he lies back down.

'Maman is here. She'll be here with you.'

'If you go to the next town south and back again it should only take three days,' Mathilde says. 'In three days you'll be back, with medicine.'

'If they have some.'

'They will. They did, not so long ago.' Mathilde looks at me, sternly. Since Dengue, since not knowing what anything is, a day is an eternity. Three days like this is torture. 'Maybe you don't have to leave, if Hugo gets better, if he gets better today.'

I stand over him, and his pale face. His tiny arms, a shadow of himself. 'I have to. I have to do something.'

We know what it means, to go back. Even a few miles south is a return. We don't ever say it, but it is a sacrifice. It means sacrificing our own safety, our own invisibility, for his.

She stops sewing. 'Why should you be the one to go? I should do it, it should be me.'

I am the one who is not afraid. Out of the two of us, I am always the one that has to be brave. 'I've done it before.'

'We had each other.' She puts her hands in front of her.

'I won't be gone for long.'

'The weather is getting worse, isn't it?' She looks out the window, she looks at my wet feet. 'It'll be colder soon. You'll have to rest, regularly. You'll have to stop. You'll have to keep warm, and stay safe.'

She offers these words of care as a way to protect herself. I don't want to say it, but she wouldn't be safe on her own. Even now, after these years. I am stronger than her. She's aware of it too, because I've allowed it. 'I know,' I say. 'I'll leave today. Before it's dark.'

She puts her sewing down and comes to stand beside

me. We both look down at Hugo. I lean down to kiss his forehead.

I turn to Mathilde. She holds my face in her hands and kisses me square on the mouth. 'Ours has been a kind of love story hasn't it? The same as anyone else's.'

'In a sense,' I say. 'I think about when we first met all the time.' I think about London all the time.

'It's wretched,' she says. 'The lot of them are wretched.'

'Do you think Mrs P meant well? Do you think they knew what they were doing?'

'Yes,' she says. 'It was a privilege of theirs to be able to rationalise it.'

'And a privilege of ours to leave it behind.'

'We've looked after each other. I loved you from the moment I saw you, and I don't think anyone could ever understand that.'

'It's okay,' I say, 'You don't have to say it.'

'I do,' she says, her face pleading. 'I don't know what this life would have been like without you. Without my dear friend.'

I want to tear my face away, feeling a lump forming in my throat like I've swallowed something dark and heavy. 'What about the last box?' I say, my voice croaking out. 'Like the boxes that make up Mrs Darling's mind, one within the other. Did I ever get the innermost box?'

Her face crumples and her mouth opens, but she doesn't know what to say.

'It's okay,' I say, relenting. 'I don't suppose anyone ever gets that.'

'You're everything,' she says, 'even so.'

I look down, her hands still holding my face. 'We're his parents,' I say. 'We'll always love each other.' She stays like that for a time, before resting her head on my

278

shoulder. She grabs onto me, and her face is angled so she can look at Hugo, over me.

I smell her hair, the whole world of it. I lean into it, I place it in my memory. I tell myself I'll come back for it.

'You're the other half of my orange,' she says.

I wonder if either of us can remember the taste of oranges.

I pack my rucksack. I kiss my son goodbye. His cold sweat stays on my lips and is caught by the wind as I leave the house. I pull my hood up to shield myself from the sky. My shoes suck into the earth beneath my feet, and I pull them back out. I hold a compass tightly in my hand, but I know the way, even in the dark.

We knew the way in the dark before. I waited for her outside that hotel, but as the minutes passed and she never appeared, I had to go back for her. I knew there was only one way out. She never questioned me for it and that made me love her more.

I left the car running before I mounted that staircase, and the quiet electric sound whirred behind me. I got there just before anyone else did. I got there just in time. I put my foot down on the pedal of a car that was fully charged and I drove us out of the city and down the empty roads. She never asked to go back to the park for her bag of possessions she'd hidden there, but she remembers them often. Even if she doesn't say it out loud, when she has a quiet day I know she thinks of her mother and that recipe for tarte tatin hidden under decking.

We reached what once was a city in the middle country. I knocked on a door of long distant relatives I remembered visiting with my grandfather, but they weren't there. We kept going. We weren't stopped for miles and as soon as we were it was too far away, and the lines of communication hadn't got to that point yet. They didn't know what I'd done. And as soon as they didn't know, I felt that I was free of it and could start again.

We took sanctuary in any religious establishment that was left (and that was few), because they would house us. As we got closer to the border the car began to sing. We listened to the noise and knew it was a whirring which meant there wasn't much time. We left the car in England, and it is somewhere there still, I imagine. We had no money or means to keep it with us. We crossed the border as though it were imaginary, but it meant a lot to us then, and means a lot still. We can never cross back.

We held onto each other like children. Mathilde had this idea that we were, in a sense, and she called out my name in her sleep and not her mother's or her grandmother's, or her own. I started to tell her about what was before and took delight in remembering with her as a witness, a stranger to it all.

Where at first I was terrified by the thing occupying space inside of me, I now became curious. It was a relief to let go of my body after all these years and give it over to someone else, however small. I gladly took the extra food from Mathilde, and made sure I rested when I needed to, and stopped along the road in a place that was safe. I began to take care of myself in a way I hadn't before, and I would sit and tell Mathilde about it at night, our arms outstretched beneath our heads, rolled towards each other. I compared my swollen fingers with hers, and the hard mound of my belly with her flat expanse that stretched over muscle and bone. Look, I said, I'm something else now. I told her I was ripe like an orange, I was plump like an apple, I was fruit and was the taste of fruit and I would grow where nothing else would grow. I said it jokingly, but she believed me. She said it was more amazing than all the fruit she had ever tasted, if she could still remember a thing like that, months later.

She rubbed my belly and pressed an ear to it. It sounds like the sea, she said, and I wondered if for her that was just another thing to be afraid of.

But the fear of death – not just of my own, but of all living things – was replaced slowly by anticipation. It was replaced by the feeling of something small bobbing to the surface, something I didn't recognise. It was a hopeful acknowledgment that my body was doing something that I hadn't told it to do, something it knew beyond any understanding I had for it. It carried on without me, as surely as the sun always appeared in the morning, however hidden and small, and left us at night, as we lit candles round the altars of churches and temples, and wherever else we slept.

I gave myself over to it, that feeling, and it spilled over to Mathilde, too. So much so that she would sit behind me, legs around my legs, and brush my hair with an old hairbrush she found, one with soft white bristles and a silver frame that had rubbed away to black. She took care of me as I swelled up like a sponge reaching water. I was never afraid. I welcomed the kindness of strangers. I didn't fear them. Not until Hugo was born.

When we left, we left everything behind. We were wiped clean. We took a vow of poverty. We went without fruit and meat. We went without one kind of love – the intimacy of a body, the weight of a person – but not all kinds. It was the price we paid for freedom, so we didn't mind. It didn't worry us so much, then, because we always just had enough. We always had each other.

Near the end, we had to stop walking. I was too big and could barely sleep with the weight of it pressing on me. That's how I knew it was coming long before it started.

Even as we sat eating cabbages and beetroot from allotments we passed, counting the weeks between us now and us then, we still couldn't pinpoint exactly when it was supposed to be ready, when it would arrive. But I knew when I was ready, when the expectation turned to irritation, my whole body willing it out of me.

Somewhere between deciding to keep it and him appearing in front of me fully formed, the miracle of it made me greedy. The wonder of it made me possessive, and I wrapped my hands around my own stomach and felt him shift, the same way any human shifted, and I knew that Mathilde had been right after all, that there were still some miracles in this world yet, things that didn't wait for you before they appeared.

I wanted to ask it: What are you ready for? Do you really want to see all this? But it did, somehow. We were in one of the last places then, a mosque, and they let us in and helped us, because they said we are all people here. They told us they could help us, because we are all people.

One of the women there said she had helped women many times before, and when she saw us, she cried in that way you do when you haven't seen someone for a long time. She kept saying over and over, imagine if you had been left out there, imagine if you had been out there.

I can't remember who was around me or stood beside me. I remember that I had cushions piled behind my back which made me feel worse and I remember the woman saying she could stretch her fingers over the opening of the head and it was ready. It was Mathilde, though, who reached her hands up inside of me and helped him out, and she said later that that is when she felt like a mother. She handed him to me and her hands were bloody. She told me it was a boy and I laughed. One good one, I said. She laughed back.

The placenta followed. We ate it later for nutrition.

I tore, and Mathilde sewed me up, the woman at her shoulder, watching. We stayed in the mosque for days, waiting for him to latch, and they gave me everything they had. It took me a long time to heal.

Mathilde's hands were bloody when she gave me my son, and that is what made her feel like he was our son, the way she brought him to life.

In the days that followed it became her time to give herself over to him. She sat with me, as we coaxed him to the nipple, taught him what he already instinctively knew. She was the one that looked after him all through the night, his face a scrunch of shock and displacement. She swaddled him best and soothed him best, and then it was her turn to be unafraid.

She told me that the baby had a serious face, like a writer. She told me about a French writer that she knew once, who wrote about misery and hope. He wrote about the people and he wrote about change. He was someone who made a difference. We decided we had that wish for him, for our son. We named him Hugo.

He was a happy baby. He smiled, and he learnt it from no one. We realised some things were innate and couldn't be taught, and that made us love people all over again. With every movement we realised something about humans that we never knew, and we always thought we knew everything. He moved and he crawled and he walked, and even though we took him from town to town to try and get further away, to try and find work, it never seemed alien to him. He never complained. When he learnt to speak, he said all the good words. He never knew a drop of French or any other language but English and he'd never know any different and he'd never mind. He pushed us, and was curious, and he pushes us still, the way he reminds us that it's normal to want something different, to want more, to ask questions. It's normal to want to know the answer. That is innate, too.

The further north of the border we got, the closer we came to using our real names again. By the time Hugo could speak, we were far enough away, we were safe. We didn't have to hide. He pushed us when we needed to be pushed, and he showed us grace, when there was none to be found.

Of all the hardest things to lose in the world, amongst all the food turned to dust, all the people you loved a memory, all the landscape you knew as well as your own body turned to mulch, hope was the hardest to lose of all. The loss of hope was always fatal, in one way or another. Gloria knew that.

Hugo gave us a shell to hide under. Staying quiet was a way to protect him, and out of the things that can be learnt, he learnt that from us. But he also made all the rest of it a mist. Our past lives were background noise and he was clear as a bell. He unravelled us, and the feelings that had been squashed down by the world we lived in, like the tin of pineapple under the floor. We pierced it open with a hiss of air. But there are some things that are irretrievable. The time alone taught us that too. I always wanted more from the world and more from Mathilde than she had to offer. But we could never find the voices to explain it to each other, because those had been taken from us too.

I sat with her once, when Hugo was small, after I'd reached out to her by the neck and pulled her face close to mine. Stop, Jaminder, she said, you're hurting me. Well, you're hurting me, I said to her, over and over, her eyes scanning my face like words on a page, like watching the world outside from a moving train, unable to find a stationary object to focus on.

I was always leaning for her like that, even after all

284

they'd drawn out of us, all the fear of ourselves they'd entrenched in us. She told me it wasn't right, but all that meant was it wasn't right for her. She couldn't understand the other side of it, and after all that time in London, I didn't either, not for a long time.

After Hugo, I had to re-learn myself. I had to look at myself, through the punctured hole of the tin. I had to accept it, and the limitations of getting older in this world, and what this life that we'd chosen, and not chosen, meant. I had to learn to put the tin back under the floorboard. I had to learn to live a life of half-formed ideas. Hugo was the one thing that was ever fully formed.

As I walk the road south I imagine that I am walking home. I imagine walking all the way to Kenya in my mind and imagine the weather getting warmer and warmer until the sky clears and it is blue like the colour of the sea in Mombasa and the smell is the smell of warm air, and I am home again. I wonder what this memory will mean to Hugo, if anything, and what his home is. When everyone else wants to go home again, where does he want to go? To the dreary town in a country none of his family has ever known surrounded by strangers? Is it the roads that we travelled upon and the buildings we sheltered in and the people we met? If he grows old, I wonder if he will ever tell someone that he wants to go home again; I wonder if he will tell them that the road is calling him again and that is where he wants to go. I also wonder that after these days, if I return with medicine or without, if he will have already passed, if he will already be home, and if so, if I could reach out a hand and follow him towards the light; if that is the only way to ever really go home again.

The night is drawing in, and I look for somewhere

to shelter. I've made it to the next village and there is a church, as there is in most, but little else. Everyone will have left here, and I don't expect to see many people. I think of Mathilde and Hugo, and they seem far away. As far away as London, in my mind. Distance in the dark means the same if they are three miles away or three hundred. Without electricity, they are as apart from me as if they no longer exist.

I settle myself in the doorway of the church, a place familiar to me now. It's warmer here, but still cold. I feel colder as I look out upon the graves and remember Mathilde telling me about her desire for blackberries to grow over her when she died; this image she had in her mind of regrowth and the taking over of nature. I can't imagine a thing like that, where we are, where all we have is rain and wind.

Did you know that oats are pollinated by the wind, in the way that fruit is not? I'm sure you know, after looking after your bees, I'm sure you know more than most. The way you clung onto them, when they were totally useless, the way you used them to look as though you were trying, when really you just cared about your own skin. That's why honey is blood. That's why I'd never taste it again even if I could.

I'm sure you could never imagine a place without fruit or vegetables, a place where there is only oats because there is only wind, and there is little sun. A place of hopelessness. A place like this.

I'm sure you could never imagine a place where nature is taking hold again, in its own way, and we have no place left in it. Perhaps we're being pushed out, and we never really belonged to it, and we certainly never owned it, not in the way you believed. There's a kind of hysterical irony to the work you did: in ruining nature completely, having made a mess of it, you returned to it, you asked it questions, you sought guidance from it.

I don't think you understood it, I don't think you were humble enough to understand – and maybe I'm not either, but Mathilde is, with her blackberries – that all this will go on without you. It will go on without all of us. And maybe that's a shame for us, that our pocket of time on this earth was wasted and if viewed from faraway said something awful about human nature. But I don't think it's necessarily a shame for the earth itself. I think it could find a way to carry on without our disturbance. I think it would quietly thrive.

I think no amount of arrogance you have could stop certain things from being true: that you are not as powerful as nature. And that's one thing you didn't win, after all. You never held the world in your hands.

Even if for a moment you believed you did.

I wonder if Father Anthony is right, and there is more after this life. I can't imagine it. I imagine this is the end of our world, with Hugo sick and wrapped up in bed and Mathilde standing over him and her telling me she loves me in her mind, in the same way that I talk to you. That wouldn't be such a bad end of the world, would it? That it ends, with my body shivering in the doorway of an abandoned village and my mind elsewhere, my mind with my family and surrounded by them and loved by them. My mind remembering a time when I could pick up my phone and call them. Now I can't so I call them in my mind, which might be more sentimental than if I actually had a phone and could send them a careless note.

I think of this end, but I think of what I must do, too. I surely must rise again, tomorrow. I must make my way back.

I wonder if I'll ever eat again, I wonder what I might taste. I think of the rose-sherbet milkshakes we had as children, the ones with the kulfi, the ones so bright pink they burnt your eyes. I think of my grandparents' hands, passing me a towering glass with a long straw and a tall spoon, glinting out the top of it. I am a child again and they are handing me a milkshake, and I can taste it. I open my mouth, and I can taste it. Then I close my mouth and lay my hands next to me on the hard, stone floor of the church's porch. I know that dream is just a dream, but it reminds me that somewhere, I had another home.

Those days are cold and fruitless. When I make my way back, I walk as many have before me: empty-handed and hollow. I still make it, the soles of my shoes rotting, and my hands worn and cracked. I walk up towards the town and imagine my return, even as I am returning: Mathilde's face next to mine, and Hugo's milky breath. I have no sense of time passing, have lost count of the days. I only know that they are waiting for me, and I never lose sight of that.

As I trudge back towards the town, I remember walking home before, time and again, back to our flat in Kilburn, after my grandparents had left me. I walked back in the darkness and felt a sense of the new world. I thought of my life as before and after; but not after the blackout, after them. I walked home down the High Road and thought of their oval fingernails, somewhere, maybe still on their fingers. I thought of the feeling of home I had lost, and how we all sat, afterwards, flicking on and off light switches and kettles. The piano still played, you didn't need electricity for that, but it didn't quite work without them. In the end, it became part of the way I survived: burning it piece by piece, including the keys, each black and white bar reduced to ash. London was filled with smog, and there were days where you couldn't see your hand in front of your face.

None of that mattered as much as how we'd all lost someone, and how mundane that became. Mathilde would ask me how I survived after that, without anyone. But there was always someone. There was always something leftover.

I carry on through the town, the streets quiet because of the rain and the dark. I walk up to our doorway and for a moment remember my hunger: I grasp at my stomach as my limbs shake. I pull myself up and through the door, my hands wobbling on the handle. I climb the stairs past Mrs Donald's flat as though I'm eighteen and have eaten a full, heaving plate of food, and I don't stop for a moment before pushing open our own door, and stepping towards the living room.

Hugo sits there, just as I'd imagined. Leaning towards the fire, his fairy tale book in his hands, quietly turning the pages. He's reading to himself, and nodding his head, and I can tell the fever has left him.

I hear a clatter of plates in the kitchen, and Mathilde's soft hum, and I stop for a moment, holding onto this sound. I wait, before they turn around and see me. I imagine Hugo saying my name, and Mathilde's soft hand on my shoulder. I pray to the ordinary, I tell myself I'll never want for anything.

I look at Hugo, and imagine that he was born in another time, fifty years ago or more; with his back to me, looking into the fire, holding his childhood trinket – he looks like any boy, anywhere.

Epilogue

I found a lemon yesterday. I wanted to show it to you. I sewed it back up together from each bit that I peeled and tore, and it looked quite good like that; it looked like a whole piece of fruit again. But then Mathilde came in and laughed at me. She did that to keep the shock of seeing a lemon off her face, I could tell. We thought everything had gone, everything but this. Everything but the leftovers.

'Fruit art?' she said, but I didn't think it was art.

I wanted to tell you, as I sewed the lemon back up, that I forgive you for spoiling my life. And as I sewed it, I thought of all the fruit you had taken, and all the things you had thrown away, when there was nothing. I thought it perfectly expressed your meanness, in the way that the far worse things you'd done could not.

I lifted the lemon up and thought about how its skin was happier than you have ever been and brighter, and how if you saw it, all you'd see is the broken peel and not the other, luminous side of it.

The yellow of the skin is how you haven't spoiled my life, one bit, and the white of the inside pith is all the good days that have gone and I can think of, that no one can touch. It is the lesson that if someone ever took something from me in the way that you did, I'd leave.

I didn't think it was art. I thought what would have been art would be the way that you looked at it, if you could see it. How I'd done it, how I'd made something.

How we'd made something, out of nothing, all three of us. How we'd done it.

That would be the art: the look on your face, if only you could see it.

Acknowledgements

Thanks to Kay, Ceris, Bob and everyone at Sandstone Press for making this book a reality. Thanks to David and Philippa at DGA for taking me on and having faith in my writing. Thanks to Jonathan at City University for showing me how to write a novel and giving me the confidence to finish it.

Thanks to Fiona, my first and faithful reader. To Kate, Freya, Maddie, Caroline, Lauren, Sarah and Van; fine readers and friends, who saw me through countless drafts. Thanks to Amrit for the stories of Kenya, and Krina for the mangoes. To all my friends, who supported me in countless ways.

Thanks to Emma, *mi media naranja*; Matt, Rachel and Les, for reading and encouragement. Thanks to my parents for a lifetime of support. To Mum for a home full of books, for seeing the writing on the wall and teaching me how to persevere. Thanks to Dad for telling me to do what I love and for taking it seriously – I wouldn't have got here without that.

Thanks to Theo, for advice on plot, politics and peaches; without you this book could not have been written.